Daughter
of the
Drowned

KERRY WILLIAMS

— HOT TREE PUBLISHING —

Daughter of the Drowned © 2025 by Kerry Williams

All rights reserved. No part of this book may be used or reproduced in any written, electronic, recorded, or photocopied format without the express permission from the author or publisher as allowed under the terms and conditions with which it was purchased or as strictly permitted by applicable copyright law. Any unauthorized distribution, circulation or use of this text may be a direct infringement of the author's rights, and those responsible may be liable in law accordingly. Thank you for respecting the work of this author.

Daughter of the Drowned is a work of fiction. All names, characters, events and places found therein are either from the author's imagination or used fictitiously. Any similarity to persons alive or dead, actual events, locations, or organizations is entirely coincidental and not intended by the author.

For information, contact the publisher, Tangled Tree Publishing.

www.hottreepublishing.com

Editing: Hot Tree Editing

Cover Designer: BookSmith Design

E-book ISBN: 978-1-923252-15-8

Paperback ISBN: 978-1-923252-16-5

Artwork: leo.nor_art

This book is dedicated to my nan.

*Thank you for retelling me Stephen King stories as a child.
Obviously, it shows!*

If you find this book,
Read IT, and love it –
Please leave me a review!
and buy book 2!

If you hate it – pass
it along to your
enemy! Perhaps they'll
love it!

Kerry x

CHAPTER
ONE

When I was seventeen, I died.

It didn't last. Though sometimes I wonder if it was my greatest misfortune that I didn't remain dead. It's especially in moments such as these, when my mom clings with red shellac talons sunk deep into my elbow, that I consider if I were to return to the water, would I welcome its murderous embrace as if an old friend? Alas, these days I dare not take a bath, let alone swim, for fear of the water taking me again.

My mother marches me around the morbid social club like a zombie. It's the kind of place where the walls remain tainted yellow by cigarette smoke, preserving it in time, its owners unbothered to paint over the past.

Mom breaks the silence between us, nestling us in a corner away from prying ears. 'Sorry I missed your birthday, Lovely.'

My muscles ache with the stiffness of receiving empty sympathies from faceless strangers, then having to return my empty thanks.

'My birthday was six months ago.' The harsh edge of my tone is an unintended one, and when tears slide down her cheeks in silent, slow, sad drips, I'm compelled to soften my words, though the rigidity in my spine remains. 'There was so much going on with Dad.'

She stares at the floor, sniffling. My words evaporate into thin air. Unable to comfort my mother in any physical aspect, I drive my thumbnail hard into the bed of its partner, the sharp squeeze of pain sailing me through the uncomfortable moment.

Her bottom lip trembles. 'It was your twenty-first.'

'Mom, it doesn't matter. You were caring for your dying husband. *I'll* have other birthdays.'

Giving me a shaky smile, she bows her head a little as if already afraid of the answer to the question she's gearing herself up to ask, the cogs all but visible in the clench of her jaw. 'Christmas is in a week. How about you come home and stay for a while?'

There it is.

My returning grin is more of a grimace. This is an emotion I'm more than familiar with—guilt. Because it took my dad dying for her to regret our unrepaired relationship. Funerals are saturated with the stuff, and it's been a long time since my parents' house felt like home.

'I have to work, Mom,' I tell her, picking at the frilled cuff of my long sleeve.

'Of course,' she says with a fake brightness.

A sharp pang of my own guilt spears my stomach.

'Do you want a drink? A glass of red wine?' She motions towards the mammoth queue at the bar.

'No, thank you. I'm not drinking right now.' I keep my eyes on my toes. 'Completely sober.'

'Oh.' It's a loaded *oh*. 'Fantastic news, Lovely.'

We descend into another awkward silence. Relief sparkles in her expression when someone new walks into the room. 'There's your uncle. I'd better go talk to him. It must be hitting him so hard. Your dad was always there for him when your cousin passed.'

The tension melts from my mom's body in infinitesimal increments as she moves away from me, her shoulders drooping, a relieved breath filling her lungs. Even in grief she's an elegant creature, her slim frame wrapped in layers of black. She embraces my uncle, the gesture full and warm, not the stilted mockery of a hug we'd shared.

I sigh. My cousin's funeral was the first I'd ever attended. The seven-car pileup had been within a year of my own not-so-tragic brush with death. His demise passed me by at the time as if it were a mirage. My grip on reality was already drifting, my relationships with my family quickly deteriorating as I became lost in a haze of psychiatric assessments and was beginning to dabble in what would become a three-year substance affair.

Rubbing my arms to warm myself against the constant chill that glitters in my bones, I observe my uncle. Our family traits are strong ones—bright sky-blue irises teamed with flaming red hair. The violent ginger of my mane was a curse to me as a teenager, though the time when I cared about my appearance has long perished. After my accident most things faded away into meaninglessness. Including my looks. I stopped caring that I'm too tall, my limbs so long that I border on imposing, my hair its own wilderness, though it's now forever worn in a long braid trailing down my spine. Keen to mask all that's noticeable about myself, I wish to fold inwards, be small. Even the blue of my eyes has dulled to grey over the last four years.

Inching my forefinger under the black fabric constricting my wrist, pushing it up the slightest amount, and thumbing the rough skin there, I wish—oh, how I wish—to be so very far from here. I allow the din of the room to wash over me, imagining it to be tribal tongues, fast and blurry as they slide around my edges. My lips part as an all-too-familiar chill settles on the back of my neck, causing every hair on my body to stand on end. The volume of the room drops as my heart tremors, its beat deregulating. Despite so desperately not wanting to see what horrors may lie behind me, the urge to turn my head rears. The false sensation of icy fingers slides over my skin.

Flee. I need to flee. Escape this crowded room and suffer my delusion in solitude.

'You always did have a tendency for the dramatic,' a voice croons into my ear.

I spin, almost losing balance, to discover its source, and I find myself caught in the amber-hazel gaze of Tino. His ochre-brown skin is as flawless as it always was, although he's lost the boyish softness of his teenage years, his manicured stubble marking him as a man now.

'Tee!' I exclaim.

He wraps his arms around me, and though I want to flinch from the sudden embrace, I resist the urge to pull away. After all, his face is the first welcome one I've encountered on this horrid day, and I should be thankful to him for snapping me out of my trance.

'Tee and Lee back together again.' His tone is all sugared warmth spoken into my hair. He pulls away, holding me at a distance to better drink me in. While his gaze is nothing but friendly, it makes me squirm. 'You lost my number? Would it have been so difficult to pick up a phone? It's been years.'

The hurt in his voice makes my heart ache. I never expected him to miss me.

'It's been *a* year. A rough one. I needed to get myself straight, and that was something to be done alone.' I shuffle about, glancing at my boots before facing his scrutiny, peering through my lashes. 'And what do you mean? Why am I dramatic?'

As if sensing my awkwardness, he releases my elbows and falls in step beside me, leading the way to the buffet, his arm light around mine. 'I saw you, back at the funeral. Standing in the rain like a Victorian widow in the cemetery. So stoic yet full of poise and grace.

Everyone was staring at you.' He chuckles. 'Glad to see you've dried off.'

The dress I'm wearing could be argued to have a Victorian vibe, I suppose, with its high neck and full-length sleeves. I was drawn to the pretty display of elaborately arranged decorative buttons adorning the bodice. It's one of the nicest things I own. I draw my thumb across one of the ruffled cuffs. 'I like this dress.'

'You look great,' he assures me, beaming with a smidgen of irony shining through, followed by a wink.

My stupid pulse quickens at his easy gesture. I'm out of practice at being around people, even Tino. It's ridiculous what a year of self-imposed isolation will do to a person.

Tino raids the buffet, towering mini sandwiches onto a paper plate while popping a sausage roll into his mouth.

My own mouth waters as I survey the spread, the delicious aroma of curry teasing my taste buds.

'Are you...?' His question trails off, his attention focused on his plate of food.

'What?' I say absentmindedly, distracted by the sight of so much food laid out, ripe for the picking.

What would be the harm in allowing myself a sandwich or two—or three? However, the risk is too great in front of all these people. I'm already caught firmly in the peripheries of all in attendance. What people are already gossiping about me takes little stretch of the imagination. The drug addict, tearaway, black sheep of the

Timms family. Best not do anything to cause a scene by devouring the buffet. I step away from the food with purpose.

'Straight? Are you all right?' he clarifies, still not bringing his gaze to meet mine.

The words do their job of distracting from the food, though I'm sure an audible grumble from my stomach gives me away.

'Oh.' I pick at the edges of my nails, wincing a little as the first droplet of blood oozes out. 'It's been hard, but yes. I've been sober for about ten months now. I'm even working. I have a job, a nice little flat. It's not much, but it's mine. Taking things one day at a time is the name of the game.'

He sets his gaze on me. 'That's great. Maybe now would be a good time for me to visit? If you're ready for a friend?' He's so full of goodness, it almost hurts to behold.

'Do you really mean it?' *After everything I put you through* is the part I don't voice, recalling his fingers grasping mine at a party where he begged me not to leave with someone he knew I shouldn't, the bloody knees he tended when he found me in an alleyway passed out, and countless other times he scraped me off the floor.

'Of course. I miss you. I wish I'd known how to get hold of you. You shouldn't have had to go through such a thing alone.'

Colour floods my face. Getting clean was even less

pretty than the partying. It's the last thing I would have wanted anyone to witness.

Tino's fingers twitch. He's clearly sensing my embarrassment.

'Soooo,' he says, 'where are you working?'

'On the other side of Birmingham,' I tell him. I'm so glad to be talking about something neutral again that my hand gesticulation is a little too wild, and I almost knock his plate of food out of his hand.

He retreats a step back to miss my attack.

I force myself to muddle on, heat rising in my cheeks. 'There's a little care home there. I work the night shifts.'

Tino drops a sandwich, his eyes going wide. 'A care home? I'm assuming you mean with elderly people?'

'Yes,' I confirm, pretending to give my attention to a nearby pot of dip, though I make no move to take any.

'Jesus, Lee, you don't make it easy on yourself. What's so wrong with getting a job in a supermarket or something? You don't always need to surround yourself with death and the dying.'

'We're all dying, Tee,' I tease, trying to ease the mood. My attempt at humour is far from convincing.

'Don't pretend you misunderstand.' His expression turns stern. 'You have to break the cycle. You can't keep doing this.'

'I'm not doing anything,' I tell him, the heat of embarrassment turning my face full red. 'It's easier there. It doesn't matter to them if I'm different. The people are sweet, and I get to hold their hands. I bring them comfort, and that, in turn, brings me comfort.' The tears pool, giving my vision a mirage-like quality.

'Lee, I'm not saying it's not a worthwhile thing to do. But you're delicate.' He's all warmth again, squeezing his paper plate between the dishes on the buffet table before putting his hot palms on my shoulders. Burning the skin beneath the thin material of my dress. He waits a beat. 'Do you still see them?' he asks in a whisper.

My voice is stuck in my throat, and the stubborn tears won't budge. I refuse to let them fall. Refuse to shrug off the searing heat of his touch. I refuse to be weak, breakable, addict Lovely. But Tino is waiting for an answer. His earnest expression urges me on as he waits with unending patience. Like old times. Denying the tears their spill, I give what I hope is a firm nod.

'Lee.' He coaxes my name forth before pulling me into a hug.

The sensation makes my skin itch. I half want to melt into him, allow myself the comfort, while my more rational side calls for me to run screaming. The irrational side wins. Closing my eyes, I steady myself, accepting the embrace, assuring myself that this is Tino. He's different. Tino was the only one who never called me crazy. He didn't let my brain damage change his friendship with me. He alone didn't recoil from the change that left me a ghost of who I was. Putting a distance between us was never something he desired. I did. His kindness was like a burning brand, too much to bear. *I* pushed *him* away.

Because I was too scared to live.

Because I was too scared to die.

Too terrified of what the accident had done to me. My brain damage had led my own sight to betray me, paving my way into insanity.

With my fingers on his waist, heating a little at the firmness of his muscles, I put my friend at arm's length once more and school my face into what I hope is a mask of indifference as goose bumps fire down the left side of my body. Creeping dread rises in my throat like bile, bitter, raking my gaze over puffy eyes, ill-fitting suits, and day-old stubble, searching for tell-tale signs of decay. An eyeball hanging from its socket or a cheek rotted through, the pooling of rancid water across the worn shagpile carpet. Anything.

'Lee!'

My hand flies to my chest, and I jump a foot away from the life-filled face of Tino, his concerned expression searching my own.

'I'm sorry, what?'

Recovering, I do a sweep of the room, smoothing the hairs on the back of my neck. *False alarm.*

'Where'd you go?' he chuckles, though his preoccupation with restacking his abandoned paper plate gives away his nerves. He peruses the selection of dips, waiting for me to compose myself.

For lack of anything better to do, I pull my phone from my handbag and give him my new number along with a promise that we'll catch up soon. A real catch-up somewhere that isn't my father's funeral.

And then I chance a glance over my shoulder.

CHAPTER
TWO

My back hits the flimsy wooden front door of my flat, my head dropping with the thud of exhaustion. An involuntary sigh leaves me. The heaviness of the day is like a lead weight around my neck, and I'm glad to be in the darkness of my own home. A tiny sanctuary. My place to hide from the world.

Not bothering to turn on the lights, I splay my fingers out in front of myself and allow my instinct to guide me across the room. Faint outlines of furniture blur to black as I navigate my way to the kitchen. I yank open the fridge door, the golden glow within illuminating the unseen corners of the flat. It could be sunlight basking on my face. These days I operate in near-exclusive darkness; truth be told, I find a neon sun suits me well.

On a regular evening, I'd be heading to work. Nights that are spent strolling abandoned hallways, checking in on residents who cry out, or making tea for those whose day has become confused with night. I love to talk to these people best of all. Already half out of this world, they speak of their mothers long passed as if they were with them yesterday. They call me *sweet girl*, and sometimes they cry because they are unable to remember. All they want is to remember. In return, I tell them I wish to forget, that remembering isn't all it's cracked up to be. They smile. Gap-toothed, wrinkled grins. I assure them that *I* will remember *them*. All of them. They're always calmer after we speak. I calm what troubles their ailing mind. It seems I've found a use in this messed-up world.

Scanning the contents of my fridge, I gaze at the Tupperware that sits in size-ordered stacks, labelled with contents and dates. Structure has been important for my recovery. It's been a weird day, burying my father. My head hurts from having to have conversations that are expected to make sense. I long to lose myself into another world of one of my residents, suspended in time and space. Exist there with them for a while. To not be Lovely for a moment.

The world is out of sync, I haven't eaten all day. My mind wanders, which is a dangerous activity for a mind like mine. A grief I wasn't expecting wraps around me, its hands hard on my heart. Melancholy seeps into my pores as I contemplate the world now existing without my dad in it. We hadn't spoken in a year. I'd removed him from my life. Our relationship had deteriorated to one solely of pain.

And yet.

And yet.

His absence from this world is devastating. Grief tightens its grip.

The tears drip and roll, shining in the glow of my refrigerator, falling like muted raindrops to the floor. The carefully erected partitions in my brain which allow me to function slip, then slide out of place.

Depraved instinct takes over, and I raid the fridge. First, cooked chicken prepared for dinner. I devour it, letting the tears slide down my face as I methodically consume each delicious bite, sucking my fingers before moving on to my precooked rice. I shovel it into my mouth until it's gone, pausing to take a long glug of milk before continuing with what's next in the fridge. A block of cheese, followed by a jar of pickles. My sobs are the only noise permeating the crunching and swallowing. I scoop out the entire contents of the butter tub with my fingers, letting it slide down my throat.

After two hours of continuous gluttony, everything is gone from the fridge, every morsel of food, every condiment. My hunger isn't even close to satiated.

When it's all gone, I cease crying.

I peer at the mess that is my dress, at its sweet ornateness now smeared with milk and mustard and juice from strawberries. *Shame*—it was a nice dress.

Closing the fridge door, I'm plunged into darkness once more. My own languid fingers coast over the smooth surface of the counter, as if in a dance of seduction. When I turn the oven on, a new lesser glow is cast over the dark kitchen space as I meander to the freezer and stack boxes of frozen food one atop another. The fleeting thought occurs to me that in the morning, I'll be irritated with myself. I'll need to go shopping again, precook and plan an entire week's worth of food. But I'm too far gone to stop. I empty an entire bag of oven chips onto a tray. Crunching through a few of them frozen, they shatter between my teeth, cooling my hot grief, before I throw them into the oven.

A psychologist once told me the compulsion to eat was to do with the trauma of my brain damage, although the extremity of the repercussions I experienced was something they hadn't witnessed before. I can eat an entire kitchen's worth of food in one sitting. My parents learned to not buy any more than a week's worth of food at a time in case I had an episode and demolished everything in sight. When I was using, things got better, one compulsion replacing another. Strange how, as things got worse, my parents missed the days when eating all their food was my one vice. Life can only be appreciated in reverse, but you have to live it forward. Someone said that to me once.

The wailing of the oven alarm breaks me out of my musings. Even though the chips are too hot and burn my mouth and throat, I welcome the blistering heat, sores instantly peeling the fleshy skin away from the inside of my cheek. Something to fight off the chill in my bones. I shove more burning chips unceremoniously into my mouth as I fling the next thing into the oven, also without ceremony.

Drip.

Drip.

Drip.

My kitchen tap is dripping, the sound like an ice pick to my skull.

The potato I'm chewing congeals into a lump in my throat, refusing to be swallowed. Closing my eyes tight, I force the food down. *No.* I stomp over to the sink to tighten the tap until my palm turns pink with the effort. Just no, not today.

Why is the food taking so long?

I grab the tray of what I believe is fish fingers out of the oven without pausing, the tips of my fingers searing in agony. With a mixture of a gasp and a cry, I throw the tray, along with all the hot food, to the floor. The tears rise again, and I crumple to my knees, my bones crunching on the hard linoleum. My burned fingers search for the food on the floor, then hastily shove it into my mouth when they find it, causing hot tears that have nothing to do with grief to cascade over my cheeks. My mouth blisters and fills with blood and scorching pain.

And the kitchen tap is still going *drip, drip, drip.*

Jamming myself against the cabinets, I cry out against the food stuffed in my mouth. I push the heels of my palms into my eye sockets until my vision is littered with stars. My chest heaves as I struggle to swallow all the food half masticated in my mouth. Sensation filled with dread rattles my every cell, the *dreaded dripping sound* slows, and my vision blurs in a hazy terror.

I'm having an episode, I tell myself, trying, against hope, to bring it under control. *Triggered by the emotion of the funeral.* My fingers slip into my hair, pulling it free of its braid as my world shivers, then shakes, all while I utter useless breathing exercises to myself.

It's not real.

It's not real.

It's not real.

I shouldn't look, but I always do. The invisible shuddering is colossal, like the belly of the earth is opening, ready to swallow me whole. But as I peek through my fingers, the world appears normal, and my kitchen remains intact.

The tremors are not real, I tell myself, forcing myself to acknowledge the figure looming into view in my home. *Get it over with, Lee.* Though I'm not prepared for the impossibility of what my eyes are telling me.

Bloodcurdling screams rip through every corner of my flat. It takes a moment to recognise them as my own.

THE STREET IS DESERTED AT THIS TIME OF FOXES AND THIEVES. I pound my palm on the familiar red front door, glancing furtively around the abandoned city's edge. I hope Tino still lives with his mom. Rain bounces off my face, the water catching the orange glow of the streetlights in an unnatural way. Alone here, there's nothing anchoring me in this wet amber world. I might be here bashing my fist against the door of a friend, or I might already be dead, lost to this world. Shuddering, I pound some more, chest flat against the wood, as if melting my way through it were possible if I wished hard enough.

The rain.

I wish it would stop raining.

I wish I could escape water.

Please be here, Tino.

Desperation floods my body. I'm glad the rain masks my frantic tears as I slump against the door, clutching my chest, my chattering teeth reverberating in the silence of the early hours. The weakest of desires to find comfort in a friend spools through me, undoes me. Someone. Anyone.

Save me.

How is it possible to drown on my feet?

The front door of the slim terrace house swings open, and Tino's mother stands in the doorway, her expression frozen as if I'm a mad person, which is a fair assessment. Keeping my hand clutched to my chest, all I'm capable of is blinking at her in the rain, with my wild hair tamed by the downpour and plastered to my face. No words come. I grimace through my tears, my teeth now clenched.

'Oh, *bella*.' Her voice is soft—as soft as a duvet I long to throw over myself, resurfacing in a few hundred years. She doesn't hesitate to step out into the hammering wetness and take me in her arms.

What it is to be held. And to be held so tenderly. I thaw, crying into her hair, letting myself melt into her embrace for a moment before I pull away. If I stay there, I might dissolve entirely.

The concern doesn't leave her face as she pulls me into the hallway. Her eyes rake over my soaked dress clinging to my frail frame, her expression turning a fraction darker, but she doesn't give voice to any of her tumultuous assumptions. Instead, she bellows Tino's name so loudly, I almost cover my ears.

In the shelter of Tino's mother's house, the world settles around me. I embrace the calm it brings. Pushing my drenched hair from my face, I've made it a few steps towards the front room when Tino's heavy tread falls frantically on the stairs.

'Ma! Ma! What is it? What's wrong?' He stops dead at the sight of me, his face changing from concern to absolute bewilderment.

I peer at him in my washed-away Victorian dress, still clutching my chest as if I may split in half otherwise. *Boy, I really nailed the drama he implied earlier*. Tino stands statue still, wearing only his boxers while regarding this strange scene. Despite all my panic, colour heats my cheeks. I haven't seen Tino in a state of undress since we were kids. His legs are so long now, balanced by broad shoulders, faint traces of a six-pack rippling within his abdomen. As we stare at each other, I sense rather than witness the embarrassment against his dark skin. He's the perfect mix of both of his parents: the same thick

Italian hair of his mom that he wears a little long and brushed to one side in perfect complement to the dark skin of his Congolese dad. His amber-hazel irises are his own. Tino's beauty hits me with a sudden shock, as if I'm seeing him for the first time now that I'm no longer tangled in the trappings of adolescence or a drug-fuelled haze.

He crosses the hall in two quick strides and takes me by the shoulders, staring deep into my eyes as if their depths will reveal my secrets. 'Lee, what's wrong? What's happened?'

The weight of his stare and the concern in his visage is almost too much, almost crushing in itself. A wave of unfamiliar emotion crashes around in my stomach as the heat of his palms sears through the sodden material of my dress. If I could melt, I would—melt away into nothing. Simply evanesce into his being.

'Lee.' He shakes me a little, sinking his head to move closer by a fraction so his face draws level with my own, making it impossible not to notice the inviting curve of his lower lip.

'Do you think it might be true?' The words stick to the roof of my mouth before leaving my lips, sounding strange in the dead of night.

Tino stares for an eternity, serious, not his usual self, absorbing my question until he straightens.

'Wait here,' he tells me before walking past his mom and taking the stairs two at a time.

She mutters something in Italian to him that's

beyond my understanding, and in return he tells her she should go back to bed. She gives me a tender pat on the arm, ushering me into their living room before ascending the stairs.

Being so alone in Tino's front room, icy coldness seeps into my skin. I wrap my arms around myself. Thankfully, the drenching from the rain made the stains inconspicuous on the front of my dress. I hadn't waited to change or grab a coat. I fled my flat and got in my car before driving all the way here like a woman possessed.

Tino appears in the doorway, fully clothed now, holding more garments clutched in his grasp, caution caught in his gaze as his eyes search my body. The sudden scrutiny makes me blush again.

'Sorry, Lee. It's obvious you have no pockets or anything, but....'

'I'm not....' I swallow hard. 'I haven't relapsed.'

He nods with a certain carefulness and steps towards me, holding out a jumper and jogging bottoms. 'You should change. You're shaking.'

I don't respond. Instead, I bow my head, burning with shame, though I've done nothing to earn it. After taking the clothes from him, I proceed to shuffle to the bathroom to change. Being in his home again is a strange sensation, so familiar, yet under the cloak of the early hours of the morning, there's a stark chill about it. Keeping the lights in the bathroom off, I peel my dress from my cool body, thankful when the downy material of Tino's jumper slides against my skin. Lifting the front of the soft fabric to my nose, I inhale. It smells like fresh laundry, all comforting warmth. When I smooth the sleeve against my cheek, the panic ebbs out of my chest. I slip on his jogging bottoms and roll the waistband over a few times.

As quietly as possible, I pad downstairs and peek into the kitchen as Tino potters around, his strong features more relaxed now in the mellow glow.

When he catches sight of me in his clothes, his smile warms me further. 'They suit you,' he says.

'Thank you. Even changing out of those clothes has made all the difference.'

'Coffee?'

'Please.'

The rich aroma of the drink settles me even further as I watch my friend move around the kitchen with a graceful ease. My psyche floats back down to earth, rooted around Tino, someone from my life before. I almost lose my nerve to ask my burning question again when he passes me my mug of coffee, leaning against the counter to better assess me.

He beats me to it when he returns to my earlier question. 'Do I think what might be true?'

I take a moment to glance at him, although I return my stare to my coffee as I admit, 'You were the only one who never called me crazy. Who didn't treat me like a pariah. I never thanked you for your kindness, Tee.'

His silence permeates the air between us. I chance bringing my eyes to his, but he doesn't respond to my thanks. Instead, he holds my gaze, waiting for me to go on.

I blow a little on my coffee, attempting nonchalance. 'Did you ever believe me, or was kindness the total sum of it?'

'Lee. I'm so not qualified,' he says, putting his own coffee to one side.

'When I had an episode—' I train my gaze on him, and for its loneliness, the distance between us in this moment could be an expanse of ocean. '—when I told you I had visions of the dead reaching out to me. Did you ever consider if they were real?'

Tino stares at me hard before dragging his palm over his face. 'What happened, Lee? Why now?'

Going back to pretending like my coffee is the most interesting thing on the planet, only my shaking body sends ripples across its surface. His avoidance of the question should be answer enough. He never believed it for a moment. He was merely being himself—too kind, too understanding.

'Please answer the question,' I probe regardless.

His pause is so long and so loaded, I assume he isn't going to answer. When his feet come into view with an urgent step, his hand forming a delicate cradle on the side of my face, my eyelids flutter closed. The caress is so gentle that for someone like me, it comes harsh against my skin, it's so alien.

His voice is just as reassuring. 'I know it was very,

very real for you. I'm not going to pretend to understand.'

'I saw him tonight, Tee.' My voice trembles. 'It's never been someone related to me before. My own dad's corpse was in the middle of my kitchen, dead and wretched and reanimated.' I tear my gaze from Tino's to stare at his chest. 'He was terrified, and his eyes.... They were so like his. It was *so* real. Something inside me clicked.' Tino moves his arms around me, and my breath catches at the grim admittance of my reality. I confess, 'What if all this time, it's been real, and it wasn't brain damage alone? What if those people needed me, and my response was what? To do nothing? To get so high that I hoped to drown them out?'

The grip of hysteria fizzes at my edges, my body shaking so violently that Tino removes the cup from my fingers and puts it on the counter before bringing me into a tight embrace. For a moment my body goes rigid before relaxing into it, and I allow myself to collapse into him a little.

Tino grasps the top of my arms to return my attention to him. 'This is all so fresh. Your dad died. You're exhausted. It's normal to grieve him.'

My body slackens a little in his grip. 'You don't believe me.'

'It's a big leap of faith you're asking me to make here. You've been absent from my life for over a year.'

Something stirs within me, a certainty. I wiggle from

his grasp, and then I curl my freezing fingers around the warmth of his own.

'I'm asking you to entertain the possibility,' I implore him. 'It was my dad, Tee. I could *feel* him. All this time, I've been ignoring them, and they need something from me. My dad needs me now.'

His eyes search mine, perhaps for any signs that I'm high or lying or possibly crazy.

I am *crazy*.

I bat the paranoia away. *It was an episode, nothing more.*

Stop. It's not the time for my brain to turn on itself.

Tino steps away from me, dragging his hand down his face. Processing. Then he says, 'Let's say for a moment this is real. Let's say you were visited by your dad tonight. If he needs your help, what comes after? How do you help the dead?'

He waits, standing in the kitchen where we both spent much of our childhood, cast in the merciful trappings of a new dawn, for me to have answers.

'I have no idea,' I breathe, and he flaps his arms at his sides in consternation. Annoyed, I pop my hip at him. 'You were the one who said you would have been there for me when I left before. My mistake to assume.... It's been so long....' The words crumble into nothing in my mouth.

Tino's expression turns to one of defeat. 'Of course I'm here for you, Lovely.' He never calls me by my real name. Then his expression turns clement. 'We'll figure this out.'

CHAPTER
THREE

Stiffness lingers in my neck muscles as I gingerly rise to sit, blinking as I take in my surroundings. The accusing stare of daylight filters in through the net curtains. What happened last night returns to me in a haze. Exhaustion finally sank its claws in, and I fell asleep on Tino's sofa after he agreed to help me figure out how to contact my dad.

My dad. My *dead* dad.

I push my head into my hands. *I'm having an episode, aren't I?*

Fingering the edge of Tino's jumper, I tease it over my wrist, my heart beating in double time. I almost don't want to look, but I should check. Maybe if there's clear evidence of a relapse, whether I'm in the grips of psychosis or not would become clearer to me. But I don't get there before the living room door bangs open, bringing Tino in. I shove the sleeve down to its original position near my thumb.

'Did you manage to sleep?' he asks, the corners of his mouth betraying a smile as he takes in my appearance.

I nod, trying to smooth out the mat of my waist-length curls that is now bunched up on one side of my head. It must resemble more of a bird's nest than hair right now. I pull my knees under me, trying to make myself small.

'Glad to hear it.'

For the first time, I take in what Tino is wearing: a black uniform complete with heavy-duty trousers, boots, and a black shirt with a thick black vest over the top. 'You work security?'

'Who would have thought it?' He grins, checking his reflection in the baroque mirror above the fireplace, sliding his fingers through already perfect hair.

'You always preferred starting fights, if I remember right,' I tease him.

'No, Lee, you're remembering wrong. I liked finishing fights—there's a difference.' He winks.

'Right.' Staring at the floor, I fiddle with my nails. 'Tee, is it okay if I stay here while you're at work?'

His surprised expression is enough to make me laugh, almost. 'You want to hang here with my ma?'

Embarrassment creeps in, and I drop my gaze. 'I'd love to, actually. I don't believe I should be on my own right now.' I wish my body would cave in on itself and disappear as he scrutinizes my person, assessing me.

What should he do? Am I going to snap, escape, relapse, run away? All fair assumptions.

You *should run far away, Tino,* I think.

My own patheticness must be tangible, because his voice is all sympathy when he says, 'Of course—please stay. For as long as you want.'

His eyes are so warm, I'd like to lose myself in them. This past year has left its mark on him, coupled with our drifting apart during my drugs love affair. He's not the skinny teenager who was always fighting my battles for me. Or trying to, at least.

He clears his throat, taking a step away from me while pointing his thumb at the door. 'I have to get to work, but stay, relax. I'm sure my ma will love cooking you a three-course meal for breakfast.'

The colour rises in my face as I recall how I ate almost every piece of food I own last night, but yes, I'm so ravenous, a three-course breakfast wouldn't stand a chance against me right now.

'When I get home, we'll talk about what to do next,' he adds when I don't respond.

'Thanks, Tee,' I say, weak with relief.

He edges towards the door, unsure if he should leave. He must give me more credit than I deserve, because he ducks his head and exits the house.

Tino's right—his mom relishes having me here. I sit with a stack of three fluffy pancakes in front of me, covered in butter, syrup, and sliced bananas with both a glass of orange juice and a cup of tea on the side. I make a pointed effort to use the cutlery, take my time, and not devour it with bare fingers like I wish to. Rose sits opposite with a careful expression, cup of coffee in hand. I don't mind the silence between us. I'm almost sorry when she breaks it.

'Was it an episode, dear?' she asks quietly.

My chewing slows as I meet her gaze. I whisper a yes.

'Stay for as long as you like.'

'Thank you' is all I say, avoiding her sympathetic expression by taking a long drink of tea.

'It's funny,' she continues after another silence, 'your uncle had a "sighting" once when he was younger —much younger. Before you were born. The ghost of his mother flashed before him not long after she passed.'

I'm unable to conceal my shock. A choke leaves my throat, my cutlery clatters to the table, and tea all but splutters from my nostrils. 'Why did no one tell me about this?'

Pushing her long hair off her face, she gazes out the window, her expression becoming distant. 'It was nothing more than a story, one that came out after a few drinks in the pub. An amusing story is all. Just....' Her eyes take on a wistful sheen. 'Sometimes I wonder how much tragedy one family should suffer.'

But I'm on my feet, scrambling around for my car keys. 'No one told me. No one *ever* said a word, Rose.'

Where are those goddamn keys? After everything I'd been through during those early days, when I cried over ghosts before I learned my lesson and stopped talking about the dead I'd dragged out of hell with me—why did no one stop and think about how my uncle had seen one too?

'Honey.' She stands now, trepidation rising in her voice. 'I didn't mean to alarm you.'

Pulling my car keys out of the crack in the sofa, I turn to Rose. 'Tell Tino I'll be back.'

I fly out the door and into my car, not bothering to buckle my seatbelt. It's over an hour's drive to my uncle's farm. I haven't been there since I was a kid—before my accident, before his son died. I didn't even speak to him at my dad's funeral. The road is long, and as the journey progresses, calm does not descend. Instead, cortisol floods my body, sending my knuckles white in their grip on the steering wheel until it's nothing but winding country roads and single-track lanes, not another house for miles. Nothing like the busy Birmingham streets I'm used to.

The farm is cast in quiet as I make my way along the seemingly endless drive, still wearing Tino's oversized clothes, my untamed hair whipped by the wind. The farm is eerily quiet. Usually there's a Timms running about, tossing a hay bale. Or at least a chicken on the loose, clucking across the yard. But as I park and ease out of the car, the windows look dark, the farmhouse cold. Only the clinking of the metal gate that leads to the fields below rings through the crisp air. I knock on the door, unsure of myself now that I'm here. What exactly am I going to ask him—*'Are you visited by the dead too? How could you leave me believing myself insane when you see them?'* The weight of the accusation sits heavy in my chest. If he shares my visions or believes it's even a possibility, he's never given voice to those beliefs, never attempted to reach out to me.

I'm just about to turn around to leave when the door opens. 'Lovely?'

I peer into those piercing blue eyes. His voice is so like my dad's that grief rubs rough against my soul.

'Jacob, I was hoping we might talk?' I squeak.

He continues to appraise me, not saying anything more, instead opening the door wide for me to come in before leading me into the kitchen. All sorts of vegetables are stacked high on the counter, potatoes and carrots caked in earth. Muddy wellington boots line the wall by the door. Signs of a busy family life are scattered across the vibrant room. The coldness of the outside was all in my head. I'm so terribly tired of seeing what is impossible for others to behold.

Jacob puts the kettle on the hob before moving to fetch the biscuit tin from a high shelf and sliding it across the table in my direction. 'I'm afraid you've missed the others. They're in Cambridge visiting Jen.'

'It's okay. It's you I wanted to speak to anyway,' I tell him as I open the biscuit tin, perusing his selection of treats.

He leans against the counter, crossing his arms before bowing his head, silently urging me on.

'I'm sorry to spring a visit on you so suddenly,' I say, turning a custard cream over in my fingers.

'It's okay, Lee. Tell me what's on your mind.'

As I crunch through the biscuit, words whirl round my mind. I attempt to conjure an explanation for my sudden visit without sounding like I've lost my marbles. 'I was talking to Rose this morning. You remember Tino's mom?'

'Of course.'

'She was saying—' I falter, remembering her question. *'Was it an episode, dear?'* I swipe at the doubt in my mind and push on. 'She told me....' My mouth is so dry, instinct screams at me to leave. 'What she said was....'

Jacob's silence is deafening.

This is a bad idea.

'Actually, Jacob, so silly of me—there's somewhere I need to be. Thanks for the biscuits.'

I snatch another from the tin and attempt to make my getaway, but Jacob cuts me off before I arrive at the door. 'You came here to talk, so talk. What did Rose tell you?'

Faltering once more, I bring my gaze to his too-blue eyes, encountering the same knowing look my father wore. 'She told me you had a vision once—something that appeared to be a ghost. Is it true?'

Jacob releases a big sigh, letting me out from under his stare. 'I did, once.' He paces into the belly of the kitchen, where he places his palms on the table, his back to me.

My heart thunders. 'How come you never mentioned anything?' I should be furious, but more than anything, I want to know how he could leave me so alone.

Jacob's head hangs, and he speaks to the table. 'Because I didn't believe it mattered. What happened to you was mere months before Brady died. By the time your parents had revealed the true extent of the problems you were facing, I was in a dark place. I'd just lost my boy. Besides, my own apparition happened such a long time ago, and only once—nothing like what you were going through. Lee, trust me, if I believed my experience would have helped you as the years went on, I'd have brought it up. I didn't want to confuse the situation further.'

Swallowing several gulps, I force the words out. 'Rose told me it was your mother.'

'Yes,' he whispers.

'Did—' My voice cracks. 'Did she appear wet?'

Jacob swivels on his heel, agog, his eyes widening. 'How did you know that?'

My chest convulses, fresh pain ripping through it. I cross the kitchen in two strides before sitting at the table and throwing my head into my hands. For the second time in two days, I cry uncontrollable, loud sobs for the last four years of a life of pain riddled with insanity and nothing but self-doubt—other than the certainty that I'm crazy. Numbness. More pain. The dead stretching their awful, dripping fingers towards me.

Every cut.

Every dose.

'Jacob, why didn't you tell me you had a vision?' I cry.

His grip comes heavy on my shoulder, clearly intended to be comforting, but I jerk from his grasp. It's unbearable to be touched right now.

'Lee, I didn't.... You were having so many episodes.... I didn't....'

'They're always sodden.' My voice shakes. 'It's how they appear to me. I assumed it was related to the trauma from when I drowned, which explained why they seem to have drowned too. But when your mother visited you, she looked wet, too, didn't she?'

Jacob takes a seat opposite, easing himself into the chair, his eyes never leaving mine. He examines me as if I've changed my very form.

'It was over before I knew it. Happened in the blink of an eye. When my mom died, I didn't get to the hospital in time, never had the chance to say goodbye to her. It rained the whole journey home. When she appeared, it was for a split second. In the moment, I forgot she was dead. I thought she must have got caught in the rain.

Then she was gone, and the fact that she died hit me all over again. When I did tell people, I described it as how she came to me to say farewell. For me, it wasn't terror—it was comfort. She came to say goodbye when I couldn't.'

Jacob slides his hands over to mine, but I avoid his consolation with a swift jolt.

'Lee, I'm so sorry. If I had known....' I briskly brush the tears off my face as Jacob pulls himself upright to regard me with mild horror, his words dying on his lips for a moment before he fumbles on further. 'All those people.... You mean to say that all this time.... How many?'

A coldness settles over me, the chill in my marrow offering a certain detachment. I shrug. 'Hundreds.'

'Hundreds,' he repeats in the barest whisper. 'Why? Why you?'

'I haven't the faintest idea. But they obviously needed my assistance in some way, yet I've ignored them. For four years I have told myself I'm traumatised, living with brain damage and psychosis. Listened when doctors, friends, and even my own family have told me I'm crazy. I have been *dying* for the past four years, chased by hallucinations no number of drugs, prescription or otherwise, had any hope of slowing down. When one word from you —*one word*—would have helped me so much. I would have known I wasn't alone. And I've been so alone, Jacob.'

My chest heaves, and as my brain spins, passing out

is a real possibility. The truth. The truth is such a weird thing. The truth will set you free—that's what they say. The truth will set me free. But that isn't the case. For some reason, my truth makes me nauseous.

It was all real.

It *is* all real.

'I saw my mother once, Lovely. I explained it away as comfort. Truth be told, I'm not sure if I ever believed in it or if my mind needed to do something to bring me peace after she passed. Something to ease the guilt.'

'Did Brady visit you?'

Jacob stills. 'No.'

His cheeks become wet with tears while I garner the courage to speak. Several seconds pass before the words come. 'My dad came for me last night. I need to help him. He…. They…. What if they need my help?'

Jacob swallows hard, and when he rises, it's so sudden, it makes me jump backwards. He gives a few sharp sniffs while nodding. 'There's someone you should talk to.'

My pulse quickens as I wait for him to go on, and I pick at the healed wound on my fingernail.

'I keep in contact with some of Brady's old friends. Most are local, but a friend of his lives in the States now.' He shakes his head, smiling a fraction as he pulls out his phone followed by a piece of paper. 'She leads a different type of lifestyle these days. A free spirit. You're not going to find answers from me or around here.'

He scribbles something on the paper before sliding it across the surface of the table to me.

I examine the information on the paper, finding a simple name paired with a phone number. 'She knows about this stuff?' I ask.

'Lorna *might* be able to help. I'm a practical man. I don't pretend to understand how everything works in this world, but I've had many people taken from my life too soon. I have to believe there's something more.'

My throat becomes coated with grief. His son and I were the same age. Brady was barely eighteen when he died. Our families were wrecked. My near-death experience followed by all the terrible repercussions of brain damage, and then Brady had a fatal car crash under a year later. Only, I got to live, while he didn't.

Examining the paper in my fingers, I scrutinize Jacob's tight scrawl.

'Speak to Lorna,' he says after a while. 'I'm sure she understands more than I do.'

When I arrive at Tino's some hours later, I check my phone to find five missed calls from him. I take the piece of paper with Lorna's number on it from my pocket, and I thumb the thick graphite of the pencil markings.

What did Jacob mean by 'different lifestyle'? Even more, do I really want to go down this rabbit hole?

I hit Redial on Tino's number, and when he answers,

I tell him I'm in the car outside and ask if he'll come out. Minutes later he's in the passenger seat next to me. Heat radiates from him, filling the enclosed space, the condensation his presence provides giving us privacy.

'Jesus, Lee, you just took off. I was so worried.'

'Sorry.' I stare straight ahead through the sweating windscreen. The street is much busier now with people arriving home from work, the jubilant shouts of children ringing through the air as they scamper home. 'I had to go talk to my uncle.'

'And?'

I pass him the scrap of paper, not needing to meet his eyes, as his stare burns into me before he takes a moment to inspect it.

'Ah, of course. This makes sense,' he says wryly and shakes his head. 'What am I looking at here? A number? Who is she?'

'A friend of my cousin, apparently. I never met her, though.'

'Your cousin who died?'

I nod.

'Sorry, am I missing something?'

Sighing, I say, 'According to Jacob, she's someone who has the know-how to help.'

'Help you contact your dad?'

'Yep.'

A kaleidoscope of confusion flitters across his face. 'How on earth does your uncle have the number of someone in contact with the dead?'

Exhausted and inescapably hungry, I give my head a noncommittal shake. 'No idea. But it's our only lead right now.'

Tino shoves the scrap of paper back into my hands. 'Well, for God's sake, call her, then. The suspense is killing me.'

CHAPTER
FOUR

The phone rings, thunderous in the quiet of the car. Maybe I should have texted her first. I have no idea what the time difference in the US is. *Are they ahead or behind the UK?*

Reading my anxiety, Tino opens his mouth to say something, but words fail to pass his lips before someone picks up.

'Hello?'

My heart jumps into my throat. 'Is this Lorna?' I ask. Tino's fidgeting is making me even more nervous.

'Who is this?' the voice asks, British with the slightest Southern US twang.

'Sorry, you have no idea who I am. My name's Lovely. I'm Brady's cousin. His dad gave me your number. I hope you don't mind.'

Silence.

I have to check the phone screen to make sure she

hasn't hung up. Tino gives me a searching glance as I continue, 'Are you there?'

'Yes.' Another silence. 'Is everything okay? Is Jacob all right?'

'He's fine. Well, as fine as can be expected. His brother died a month ago.'

Lorna takes a sharp breath. 'I'm so sorry for your sad news. Was it your dad?'

'Yes, it was.'

'Sorry for your loss,' she tells me, but the way she says the words makes it sound like a question. 'Jacob asked you to call? Email is usually his preferred method of communication.'

My throat's as dry as the Sahara. Telling my awful truth to a stranger, a lone voice at the other end of the line, hits me as a horrible idea. Then again, there's nothing tangible about her, so what do I have to lose? 'He said you might be able to help me.'

Silence again. Tino nods in encouragement.

'I'm no grief counsellor.'

'He came to me,' I blurt out.

'Who?' she asks, dumbfounded.

'My dad.' I clutch my chest, and an icy breath ghosts my ear, making me glance into the rear seat. Thankfully, the world remains peaceful. 'I saw him after he died. It wasn't the first time I've had a vision of someone who has passed.'

Her silence continues, and I flail, clutching at straws. 'Jacob told me you might help. I hate to bother you with this—it must sound beyond ludicrous—but you're my sole lead.'

Another silence follows that's so loaded, I almost hang up right there.

I swallow. This is stupid. So stupid. I'm about to tell her I shouldn't have bothered her, that I have brain damage, so I get confused sometimes, when she talks again.

'Hold on a second.'

'Sure.' As soon as the word leaves my mouth, I jump out of my skin as she yells a name in my ear.

The line goes quiet for a while. I raise my eyebrows at Tino, who cocks an eyebrow of his own.

He grins a little. 'You're terrible at this.'

His statement throws me off balance, bringing me back to earth with a bump. 'At what?'

'Asking for help.' He shakes his head, his mouth stretching into a wry smirk.

'Well....' I finger the edge of my jumper—Tino's jumper, rather. 'I don't exactly have a good track record for receiving it.' A wave of guilt washes over me as his expression turns stony.

'What's happening?' He nods at the phone, breaking through the awkwardness.

'She's gone to talk to someone.' I shrug.

Her voice finally returns at the end of the line. 'Are you there?'

I return the phone to my ear. 'I'm here.'

'You wish to communicate with him? Your dad?'

The directness of the question, the matter-of-factness about it, shocks me. Never once has it been phrased in such a casual way. *'Oh, you have visions of the dead? What do they want?'*

'Yes,' I answer, my own desperate conviction coming as a surprise to myself.

'Okay. I'll help you. Well, I'll try. In theory.'

This has me reeling. It's the response I didn't dare hope for. The result leaves me somewhere between happiness and nausea. 'Really?' Instinct causes me to glance at my phone in disbelief, and somewhere in my brain, a voice screams, *'It's a trick, it's a trick, it's a trick.'*

The sunshine in her voice beams through the phone line as she confirms, 'Really. Well, not me as an individual. But I'm friends with people who are in touch with the other side. Now, you have two options: either I refer you to an acquaintance in the UK, someone legit, or, if you're in need of a friendly face, you're welcome to come to the States. Lis and I have plenty of room.'

'You believe me?' I whisper. 'No questions asked.'

'Sure.' The word is laced with a nonchalance I have no understanding of. 'I've heard stranger things.'

Her words sink into my body. She's heard stranger. She believes me. I'm not crazy. I close my eyes. *I am not crazy.*

'Are you sure it's okay if I come to you?' I ask.

'Of course. I'd love to meet a cousin of Brady's. Truth be told, you won't find a better practitioner than here in New Orleans. I'll send you the details to this number, but don't worry about a hotel. As I said, you're welcome here. Text me all your flight details when you have them, and I'll come meet you at the airport.'

Beyond stupefied, I mumble a thanks, catching myself in time as Tino's expectant expression snags my own. 'Lorna, is it okay if I bring a friend?'

'The more the merrier,' she chimes before ending the call.

I stare at my phone for a full minute. She believes me. She didn't even need convincing, just, *'Yes, you have visions of the dead. You need help communicating with them. I'll help with that.'* A practitioner—the name for someone who communes with those who've passed.

'Lee, talk to me. What's happening?'

'I'm going to New Orleans.'

An emptiness resonates around my words, but inside, my emotions are crashing, flooding through me. My brain struggles to cope. I barely register what he's saying to me, his words taking on an underwater quality. I fiddle with the edge of his jumper I'm still wearing, pulling a thread free as I interrupt him. 'Will you come with me?'

His brow knits with frustration, as I haven't been listening and have answered his question with one of my own. 'What are we going to New Orleans for?'

'According to Lorna, she's in touch with someone who might help me commune with my dad. She called them a practitioner.'

Tino sinks his head into his hands. 'What's happening right now?'

With a tentative hesitation, I place my hand on his shoulder, offering what I hope is reassurance.

'She believed me, right off the bat. Didn't question it at all. This is something I have to do. I need answers. The last four years have been hell. But—' I retract my hand and pull at the loose thread again. '—you were right. I'm fragile. I'm so broken, Tee. If I go, if I find the answers to what's been happening to me, maybe I'll find my broken pieces. Maybe I'll piece myself together. Be whole again.'

'Shit,' he mutters before finally lifting his head from his palms. 'When are we leaving?'

As much as I would love to live the rest of my life in Tino's comfortable clothing, I need to face my flat, shower, and wash away the last forty-eight hours before trying to get my head around the notion that I'm going to travel to the US to stay with a stranger in an attempt to talk to my dead dad.

Despite my assertion to my uncle, a dark pit ate its way into my stomach on the way home, a fear that I might not like what my dad has to say to me. We weren't on the best of terms in life, so why would that change in death? Was there some great truth he discovered in the afterlife that has redeemed me in some capacity? Does he repent for not believing me? Will he apologise? Tell me he loves me?

Would he rescind all the unkind words spoken between us?

Could I forgive him for them?

After all, he wasn't the only one—no one believed me. After a while, *I* didn't believe me. My lack of belief in my own visions didn't stop them from coming, though—didn't stop my world from tilting. Every time they did, it was like drowning all over again, the saltwater of the sea filling my lungs once more. Drenched skin, dripping, with wrinkled fingers reaching out to me. Flickers, blurs, remnants of people who once walked this earth. Their lips open but no words coming out, mouths flapping like suffocating fish with deep dead eyes. When the apparitions first appeared to me, I would scream, demand they tell me what they want, only for stagnant water to bubble at their lips.

But as time went on, I changed. The prescription drugs made me go underwater with them, too drugged, too stripped of my emotions to scream, but nothing was strong enough to dull the horror. I found new ways of drowning them out, to graciously accept my madness. To witness in a stupor when the world shook, came apart at the seams for one of the dead to crawl like a spider out of the crack, the sweet relief of heroin flooding my veins as they advanced. Mastering a fake calm, I didn't shake as much, was less compelled to scream at them to return to whatever hell they came from. Instead, I observed the rot-filled water dripping around them, the unfathomable desperation in their expression with a more stoic sort of terror. I found myself clutching onto the seams of life, too scared to die for fear I would become one of the withering dead. Better to be an addict than insane in the eyes of those around me. At least they understood addiction.

When the relief drugs brought me wasn't enough, it became all too apparent how much more harrowing life was about to get. There are worse horrors in this world than being visited by the dead.

Through the ether of bad decisions, a vague notion had come to me that enough was enough. I left my life of denying my awful visions behind to get clean. I carved out a sort of existence for myself. Keeping myself structured, I lived a life of strict routine. It didn't stop the hauntings, but I was coping. It was *my* life.

And now all of that's blown out of the water.

'Lee?'

How long have I been standing with my key in the front door?

Staring.

Thinking.

Waiting.

What am I waiting for?

'Lee?' Tino asks even gentler this time.

His sympathy is almost too much to bear. I tear my gaze away from him the second the *'I'm so sorry for you'* sentiment leaks out of him. 'I don't want to witness my dad all wrung out again, Tee. Not like that. Not like *them*.'

'You don't have to be the one. Let me go in and grab your stuff. I'll be out of there in five minutes. There's a hot shower at mine, plus all the coffee you can drink. You don't have to face your dad, or whoever else is in there.'

'It's my flat.' I grimace. 'I have to go in at some point.'

'Why?' He grins, leaning against the doorframe. 'Let me wait on you. I'll fetch your stuff from inside as and when you need it.' He glances around with a dramatic flair. 'It is a rather nice hallway.'

Laughing, I relax my hand off the key, slouching my body to turn enough to drink him in. The humour in his smile changes to one of warmth, pure and stunning. He gives a light shake of the head, moving his body in front of mine as if to protect me before turning the key and opening the door.

Although Tino offers no actual protection if my dad does make an appearance, his gesture comforts me. He takes cautious steps, peering around the flat as if someone might pop around a corner at any second.

Laughing a little, I place my palm on his shoulder to move past him. 'You may be starting to believe me now, but your support doesn't mean the dead will be jumping out at you. What I have isn't catching.' Stopping to give him a dramatic turn, throwing my hair over my shoulder in the process, I feign shock. 'Or, who knows—maybe they will.'

Tino's eyes stretch with fear.

A deep belly laugh escapes me. 'You should see your face.'

'So not funny,' he retorts and straightens, regaining composure.

'It's a little bit funny.' I half smile. 'Okay, sit tight and watch TV or whatever. I'm going to take a shower. I'll be as quick as I can. I'll pack a few bits, travel light.'

He nods, walking further into the flat, taking it in for the first time. There isn't much in the way of belongings to inspect. I don't own much stuff.

I've only taken two steps into my bedroom when his voice cuts through the silence, bellowing, 'Oh my God, Lee! What happened here?'

Panic flooding my system, I dart out into the front room and then the kitchen to find him surrounded by empty containers and jars, a whole stack of food defrosting into a big heap on the counter.

'Oh, crap. I forgot all about this,' I say as I spot a few stray fish fingers on the floor.

'What is this?' He lifts a box of oozing Cornettos.

Shaking my head a little, I come to rest my hip against the counter. 'Before the apparition, I was super hungry when I got in. I was eating.'

Tino arches an eyebrow, turning an empty jar of mustard in his palms.

'It's an addict thing, apparently,' I say by way of explanation.

He returns the jar to the crowded countertop and prods at the now-empty tub of butter. 'Not so sure about that.'

I cock my head, for the first time considering everything that happened after my accident in a new light. 'Do you believe it's connected?'

'That's a subject I have no authority on.' He takes in the state of the kitchen. 'But this is something to behold, for sure. You never made it a secret from me, your compulsion to eat. But seeing it, really seeing it, is something else entirely. This never happened before your accident?'

Shaking my head, confirming that my near-death experience is indeed the epicentre of my woes, I almost taste Tino's acceptance growing in the air. Against all his better judgement, against what's rational. He's not indulging me now. He's beginning to believe the horrors of my life are more than delusions. A little braver, I take a step towards him as he drags his line of sight from the empty boxes and jars, his focus settling on me.

'Where did you go?' he asks, his voice a whisper laced with so much compassion, I almost die inside. The heat of his words fills me from my head to my toes. 'When you died, where did you go?'

The question makes me shake in response as his fingers trace mine. A moment of silence envelops us before he takes them in his own, holding them like they're made of glass. A touch I don't want to recoil from. The opposite. Perhaps the heat of him will finally warm me up some, chase away the stark cold that haunts me.

'I haven't the faintest idea,' I say through the lump in my throat.

To be believed.

It is a new type of sweetness. A new type of torture.

CHAPTER
FIVE

Something claustrophobic lives in the New Orleans air. Now that I'm here, anticipation saturates my pores and nerves shake my bones.

My manager at the care home where I work was understanding of my need to take some more time following my dad's funeral. Luckily, my work comes with a prerequisite of compassion in its people. I was granted three weeks of leave, allowing me to spend Christmas, the best one I've had in years, with Tino and his wonderful family—although I'm plagued by guilt because I haven't spoken to my mother since the funeral. She isn't even aware I'm leaving the country, as any attempts to explain to her what I'm going through would have resulted in her having me committed.

The Ngoy family Christmas was a joy. I, a willing outsider, observed their easy happiness with glee. Luckily for me, Rose cooks enough food to feed a small army. She even bought me some last-minute presents. A thick cream cable-knit cardigan and a beautiful leather-bound notebook, which she encouraged me to write my thoughts in, telling me journaling helps her untangle her unquiet mind. I already miss her calming aura.

However, now that we're here in America, running away presents itself as a preferable plan. Communicating with my father where he is now is terrifying for so many reasons. That he may have nothing good to say is one thing. That the larger part of myself believes this is some kind of elaborate trick, a prank someone has organised to send me into a spiral revealing the craziness inside my soul ready to strike, makes it even scarier.

In the few days of waiting for our flight, the dead have been conspicuous in their absence. It's made me jumpy. I can't shake the feeling that I followed a wild-goose chase across the Atlantic and I *should* be committed.

Standing outside the Louis Armstrong Airport terminal, the cool winter air biting my cheeks, I think I might be sick.

Unsure of how to arrange my face, I approach two women holding a cardboard sign with my name on it. I'm not sure what I was expecting, but they aren't it. Tino gives me a furtive glance before also making his way over to them.

As we approach, one of the girls, Indian-looking with rich olive skin, shiny black hair, a short fringe, and wicked eyeliner, beams at me. She glances at my hair, then my face. 'I should have known,' she laughs. 'You can only be Lovely. The ginger gene is strong in the Timms family.'

For some reason, her words make my skin flush. Lorna's exuberant expression falters a fraction as I struggle to find any hint of my own voice. Saving me the trouble, she introduces us to her girlfriend, Lisette, who is shorter, curvy, with a cacophony of brown curls around her face, and has a thick Cajun accent. They're both gorgeous, their beauty matched only by the confidence they both radiate. As Tino introduces himself, unable to mask his own stunning presence, with his immaculate dark skin and hazel eyes that glitter at them, a sour flavour of intimidation tangs on my tongue.

Lorna rounds on me, full of expectation. Of course, she'd invited me here because she was a childhood friend of my cousin. From what I remember of him, he was full of life, quick to make friends with anyone. Nothing like me.

'Thank you doesn't begin to cover it,' I say, giving my gaze to my feet.

Lorna steps forward, reading my awkwardness, sliding her arm around my shoulders to lead me towards the car park. I resist the urge to shrug it off.

'It's great to have you here. We've been trying our best to do some research before you arrived. Marie—you'll meet her soon—told me it's unusual for someone to communicate with the dead without an instrument.'

'An instrument?' I peer into her honest brown eyes, searching for a sign that she's making fun of me.

If she notices my concern, she does nothing to give it away. Instead, she carries on following Lisette, who gives no indication that this is an unusual conversation. Tino walks at my side, listening with rapt attention.

'Yep, an instrument. A Ouija board is the most common type these days. Even then, not many people have the skill to use them in reality. It's not so much the board, you understand, but the planchette and the person.' She gives me a side glance, shaking her head. 'Sorry to ramble on. I don't mean to bore you. Marie is excited to meet someone with the ability to communicate without an instrument.'

'Oh.' Warmth spreads across my cheeks, and I pretend to find my shoes interesting. '"Communicate" is a bit of a stretch. Plagued by visions of them is a more accurate description. They don't speak.'

'Even so.' Lorna's expression turns contemplative as she reads my preoccupation with the ground. 'You're not used to this, are you? Speaking about your abilities?'

My voice becomes lost. The truth is, I hadn't anticipated a scenario where I might need to explain all that's happened to me—the accident along with everything since—as if they were facts.

'I guess I'm still waiting for the punchline. Wondering when you're going to tell me how this is all a mistake or a terrible joke. That obviously, there's no way to contact the dead, and this is all in my head.'

Lorna releases me as we close in on the car, her brow furrowed. 'Why would I do such a thing?'

'Because this oughtn't to be possible,' I want to answer. Another feeling nips at the edges of my being, an uncomfortable sensation akin to denial. In the face of all my awful recent years turning out to be real, there is this lingering sensation that what I might discover may be worse than mere madness.

Panic coming on, I glance to Tino for support, but I find my friend's expression bears more resemblance to shame.

'Because *we* didn't think it was real,' he explains to her, filling in my blanks for me. 'Lee wasn't born with ghosts following her. We grew up together, just like any normal kids. There was an accident, and then the visions came after. We believed they were a symptom of the lack of oxygen. The doctors explained it to her as brain damage. We're from a council estate in Birmingham. We don't have practitioners of the dead,' he scoffs. 'No one believed it was real. Even me. I didn't believe her.' He hangs his head. 'But Lee's dad passed, and when he returned as an apparition, everything changed. Now we need to know—*Lee* needs to know if there's something her dad needs from her.'

'Oh, you poor thing,' Lisette breathes, pulling me to her chest and hugging me tight, restricting my air. I rest my cheek on top of her head, her velvet-like hair forming a cushion. 'Don't worry, we're going to help you get the answers you need.'

The hot heat of tears rises, but I don't let them spill. I try not to let the ache in my heart split me in two. Where were these people four years ago? Lorna even knew my cousin.

'How did you get involved in all this stuff?' I ask to distract myself. 'If visions of the dead are unusual even within the world of the weird, why is this happening to me?'

Lisette releases me, raising a knowing eyebrow at Lorna, a gesture I fail to place. The expression causes a tingle of dread. Tino catches the exchange too.

'What? What was that?' he asks as Lisette disappears into the driver's seat.

Lorna almost rolls her eyes. 'Well, for starters, if the last few years of my life have taught me anything, it's this: anything's possible. Second, you're not the first unusual person I've met in the world of the weird. Believe me, he's weirder than you are.' She winks and vanishes into the passenger side.

Tino gives me a noncommittal shrug, and we follow suit, jumping into the rear of the car.

'You're friends with someone like me?' I ask.

'Not like you, per se, but different too. Only, he was born different. So your accident being a catalyst is interesting and something we'll have to talk to Marie about—what it means, if it means anything at all.' Lorna turns in her seat to direct her question. 'When was your accident, by the way?'

'Four years ago. I was seventeen at the time.'

In the rear-view mirror, I catch Lorna's eyes darting to Lisette, who returns the glance, something silent passing between them.

'What's wrong?' I press, my heart rate going double time. There's something they're not saying. Something that makes my skin feel too tight.

'It's nothing. Just interesting is all.'

'And your friend? Will I meet him too?'

A muscle in Lisette's neck twitches. Hurt dances in Lorna's expression, in the lines around her mouth, barely concealed. Her pain brushes the fringes of my body, a new sensation that I've never experienced before. It melts against my skin, and I shudder.

'I'm afraid not. He's missing in action, so to speak.'

Lisette gives Lorna's hand a reassuring squeeze as she puts the car in Drive. I want to ask more questions about her friend—how he's different, why he's missing—but I get the distinct sensation that it's a sore subject. I don't want to push the matter, as well as being certain I have no desire to relive the extreme wave of pain Lorna endured at his mention.

The New Orleans skyline is a wonder, the evening light starting to seep orange. It's such a beautiful place, like nowhere I've been before. When we used to go on family holidays when I was young, it was always to a beach.

'When did your friend go missing?' I find myself asking, still marvelling at the sunset.

'It was about six months ago now,' Lisette answers.

'I'm so sorry,' I say quietly. 'I hope you hear something soon.'

Lorna doesn't say anything, her jaw tensing. Lisette's glance towards her girlfriend betrays her nerves.

Biting my tongue, I fall into an awkward silence. I'm saying the wrong things, asking the wrong questions. Unsure as to why I have any empathy for her friend, I let out a long sigh. Maybe I feel a slight sense of recognition because he's different. I wonder about Lorna's pain over the subject and what events surrounded his going missing. Did someone take him? Or I could be reading the situation wrong. Could she have sent him away? Perhaps she's relieved he's gone, as I assume my parents were when I left. Lorna seems so open, but this is one door firmly locked shut and sheltered from the world.

'Hey.' Tino slides his hand into mine. 'Are you okay in there?'

I give the ghost of a smile. 'Getting there. Talking about this stuff as if it's normal is strange. Like the last four years haven't been a terrible hallucination.' I glance at Lorna, who is now in conversation with Lisette, before lowering my voice. 'Lorna's a friend of my cousin. If I had known her back then....'

'There's no use in dealing in what-ifs, Lee. We're here now, and that's what matters.'

But my whole world seems to have devolved into one giant what-if. If I'd have known my hauntings were real four years ago, who would I be now? I think of the things I've done and shudder. Those past acts that now lurk in the dark recesses of my mind are just as haunting as any ghost. Is there any way back from the person I very much am?

Lorna and Lisette's apartment, situated on the corner of a busy street above a bustling convenience store, is unlike any home I've come across in England. The kitchen and living area share the same space, the same as my tiny flat, but their space is light and airy with large windows and plantation shutters. The last trappings of light stream in, fractured by crystals hanging in the windows, sending rainbows of colour cascading around the room. Lots of potted plants line the windowsills, and some unpacked boxes are still strewn around the place. The apartment itself is sparse of furniture; a round black coffee table sits in the centre of the living space in front of a low grey couch, a range of books stacked high on either side forming little makeshift side tables. Some have scary titles concerning the occult, while others are beautiful collectors' editions of Jane Austen or Oscar Wilde interspersed with some trashy-looking romances. A weird mix.

'Have you guys just moved in?' Tino asks, taking in the new surroundings, clearly also finding the space lacking in belongings.

Lisette nods, beaming at her girlfriend. 'Almost two months now.'

Tino's gaze flits between them, a tiny tennis match of sorts, both of us realising in unison that they're very much in the honeymoon stage of a relationship. 'Congrats,' he says with a grin.

A wave of guilt crests through me. I'm bringing baggage to their door. 'Sorry to be troubling you both with this. I'm sure you'd rather be enjoying your new place.'

'Please.' Lorna closes the distance between us and rubs my shoulders. 'I asked you to come. Seriously, things are way too quiet around here anyway. We moved out of Lisette's old place because we were driving her roommate crazy.' She laughs, her whole face lighting up. 'You'll meet her soon. But I'm sure you guys want to rest. We'll make some dinner, give you some time to unpack. We only have one spare room, if you don't mind sharing?'

My insides turn to ice as I freeze, the handle of my bag slipping through my fingers before clattering to the floor. Even Tino appears shocked at the terror radiating from my expression.

'Oh, I'm sorry,' Lorna says. 'I assumed you two....' She trails off.

Assumed we were what? Together? Colour floods my face.

'It's okay,' Tino laughs, moving to give the cushions on the couch a dramatic squeeze, trying to give the illusion of cheeriness. 'Even more comfy than my own bed.'

His tone betrays the tension there, a slight sting where I've wounded him.

More guilt. 'I'm sorry.' My apology dies on my lips. So stupid of me. It never crossed my mind to ask about the sleeping arrangements, but the idea of sharing a bed with Tino fills me with dread over how his eyes might roam my skin in the dark when I'm at my most vulnerable.

Lisette chimes in, 'Marie has space. One of you could settle in over there? I'm sure she won't mind.'

'It's no trouble,' Tino assures her, his acquiescence far more genuine this time. 'I'm fine on the sofa.'

Lorna and Lisette exchange a wide-eyed glance meant only for each other. For some reason it makes my skin crawl. They believe me when I say I have visions of the dead—however, when they're actually in my presence, they perceive me as strange.

I take my bags to the spare room for a moment of refuge. Sitting on the edge of the bed, I stare at the wall, glad of a few moments alone. I hope Tino isn't offended by my reaction at the notion of sleeping next to him. For him it might be an easy arrangement. Why would he care about resting side by side with a person he's been friends with since childhood? My own foolish brain can't help but contemplate all the girls he might have slept next to.

Lorna peeps around the door. 'Everything all right?'

'Of course.' I smooth my palms over the soft sheets. 'My fault for overreacting. Intimacy is a little scary for me. I don't like being touched,' I lie.

Lorna lets out a relieved breath. 'I'll have to bear that in mind. I'm a pretty tactile person myself. Please let me apologise. I assumed you and Tino were in a relationship. My mistake for not clarifying.'

'It's okay.'

Lorna tentatively moves into the room. The scrutiny of her gaze makes me uncomfortable, so I stare at the beige paint of the wall again. Beige paint jars against Lorna's psyche, in my opinion.

'You're pretty closed off, aren't you?'

The directness of her question throws me off, forcing me to meet her round brown eyes again, the hint of a smile always on her lips.

'I guess it comes with my illness.'

She chuckles a little, sitting next to me and bringing her feet under herself to better appraise me. 'My friend who I told you about before—he was the same, to some extent. There was always some secret he was keeping, always something he wouldn't say.'

My heart thumps in my chest.

She continues, 'I guess what I want to say is, it's okay to trust people sometimes. His secrets never did him any favours. Trouble followed him everywhere.' The warmth of nostalgia blooms across her face.

'Sounds about right,' I laugh, the tension in my muscles easing. She's too easy to be around.

'But—' She leans forward as if peering into my very soul. '—even he had someone. You're around friends, Lovely. It's okay for you to rely on others.'

Against my wishes, tears rise.

CHAPTER
SIX

The scene before me is unlike anywhere I've seen before, the dark interior at odds with the glistening daylight streaming in through the shop windows. Crystals line the shelves, decks of tarot cards are laid in elaborate displays, Ouija boards are stacked in boxes, and voodoo dolls of different shapes sewn in bright shades with contrasting stitched eyes adorn the shelves. The shop is warm. A sweet scent of incense hangs heavy in the air.

The absence of the haunting dead these past few weeks has instilled a nervousness in me, as if some unknown entity looms on the horizon. Despite the heady atmosphere of the shop, my bones shake within me. My regard is drawn to the shop's patroness standing behind the counter, her hair in short braids, her skin dark and cheekbones angled to the point of being dangerous. Yet she appears a tad angelic in a black top with long bell sleeves, her ears decorated with silver piercings.

'This is Marie, Lovely.' Lorna gives me a gentle shove further into the shop.

Tino sticks by my side while Lisette strides over to Marie to plant a kiss on her cheek in greeting. 'Marie, this is Lovely, who we've already spoken about. And Tino, her friend.'

Marie beams at us both, dropping into a sort of curtsy. 'I hope I'll be of guidance. It's a rare thing to meet someone in touch with the other side.'

She extends both hands to me, her eyes dazzling and expectant. Hesitating for a fraction of a second, I then offer her my own slender fingers. Not wasting a moment, she turns them over in hers, then sets about examining my palms, her brow furrowing as she caresses the lines in my skin.

'I'm hardly in touch with it,' I try to joke, my trembling hands betraying me. 'It springs itself on me from time to time.'

Tino offers a nervous grin, instilling a modicum of confidence in me.

'So much pain,' Marie whispers. 'Yet—' She smooths the deep line from my middle finger to my pinkie. '—there's deep love here also.'

A snort escapes, surprising me. Palm reading is as crackpot as I've always believed it to be. The brusque noise startles the woman cradling my hand.

'You don't believe me?'

'I mean no disrespect. My life has nothing close to a "deep love." I've been on my own for years,' I explain, unable to bring myself to chance meeting Tino's eyes. We only lost touch for little more than a year, but my isolation spans much longer than those twelve months. Though I've never been aware of Tino's relationships, my treacherous brain imagines all the girls he must have touched tenderly in all the ways I haven't been.

She softens. 'You're still young.'

Unsure how the topic of conversation has steered towards my love life, I give her a noncommittal gesture, the flush flaring through me unexpected and wholly unwelcome. I search for Lorna, hoping she'll save me from dying of embarrassment.

'Where do we start?' Lorna asks Marie, holding in her amusement.

'The space has been prepared. You carry on.'

I follow Lorna behind the counter and through a door as Marie turns the Open sign of the shop to Closed before locking the front door. Tino brings up the rear as we make our way upstairs to an apartment much bigger than Lorna's and filled with stuff. A large coffee table is surrounded by a plump sage green sofa and two gorgeous high-backed Chesterfield armchairs. There are four large windows with overflowing boxes of fragrant flowers and fruit climbing the inner wooden frames. A dining table is situated under one of the large windows, holding at least twenty burning church candles that illuminate the space, as the shutters have been drawn, throwing into relief the occult artwork that adorns the walls.

In the middle of the coffee table is a worn-out Ouija board adorned with a sun and moon in the two top corners, the black lettering faded. Dread washes over my skin at the sight of it.

Tino stops at my side. When my eyes meet his, panic overcomes me. 'This is a bad idea,' I whisper to him.

'Do you want to leave?'

Nausea rolling round my stomach in torrents, I move to make a sharp exit.

Marie's voice comes from behind me. 'Tell me,' she intones, 'how is it you died?'

Her words send a rush of adrenaline through my system. I'm frozen in horror. All I do is stare, choking on my words the way I once choked on water. She moves around me into the room to study me better.

'How do you know such a thing?' Tino asks from beside me, accusation pulsing through his tone as he tilts his face towards Lorna and Lisette. 'Did Lorna tell you?'

'Death is clear in her palm.' She gestures towards my shaking fingers. 'A rebirth will sometimes cause an individual to return different.'

Tino positions himself a little in front of me, as if to protect me from Marie's appraisal.

'Your fingers are long, your skin clammy. Your natural element is water, but if I had to guess, I'd say you drowned.'

My breath jitters out of me, and my head swims to

such an extent that I have to lean my forehead onto Tino's shoulder to steady myself, but Marie steps around him.

'When I was seventeen,' I confirm. "In the sea off the coast of Wales."

'What do you recall of it? Of the other side?'

Tino evades her pacing, keeping the barrier of his body against me as my words come out with a tremble.

'Nothing. There was only pain. Water filling my lungs,' I reply, placing a steadying palm on Tino, who becomes still. 'The next thing I knew, I was on the beach, ice cold, shivering but alive. They tell me I was gone for three minutes.'

Marie stares hard at me for a moment. Minute vibrations reverberate at her edges, something which scares me while drawing me to her at the same time.

'There is what we know and what we *think* we know,' she says after a pause.

'You don't believe me?'

'I believe you do not want to remember.'

I try to protest, to explain that I have brain damage from the lack of oxygen, but she raises a hand to stop me. 'I understand some gifts are hard to accept.'

'Gifts?' The notion of my torture being a gift makes me want to scream. 'Marie, this is no gift. It's a nightmare, a living nightmare. The dead are here to torment me for not dying. They are angry, so angry, because they have been torn out of this world. They want to bring me down with them. The dead hate me for being alive!'

My chest heaves, and the hint of a smile pulls at Marie's lips as I clasp my palm over my mouth so hard, the slap reverberates around the apartment. My eyes widen, and Marie lets out a laugh. Being here, with her, this practitioner, the barriers to the known world and the unknown are already beginning to break down around me.

'You're aware of more than you wish to believe. It's a case of accepting it.' She turns serious. 'My dear, what else were you to do? Just acknowledge your ability to speak to the dead and carry on with your life as before? You protected yourself, built walls, told yourself a story of who you are, someone who has brain damage whose visions aren't real. Because despite how much the lie hurts you, it makes more sense than reality.'

The dangerous promise in her words almost causes me to demand that she stop. Part of me wishes more than anything for her to cease, while the other part, the side that longs to not be afraid, to not be broken or weak, wills her on. Fear has lived in my veins for so long, I worry about jumping off this precipice and embracing a world of the dead. There'll be no going back. However, continuing to drown in denial isn't a life worth clutching at.

Marie draws next to me, coaxing, 'If you want answers, you must be open to them. Because the reality —your reality, Lovely—is that you died. Your own eyes have viewed the marvels of the other side. It's okay to *remember*.'

The moment stretches on, but no light switch is flipped. The pain in my chest doesn't ease. I remain scared and alone, wondering if I'm crazy.

'Those memories are lost to me.' My words come heavy with apology.

'Open yourself to this world.'

She takes my elbow, leading me further into the apartment and ushering me closer to the coffee table, where Lorna and Lisette are sitting cross-legged. Marie positions me, then motions for Tino to sit opposite. He's pretty pale, too, his vision fixed on the Ouija board. Marie sits in front of the board, taking her time, giving her attention to each of us in turn and surrounding the board with an airy sort of omniscience before settling her sights on me.

'You are here to speak with your father?'

I agree with an incline of my head, not daring to speak.

'What was his name?'

'Isaac Timms.'

Marie takes something metal out of her pocket. It has a large hole in the middle and rubies encrusted around it. She weighs it with care in her palms before turning to me and Tino in turn. Our other companions need no instruction.

'Rest your fingers lightly on the planchette and embrace the fluidity of the moment. The spirits will flow through it. I alone will harness their energy. You're in no danger here, Lovely. Let me do the talking. If anyone breaks contact, my connection to the spirits will be lost. Do you understand?'

We comply. Tino's visage matches how I feel, a satin sheen of sweat beading on his skin. My stomach's a raging storm, crashing about like an ocean. Yet I comply, placing my fingers on the planchette, expecting to be drawn in by some cosmic connection in the moment. But rather than cosmic connection, when the skin of my digits touches metal, my clammy fingers slip upon the smooth surface. Lorna, Lisette, and Tino all follow suit, everyone's focus fixed on Marie. She rests her fingers on her instrument with a tentative grace, drawing a deep breath before closing her eyes. I find myself doing the same.

'Carline? Are you there?' she calls out, hints of a French accent more pronounced now that I'm deprived of sight.

No visions appear before me, and only the throbbing of my own heart thrums in my ears. My lips part in the barest gasp at the infinitesimal movements beneath our fingertips. When I gather the courage to peer at the board, catching the planchette slide to *Yes*, Marie radiates with an unearthly satisfaction.

Marie continues, keeping her voice clear. 'We search through the ether for one called Isaac Timms. We believe he lingers between the planes. Come, spirit—your daughter is here.'

The metal vibrates through me, sending a chill over my body right through to my bones. I peek around to check if anyone else has felt it, but they're all staring at the planchette. A woody scent fills my nostrils, something in my brain recognising the name of it as Amyris, and I hear the crackling of fire as the plant is ground to extract the oil. Something old. A memory of a bygone time.

Engrossed in a memory not my own, my attention is distracted from the planchette, which is on the move again.

'Halfway?' Marie asks. 'Isaac Timms is halfway?'

The planchette moves to *Yes* again.

'Halfway? What does it mean?' I ask, pushing the scent away from me.

Marie frowns. 'I'm not sure. Messages from the other side are not always clear. We need to ask the right questions. Can he be reached?' she pushes.

The planchette vibrates again, and the smell of sandalwood almost overwhelms me along with the fire's smoke, making my eyes water. The planchette moves, the vibration combined with my clammy fingers making it arduous to hold on to.

H – E

H – A – S

A

M – E – S – S – A – G – E

F – O – R

H – E – R

'He has a message for Lovely?'

The planchette moves to *Yes*.

'Deliver the message,' Marie instructs.

R – U – N

R – U – N

R – U – N

The planchette rushes wildly across the board. Our chests heave as it spells *run* on loop.

'Carline, stop!' Marie commands.

The planchette immediately stops in the middle of the board, the vibration making my bones shake, the smell of fire and Amyris getting to be almost too much. My brain is swimming in memory: the villagers came to her, and she is making something with the Amyris—a potion.

'We wish to talk with Isaac,' Marie demands.

The planchette is on the move again. My vision is still clouded with wetness through the clinging smoke as I struggle to view what is being spelled.

H – E

I – S

C – O – M – I – N – G

The earth shudders. Tilts. My vision is vibrating, the smell of smoke evaporating.

'No!' Whipping my hands away, I sever the connection with my recoil.

All eyes turn to me in alarm.

'We were getting somewhere,' Marie laments.

'Lee?' Tino is on his feet, staring on in horror.

Scrambling to stand, I try to steady myself. The shaking walls of my vision are all an illusion, yet the sliding sensation has me in a chokehold as I stumble away from the group. There isn't much time, and I have nowhere to hide. Frantic, I attempt to get a grip on something solid. All too late—the world has gone underwater.

He shimmers into view. Drenched, skin blue and fingertips dripping. Cowering, I manage to skuttle into a corner, my knees hunched in front of me. I don't want this vision, his empty expression, his open mouth.

No.

'Lee. Lee!' Tino is in front of me, grabbing my hands, holding so tight, it might crush my bones.

Marie slides next to him, her presence made known to me when she attempts to wrench my head from my knees. 'Is he here? Right now?'

I nod into my knees until I see stars. Though he's not currently in my line of vision, his being here sinks into my skin, where his death slides cold beneath my flesh.

'Talk to him. Listen to me, Lovely. Speak with your father.'

Shaking so much that breathing becomes difficult, I lift my head a fraction to meet Tino's panic-stricken eyes that are quickly replaced by Marie's fierce ones. I force my head high and compel myself to witness the awful apparition before me.

The ghost of my father.

A sob escapes my lips, tearing at my chest. 'W-What do you want?' I manage.

My dad's lips part to speak, to tell me what has kept him from going on and finding peace. When he opens his mouth, instead of words, dreaded water bubbles out in a stream.

Terror washes through me. My teeth chatter, icy fingers clawing at my throat, robbing me of my breath.

I drown.

I drown.

I drown.

It's not real.

It's not real.

It's not real.

Desperate, I bury my eyes in my knees again. *I'm crazy. I can't talk to the dead. This isn't my dad.* I never got to reconcile with him. I caused him so much pain.

My own tears cascade out of me.

Hands pull me to my feet, and I sag into them.

Against every instinct, I force myself to face the apparition once again. Drawing myself upright, I peel back my lids and become captured by my father's gaze. His expression filled with fear, sorrow drips from his pores. Swallowed by guilt, I tremble.

'Daddy?'

It's a name I haven't called him since I was a girl. At the expression of tenderness, I witness a change in him, watch as his spirit, his soul, takes a swallow of air, clearing his water-clogged throat. He staggers towards me, transforming into a figure resembling a little more the father who lives in my memories.

'Lovely.' His voice is underwater, too, but he now has words, at least. 'He's coming for you. You s-should run.'

'I-I don't understand,' I stutter. 'Who's coming for me?'

Tears of decaying water drip along the cheeks of my father's spirit. 'I'm so sorry—for everything. I'm glad I have this chance to tell you I love you. I always loved you and I'm so sorry.'

Wishing to hug him one last time, I stumble forward. My open arms swipe air.

He's gone.

CHAPTER SEVEN

My heart hammers, a caged bird desperate to escape, as I stare at the spot where my dad stood. Where he spoke to me. I'm falling. Falling on my feet. Tino's saying something to me, but his words are lost in my ears. Marie stands in front of me, her palms clasping onto my shoulders. I wish they weren't.

My dad was here.

He spoke.

The dead speak to me. No longer awful spectres bent on mere haunting, they have words, a purpose, a need.

My dad was always so alive until the cancer claimed him. He had deep lines at the corners of his mouth evidencing his smile, electric blue irises, trademark flaming red Timms hair. Squeezing my eyes shut, I imagine him pulling me into a hug while I wrap my arms around myself.

'I always loved you. I'm so sorry.'

Needing to be far from this place, I dart out the door and race through Marie's shop until my feet are hitting the New Orleans pavement as fast as they'll take me. Giving no thought to those stood shocked at my retreating figure as Tino calls out behind me, I plunge deep into the crowd. Though the day has turned dreary, the weak sun's an assault after the dark of Marie's flat.

Before long, my name dies in the breeze. I've lost him. Clutching my hands to my chest to keep my insides from spilling out into the dimming streets, I flee further from my friends.

My brain is a riot, remembering how my dad appeared like I've never witnessed one of the dead before. Talking, weeping. But it wasn't better. It wasn't closure.

Suddenly, the relief of being believed doesn't ring true, and I wish to take it back. I want it to be a figment of my imagination. I do not want this. I don't want the reality of being not only a haunted person but also charged with some otherworldly mission.

I don't want to see them.

Hear them.

The fact that they're real, and even in death are plagued by pain, makes it worse.

They need to go away.

I turn down a narrow alley, kicking glass bottles. I trip, stumble before falling to my knees, and the sharp pain of grazing my palms on the rough ground brings tears to the surface that have nothing to do with physical pain. I don't have the energy to get to my feet, to fight the tears. I let the sobs escape me, shoving my back to a filthy wall. Tears fall in torrents, hitting the tops of my knees. What I wouldn't give to not be myself anymore.

A rough American accent sounds above me. 'You okay there, miss?'

Removing my eyes from my knees, I peer into a not unkind face, tattoos adorning his rugged skin. His gaze rakes over my long, unruly hair, tear-stained face, and trembling hands. He crouches to draw level with me before glancing to the busy street bustling metres from where I'm slumped in the alley.

'You should be careful around here,' he says, his voice hard, the words a borderline threat.

Somehow his harshness is easier to deal with than any kindness that Tino has so far offered me. I lean my head against the alley wall, wiping the tears from my face. 'I'm in pain,' I tell him. 'I want it to stop. Will you help me?' My voice is dry, and my pulse does a double beat over what I'm asking, horror and hope in the pure desire that overwhelms my frayed nerve endings.

He stares, working his jaw. 'What is it you want?'

'Heroin.' I swallow. "Anything."

'Shit,' he utters under his breath, stroking the back of his head. He gives me another once-over. 'Sure. I'll be your hero.'

Relief coupled with fear floods my body, though I'm too far gone to change my mind. Desire for it flares inside my chest. To be numb. To shut off what I am, forget who I am.

I get to my feet as he straightens his stance. He's as tall as me, his gaze continuing to roam my body in greedy lust. I recall how I fled Marie's apartment without any of my stuff.

'I don't have any money,' I tell him with hollow words.

He runs a hand over his mouth, stepping a pace away to take stock of my body. His gaze is ravenous in a way I'm familiar with, though it never fails to make my skin crawl.

'You want to work something out?' His face cracks with devious intent as he motions for me to follow him into the depths of the alley.

This is good. I begin the mental process of disconnecting, erecting walls in my brain. Shutting myself down piece by piece so my body will comply, doing what needs to be done so I may get what I long for—peace. My body is not my own. It's a tool to be used.

Life's better when you feel nothing, Lovely.

This relief is a weird thing. It brings with it a strange sense of familiarity. To regress, returning to a time when the dead weren't real. Only a fool believes they may claw themselves free of the nightmare of their fate. Instead, it's one hell for another. At least *this* damnation is one I'm accustomed to.

Following a little behind as he takes corner after corner, I don't bother attempting to memorise the way we came. Where we're going is even more grey than the dying day. Dreary, piss-stinking, rubbish-filled alleyways pass beneath my unsteady footsteps until we come to the entrance of another street, where he talks to someone standing on the corner. They glance in my direction for a second before giving him a nod and slipping something into his palm. My veins burn for it.

His body half turned to mine, his face cracks in a menacing grin as he drinks in the greed of my consuming need for what he holds. His fingers clamp on the tender skin of my underarm, claiming me. 'I know a place,' he says, leading me forward.

When I shrug out of his grip, he observes me out of the corner of his eye. 'You're not from here, are you?'

I shake my head.

'What's your story?'

'I don't have one.'

My gaze fixes on my feet, and he laughs. It's a grating kind of guffaw. Pushing me up a nearby flight of stairs, he trails me so close that his hot breath tickles the back of my neck. 'Do you have a name?'

'Love,' I tell him, because it's a lie close enough to the truth. Giving him my full name adds to the violation, while telling him *Lee*, which is what Tino has always called me, is inconceivable. *I'm a different person*, I tell myself.

'Your name is Love?'

'Correct.'

'Great name.'

Not earning a response, he reaches past me to open the door to a dingy apartment smelling of cigarette smoke, the walls starting to yellow, all the shutters drawn. A heavy-set man lounges on the sofa, watching a game show on the television, volume turned up. He doesn't acknowledge us, just says, 'Grey.'

The guy I'm with, Grey, glances around. 'Which room is free?'

'Two,' he tells him without taking his eyes off the television.

Grey nods, already leading me to a bedroom, although to name it a bedroom is being generous. It has stripped-back wooden floors, a small bedside table, and a single mattress in the corner. I stride into the centre, then turn to look at him, testing the walls in my mind, detaching myself from my body.

Curiosity seeps out of Grey. 'Are you a lost soul, Love?'

His stance is firm by the door, blocking any escape. I remind myself this is where I belong.

In hell.

'Do you have it?' I ask him.

'You first.' He gestures to the mattress behind me.

As a sign of good faith, I suppose, he takes the small packet out of his pocket and places it on the table by the mattress. He approaches, cautious, his hands raised while my stomach twists. 'You look like you should be full of fire,' he whispers, twisting a tendril of my hair that has fallen around my face.

'Sorry to disappoint you.' I steel my heart, my fingers fumbling to unbutton my shirt, but I falter. 'I have scars.'

His eyes fixed on my fingers, he whispers, 'I'd be more surprised if you didn't.'

I tell myself this won't be that bad. He's allowing me to undress at my pace, at least, not pawing at my clothes, not tearing them. I've lived through worse humiliation. He won't be so harsh. And I disconnect. Tell myself I don't feel it. I won't feel it.

My focus is somewhere else, pinned to a cracked point on the wall, while I stand bare before him. I tell myself I don't notice him looking at my scars. Pretend my pulse is steady while his instructions remain distant as I lie down on the mattress. *What I'm allowing is worth it. What I will gain will make it worth it.*

My gaze remains on the crack in the wall. I become one with the dark crevice, allowing myself to fall far into the well of lies which I tell myself. *I don't feel his palms against my skin. I don't notice him pushing my face into the mattress. It's not his quickening pants condensing against the skin of my neck. In fact, I don't feel him at all.*

The walls of my mind remain strong, keeping Grey and what he's doing out. Only glimpses of Tino creep in, which serve more to make my heart ache, not my body. I push out all memories of the dead reaching out to me in their desperation, as well as my father's declaration of love. I disconnect until the next thing I allow myself to be aware of is sweet oblivion running through my veins. There's no escaping this bliss.

At some point, Grey leaves me still naked on the mattress, lingering somewhere between worlds. But the pain's gone. There's only numbness. There's nothing else. Rolling over, I fall into a deep sleep.

Grey visits me in my dreams. He's telling me how I'm safe here, that he'll take care of me. The sunshine in my veins makes me believe him. The next time someone comes into the room, it's not Grey but someone much taller. Heavier.

Through the glorious haze, a different sort of dread sets in.

My limbs are leaden as the stranger's weight shifts onto the mattress, and I'm too clumsy to make any attempt to escape. Not fully in control of my actions, my hands flail, wild as this new man seeks to pin them above my head. My nails connect with skin, scraping my attacker's face, and I'm rewarded with the sharp sting of a slap across my cheek that knocks me half unconscious.

The fight leaves me, along with my chance of building my walls of disconnection. The pain is quick and brutal. Squeezing my eyes shut, I lie once more, tell myself none of this matters. My body is not my own. Yet tears escape. He's too substantial and solid on top of me to allow me to pretend. I feel what's happening all too much.

Grey returns when it's over to find me whimpering. He doesn't touch me again, just gives me more to take away the pain.

My dreams transport me to the water, where the hands which slide across my skin are not calloused and rough and unwelcome but cool and caressing. My name is being called, and it's heavenly. I want to follow—trail its call into the depths of the ocean.

Awaking with a jolt, I'm alone in the dark. Although they're invisible to me, bruises blossom across my skin, their ache echoing in places I wish to ignore, my limbs too hazy to move. My naked body prickles with cold. As I peer into the dark, the shape of the cabinet next to me takes on a ghostlike appearance. I trace my fingers across its grainy texture to ensure it's real.

Another crash from the next room tells me what's woken me. Angry yells, then a woman's voice rings out in distress, followed by a loud, painful slap. Something breaks, and the woman's sobs reverberate through the thin walls. I scramble into a sitting position, fear snapping through me as I clutch the thin sheet over my bare skin, still barely able to view anything in the dark.

A gunshot is fired, and fear swallows me whole. My feet are unstable beneath my weight as I attempt to stand, the remnants of my last hit floating in my veins. Who knows how much time has passed?

Light pours in through the door as a man I've never

met before bursts in, taking in the sight of me cowering on the mattress. Striding across the room to point a gun at my head, he's wild and furious. Grey rushes in behind him, shouting, 'No!' and pushing his gun-wielding hand to the ceiling. The pistol goes off. A smoking hole is left in the wall next to me. I scream, dropping my useless sheet. My knees give way, and I collapse to the mattress, covering my ears, the ringing and terror pulsing through me.

Forcing myself to raise my head, I watch as the gun-wielding man hits Grey with the butt of his weapon, sending him flying into the wall before unloading a bullet into his chest. I scream again—scream and scream. It's a foolish thing to do. The man rounds on me, his pace too confident and slow, his heavy boots ominous as I push myself away to cower against the wall. He lowers himself to my level, his gun-free fingers snatching my face so I'm forced to meet his glare, shaking with such violence that his face vibrates in front of me.

'Aren't you a pretty thing?' His expression turns malevolent as his eyes explore my exposed body, the scars on my arms. 'How poetic, to take one of Grey's girls.' Forcing me to my feet, he growls, 'I own you now.'

His grin is pure evil.

He pushes his mouth onto mine. Tasting smoke, I resist with everything I have, clawing at him until he's shoving his gun into my mouth. Blinking rapid fire, the tears stream down my face as he snarls at me, 'Stop fighting, or I'll shoot you in the face.'

So I stop. When I hear him unzipping, I try to close my eyes, but he commands me to open them. There's no disconnecting from this—the light is too bright. I am spilling terror. My vision has nowhere else to land except to stare into his triumphant, sadistic expression, which is consumed with fury and the desire to witness the exact moment he claims my body reflected in my own, to observe that pain while I still have his gun in my mouth.

I'm going to die—this time in a manner so very far from the blackness of drowning.

This death will be harsh with garish colour and violent presence.

An even brighter light flies through the room, sparking against us, sending my would-be rapist on top of me with all his weight, the gun sliding further into my mouth, making me gag. His expression becomes dazed as an invisible force flings him off me. Too quick for him to get his bearings, he's hurled again into a wall with a crunch, freeing me from him.

Relief washes over me to have him away from my vulnerable, exposed body, but the light's still too accusing on my skin. It takes a minute to blink in that Marie is the one seemingly holding my attacker to the wall by an invisible force. A second minute to register Tino's fist clocking him hard around the face.

Tino's here.

The fury in his face dies the instant he turns to me, stumbling to his knees.

'Lee.' My name cracks in his mouth, though his eyes don't meet mine. Instead, they roam the wrecked state of my body. The emotion clinging to my friend is not the same as Grey's or my attacker's. There's no desire in him, only pity.

I sob.

The sound, more animal than human, rips through my chest as Tino covers me with the sheet before taking off his hoodie and wrapping it around my shoulders with care, allowing me to slide my arms inside. His freshly laundered smell fills my nostrils, making me cry even harder.

'It's okay. I've got you.' His voice is the gentlest whisper as he slides his arms underneath me to lift me from what the light reveals to be a filthy mattress.

Clutching the front of his T-shirt with so much desperation, my nails rip straight through it, I bury my head in his shoulder.

'I don't want to die,' I wail, still tasting gunmetal in my mouth, the bruising of the heavy man who came to my room lingering on my thighs, the sensation of Grey pushing my face to the mattress. I weep.

Grey remains slumped on the floor, bleeding out. Marie calls 911 for an ambulance before we sweep out of the apartment with me in Tino's arms, crying into his shoulder, 'I'm so scared of living with what I have, but I don't want to die, Tee.'

CHAPTER EIGHT

My aching muscles are sunk into the comfy mattress, a thick blanket causing my blood to boil as I come round in a daze, my hair plastered to my forehead. I blink in my blurry surroundings, trying to recall what happened. Tino's face comes into view, his amber-hazel eyes peering at me, his palm searing as he smooths the hair from my face.

'Lee.' He says my name with such delicacy, as if it's a delicious secret.

My stomach rolls. 'I'm going to be sick.'

Lurching forward, I find Tino is prepared, moving a bucket in front of me to empty my guts into. Heavens, my insides are so hollow, I can't imagine what I have left inside me.

My head lolls about. I allow it to crash with a dull thud onto the pillow, and I fall back under.

Waking again, I discover it must be morning. The sunlight glows against the shutters.

Reaching my arms into a glorious stretch, I soak in my surroundings. I'm snug in the luxurious double bed in my room in Lorna and Lisette's apartment. Tino is asleep in the armchair in the corner.

As if sensing me rousing, he follows suit, giving me a sleepy smile. Despite everything, all the aches and pains in my muscles, the smile of my friend warms me.

He gets to his feet and comes to sit on the edge of the bed, his face soft with sympathy.

'Have you been watching over me?' I croak.

'I was so worried.' He glances at my open hand but doesn't take it. 'How are you feeling now?'

'Hungry,' I murmur, sure the empty pit in my stomach is hunger. It's always hunger.

'Shall I check if the girls have something to rustle up?'

I take a moment to allow my emotions to swallow me rather than put up my constant fight with sensation. I almost died. Again. This time through my own stupid decision. Defying death, living with this power, is my only option, I can't continue to block it out. Finding a way forward is a must. To accept the cards I've been dealt while figuring out what it means. If it has a meaning at all.

While that thought, a will to live, is something to

cling on to, the remnants of poison fizz around my edges, adding to my hollowness. I have to avert my gaze from Tino's, recalling what he dragged me out of. Tears rise, unstoppable, and my words bubble on my lips. 'I cannot.... I can't even begin to say how sorry I am....' My breath becomes hard to catch.

'Hey...,' he starts, trying to take my hand, though I withdraw it to swipe at incessant tears. 'We pushed you too soon. Let me get something for you to eat. You'll feel better then.'

'No.' My words border on slurred, thick with crying. 'I need to eat a *lot*. More than is fair to ask them to make.'

'Then I'll go get you something. Whatever you want.'

He smiles, and I force myself to give him a weak one in return. The lingering effects of the drugs make it hard for me to lift my head, so I keep it sunk in the soft pillow. Knowing what I'm about to say will not be pretty, I tell him, 'I need fast food. Burgers, chips—or fries, I guess—lots of them. Ten burgers, with cheese.' My stomach rumbles. 'At *least* ten burgers, with fries. And anything else that's fried. Maybe some ice cream, too, or a milkshake, plus a Coke.'

Tino's eyes widen.

'You said whatever I want,' I remind him, my voice quiet.

He only nods before he goes to find me a gargantuan amount of food.

As soon as he's gone, I lean over the side of the bed and vomit all over the floor. My head spins, and I'm so weak that I don't have much choice but to fall back into my pillows and swiftly lose consciousness.

When I come to, the room is dimly lit by the table lamp, and the sick is gone. Now the nausea I feel has everything to do with shame.

Tino peeps his head through the door. 'You're awake.'

'I'm so embarrassed.' My voice is a scratchy mess, like nails on a chalkboard. 'Did you...?'

He shakes his head, not letting me finish. 'Lorna. She said she volunteers at the homeless shelter and has seen far worse.'

'I'm worthless.' I cover my face with my palms.

'You're so not.'

I drop my hands to stare at my friend. He hasn't the faintest idea what he's talking about.

'So,' he says after a time, 'your food went cold.'

'It doesn't matter. I'll eat it all.' He turns to leave, but I stop him short. 'And thank you. For the food and... before.'

When he returns with three bags of food, I munch through burger after burger with a skilled methodology. *God, it's so good to be eating.* We don't talk. Tino sits on the bed, a casual observer, as I devour the massive amount of food. His eyes are tinged with alarm as I near the end of my feast, tipping the last dregs of the ice cream straight out of the tub and into my mouth. Strangely, I'm not embarrassed about consuming so much food in front of him. It's more like relief, allowing him to witness a side of me which I've tried to keep so hidden.

I wipe my mouth before studying him, readying myself for whatever words of reproach he's going to send my way.

'I didn't get you enough,' he says instead, his concerned expression trailing over the mountain of burger wrappers covering my bed.

A real laugh escapes my lips. 'You brought me enough, Tee. I'd never stop eating if you let me carry on.' But his serious visage remains. 'I actually enjoy the food. It's a compulsion, for sure, but also…. It's hard to explain. I feel weak when I don't eat that much—like after having died and come back to life, I need to eat everything to keep my body going. It's as if having a near-death experience triples your required calorie intake.'

I stare at him as he digests the words. I surprised myself with how easily they came. Marie's earlier words ring true. *'There is what we know and what we* think *we know.'*

'Thank you for sharing that,' he says softly, his eyes falling to my arm, my scars on display. There's no point hiding them any longer—he's seen me naked now. My cheeks redden at the memory, all my vulnerability exposed for him to view. How I clung to him so hard, I tore his shirt.

'We should talk about what happened,' he prompts.

'Do we have to?' I whisper.

With the gentlest motion, he slides a forefinger across the smooth surface of one of the scars. The simple caress sends goose bumps all over my body, and I move my arm out of his reach. 'You did those to yourself?'

As I confirm the truth, my attention stays firmly on him, cataloguing his reaction. He sniffs.

'The pain has had to come out, one way or another.' I bite my lip. 'Tee, I've spent four years believing I should have died that day. I've been doing anything to keep the dead at bay, to run away from the pain. Running's no longer an option. I must figure this out. What's happening, and why is it happening to me?'

Tino nods, moving again to slide his fingers into mine. Though he means comfort, his sympathy is unbearable. I snatch my hand away. 'Don't,' I tell him, keeping my voice steady. 'I don't want your sympathy. I've done horrible things.'

Chancing a glance at him, I find devastation written across his face. 'I wish I'd been there, to protect you. I've failed you.'

Disbelieving, I lurch even further forward, slamming my hand to my chest. 'This blame is my own. I made these decisions. I need to live with what I've done.'

He moves closer, cupping my face with his warm palm. 'Let me take it all away for you, replace all of those horrible memories—replace them with something good.'

His eyes burn into mine, my protector, but right now, I can't bear the gentle movement of his skin against my own. It's too painful. I push his caress away.

'Tino, stop. This body—' I motion towards my exhausted limbs reclining in bed, now comfy in cosy pyjamas. '—it's beyond broken. I've filled it with poison, whored it for the stuff, to keep me in a stupor so I could be rid of the wretched things I felt. How can you bear to touch me, knowing what I've done?'

He recoils, horror tracing the planes of his face.

Now that I've started, saying the words out loud is cathartic, so I plough on. 'There are countless times I've put myself in situations similar before, when I've used my body in such a way. Willingly. Willingly giving myself as payment. I don't know any other way. I've never been held with kindness. Not once. Let alone with love or anything even resembling good. My so-called luck had to run out at some point.'

'Lee, I never knew...,' he whispers, maintaining his distance now.

'Of course you didn't,' I say softly. 'No one did. I need you as my friend. Your strength is vital to help me through this. But you—your touch—is too much right now. It's too painful.'

'Holding your hand is off the table?' Though he tries to hide it, emotion makes his voice raw.

'It is. Sorry.' Guilt laces my words for telling him, my only friend, that holding my hand is too much when I have given so much more to so many, but I need to take ownership of my body as well as figure out the mysteries of the dead.

Lorna and Lisette are beyond supportive, even though my ability to eat mountains of food unnerves them. I've decided that I need my strength for what comes next, and for whatever reason, that means consuming a lot. Hiding this part of myself is over. In a way, it's good for me. When I died, I came back different, but the girls have never met that woman, so they do not mourn her. I try to explain how it's linked to my death, or at least I think it is. In what I'm becoming to realise is true Lorna fashion, she dives into research about near-death experiences.

She doesn't find much. It irks her. Irks them all. I'm a mystery.

Lisette begins buying me entire key lime or cherry pies to eat as dessert for myself. Refusing my offer to help with the food bill, she winks and tells me that 'all that is true of this world is not yet written.' A creeping suspicion leaks into me. One I have to force down. It is kindness only, and I am unused to it.

Tino stays close. His care not to even graze my skin stings almost as much as his caresses. But I push that down. He's too good for me, I have to remind myself. Along with the fact that it's possible for someone to do exactly as you asked them to do even though it's the last thing you want. To use Tino in such a way would make me just as bad as every person who has ever laid their hands on me.

As the days pass, my strength returns, and with it

comes a desire to rebuild our friendship. Perhaps I might work up to physical contact. I'm also aware my first week in New Orleans is almost over, leaving me with a mere week left in the States. Lisette keeps her eye on the news for any update on Grey and what went down in that shitty apartment, though she finds none. In my experience, past interactions with the police have left much to be desired. I'm in no hurry to test that with American officers, and something in the glint of Marie's eye when I say it tells me that the word of an addict doesn't hold much weight here either.

My bruises heal slowly. I'd never thought about the practical side of my trip, so insurance was not something that even crossed my mind; the call of my ghosts was too strong to consider a hospital bill racking up hundreds of dollars. I've never sought medical help before, all too afraid of the padded room I might find myself in. The help I need defies any explanation of logic.

As the winter sunlight pours in through the wooden slats of the shutters, I take a moment to enjoy its warmth, pondering what it is I want in truth. I told Tino how I need to stop running from what's happened to me, but the reality of what that means is so terrifying, and I'm tired of being scared.

I dip my toes out of bed. The cool wooden floorboards chill the soles of my feet as I pad to the bedroom door. Creaking it open, I spy Tino on the sofa, talking to Lorna. He's all easy smiles and charm, filled with warmth. His very skin radiates his personality. Nothing like me. I'm as cold as the blue of my eyes. As stark as the pale of my skin. I ease myself around the door, fixing my gaze on Lorna.

'I think I want to return to Marie,' I announce.

Tino's head snaps in my direction as he sucks in a breath.

'Of course. Let me throw some clothes on.' Lorna flounces off to her bedroom with an effortless grace while I move to fiddle with the fringing on the back of the sofa.

'Are you sure you're ready for this?' Tino's words are full of caution.

'My time here is running out. If I want real answers, I'm not going to find them by hiding out here and eating cherry pie. I feel better. At least now, I'm certain....' I falter.

'Certain?'

Continuing to pick at the fringing, the words rush out of me. 'I'm certain I don't want to die.' Colliding with the lump in my throat, the words don't ring true. My emotions all but drown me. 'It'll be different this time,' I tell him, turning to pace back into my room to get changed before he has a chance to say anything else.

The walk to Marie's magic shop is bitterly cold. Tino wears the weather as tension in his body. I sense it from the square in his shoulders as he walks. The last time I was here, it triggered a relapse which almost got me killed, so perhaps his tension is well warranted. I shouldn't have brought him with me. I'm putting my old friend under undue strain. But I must admit, I'm glad he was there that night. That despite his worry and caution, I draw strength from him being around.

'Lee.' Marie welcomes me with a broad smile as we enter the shop, moving out from behind her counter to cup my cheeks with warm palms. 'You look so much better. I'm so happy you were strong enough to return.'

'Thank you.' Moving out of her grasp, I aim for a resolute appearance. 'Being honest, Marie, I have a slight agenda in being here. I need your help.'

Caution radiates from her, though she nods for me to continue.

'Maybe trying to make contact with my dad was running before I could walk,' I admit. 'I've spent years denying to myself that this ability I have is real. What you said before, when I died, how I'd seen the other side, and it was okay to remember. What did you mean by that?'

'Chère, it's no mystical musing that those who suffer trauma repress memories.' She leans an elbow against the counter while I steel myself to meet her eye.

'Meaning you'll help me recover those memories?'

A flicker of curiosity sparks in her eyes. 'Memories of what, to be exact?'

'The other side,' I whisper and, Tino drops the crystal ball he's been messing with.

Lorna, who has been quiet, pipes up. 'That's hardly walking, Lee.'

But the curiosity in Marie's visage lingers. It catches in my chest—all the possibilities of what this might mean to a medium, someone who is in contact with the beyond but has never been able to touch it.

'Have you heard of it before?' I push, emboldened.

Marie shakes her head a fraction. 'Only the same stories I'm sure you're already familiar with—white lights, tunnels, loved ones waiting on the other side.' She tilts her head. 'What is it you do recall?'

'Nothing. Just icy water clutching me, pulling me under. The crushing cold. A creeping terror. And blackness....' I pace. 'Then I was awake again, on the beach. A passer-by had gone in to rescue me, and he was the one who performed the CPR that saved my life. I wasn't breathing when they pulled me out, and my skin was turning blue. The whole thing was over in three minutes.'

Marie's brow furrows. 'You were in the sea? Quite far out?'

'Yes.'

'But you weren't afraid of the water?'

'The opposite. I loved the sea. Swimming was my favourite pastime. Before.'

'You would have said you were a strong swimmer?'

'Yes,' I answer, although it sounds like a question.

'What are you getting at?' Tino asks.

But Marie doesn't answer. She just frowns again

before moving behind the counter and rooting round in the void beneath it. Tino and I exchange a baffled glance. Even Lorna gives a perplexed shrug of her shoulders.

'Marieeee.' I tease out her name, moving over to the counter to try peering at what she's up to, balancing on one foot. 'Mind sharing your thoughts?'

She pauses her rummaging to glance at me. 'Why did you drown that day?' she queries before continuing with her search, her face lighting from within when she locates a small wooden box.

'Bad luck. I got caught in a riptide.' I tilt my body over the counter to peek at what's in her grasp. 'What's that?'

Marie straightens. 'You said the water was clutching you. Pulling you under. Your own words.'

'It was a figure of speech.'

A sly grin spreads across her lips, suggesting she believes it to be more than a turn of phrase.

'Are you suggesting someone pulled me under?'

'I'm suggesting some*thing* pulled you under.' She places the box on the counter and leans a little closer. 'Wherever you went that day, Lovely, the dead followed you into the land of the living. If you want to remember, I may have a way. But to give you sight, to see that in your past which your brain wishes to forget, is not without risks.'

'What's in the box?' I ask again, nervous excitement quavering my voice.

'It's deadly nightshade.' Marie glides the box across the counter with the barest tips of her fingers, halting it in front of my person in time with a juddering beat of my heart.

'Sounds like poison.' Tino comes to stand next to me, too careful that his shoulder doesn't graze mine.

'It is.' Marie stares at him. 'Named for Atropos herself.'

'Lee,' Tino implores, although I don't spare him a glance, 'haven't you had enough of poison?'

The answer he wants doesn't come, though. Instead, my fingers graze the rough splinters of the wooden box. That's the thing with addiction—one ceases understanding what's good for oneself. There's something enticing about the notion of *more*.

'What are the risks? How would it work?' I ask, my voice barely sounding like my own, my vision fixed on the box. I slide it around to peer at the innocuous-looking berries inside, the certainty of my agreement already ringing true in my mind.

'The spirits gravitate towards me and you both, Lovely. The openness the nightshade would grant you poses risks, namely possession.'

'No. No way.' Tino rakes his fingers through his hair, shaking his head. 'Possession? Are you kidding me?'

'Go on,' I mutter to Marie against his protests.

'There are things to be done which mitigate the risk,' she explains in an attempt to placate him. 'I would burn cedar.' She returns her attention to me. 'Possession aside, taking it slow is essential. Make a tincture. Use a dropper to administer low doses directly into your eye.'

My pulse speeds up at the notion.

'It *is* poison, Lovely,' she continues. 'You would experience the quickening, but I would talk you through it. Guide you through the ether. It'll be like brushing against the other side. It should allow you to *see*. It should return your memories to you. Where you went and what happened to you while you were there.'

My knuckles ache from gripping the counter. Marie's eyes are enough to dazzle, so close to contact that she can dip into the ether as if plunging under the water's surface and glimpse what comes next. To live in parallel the last moments of a drowning girl.

'Let's do it,' I tell her, earning a groan from Tino beside me, his concern tangible from the knit of his brow. He's certain of my fragility. He must believe this is a one-track plan to another catastrophe. 'Tee.' I place a gentle palm on his arm. 'I'm running out of time.'

'These risks, though. Poison? Possession? This is crazy.'

I snort a little. 'Crazy has kept me company for years. Why stop now? It's just a different poison, that's all.'

'Lee.' He breathes my name, his eyes desperate in their pleading. 'Don't go where I can't follow.'

My heart—it stops, or it explodes. Strange how those two sensations are so akin. His expression is enough to kill me all over again. The heat there warms a sensation deep in my insides, something I am loath to acknowledge. I must remind myself that I need to not feel those things. Not for my friend who is only afraid for me, who has witnessed me destroy myself piece by piece.

I drop my hand. Try to smile. 'I'm not planning on going anywhere. Marie will ensure my safety.'

Marie gives his arm a reassuring rub from across the counter. 'I will do everything in my power to protect her, chère.'

His Adam's apple bobs as he turns away from us, retreating towards Lorna, who is on the other side of the shop, playing with a tarot deck. In that moment, I long to stop him, to throw myself into his strong, protective arms and forget myself in the smell of his freshly laundered clothes, asking why it is he always smells that way.

Instead, I ask Marie, 'How soon will we start?'

'Tonight, I shall make the tincture, then let it rest in the light of the moon. We begin tomorrow.'

CHAPTER NINE

Smoke swirls, taking on a life of its own and filling the furthest corners of Marie's flat. Marie moves about within it, lean and elegant. The dilation and soft delirium that the deadly nightshade brings allows me to observe what is different about her —a hue in her aura, a higher vibration fizzing around her edges. Above her shoulder to her right, a red-tinged patch hovers, a bobbing glimmer of *something*.

I slide from my place on the sofa and slink across the room to her as if performing some sort of languid dance, my limbs not quite in coordination. My fingers swipe the air by the glimmer, though nothing happens other than a faint waft of sandalwood filling my nose. I'm transported to hot sticky nights on an isolated island, the musical noise of a language I don't understand in my ears, its chants rising and falling in heady fervour.

'What is it that the nightshade reveals to you?' Marie's words echo about my brain.

My tongue drags along the dry cracks of my lips. 'There's something floating by you.' I shake my head. 'A glimmer. It smells of sandalwood and ancient, forgotten nights.'

A chance of a smile dances across Marie's face. 'Carline. My spirit guide. She was a practitioner in Haiti, in my native land. Her grandmother was a healer who sold potions, cured the village of their ailments. They're ancestors of mine from a time when demons roamed the earth more freely. She would dance in the light of the fires, and the spirits would dance with her.'

I almost sense it, the ebb and flow of those wild nights where magic filled the air with the cackles of the flames. The smoke of the cedar unfurls around the room, winding around my fingers.

Marie takes me by the shoulders, whispering instructions, guiding me, walking me along a path in my mind's eye, leading me, once more, to the waters where I drowned.

The beach in Wales. The heat of the late-spring sun. It was unseasonably hot. The water was beckoning for me to take a dip in its cool waters.

The sea was fresh; I relished it. I always enjoyed the water. I swam right out, checking the shoreline every so often to see my mom and dad sharing a flask of coffee on the beach. For a while, I floated on my back, content, gazing at a sky sparsely adorned with clouds. When I had my fill of lazing in the calm waters, I began my swim to shore.

The next moment, I was choking.

Struggling.

Kicking. Frantic. Trying to keep my face above the surface.

Panic.

Darkness.

Blankness.

My next moment of awareness was of ice chilling my blood, sand sticking to my freezing skin.

Marie's palms remain on my shoulders as I splutter out a cough, my mind free of the nightshade. Marie's spirit guide is no longer visible to me.

'Sorry, Marie.' I plonk myself on the sofa and take a glass of water from Tino, who's been observing, and down it in three gulps. 'It didn't work. No new memories have returned. It's all the same—drowning, panic, and darkness, followed by coughing sea water from my lungs on the beach. Whoever said drowning's euphoric is full of shit.'

'Worry not—it was our first try. We should try again tomorrow.'

'Maybe I need a higher dose?'

Tino stiffens beside me.

'No,' Marie vows, firm but sympathetic. 'The dose is fine. It's the path. Trust, chère. These are uncertain waters which we tread. Caution is the best way to proceed. Today was a lesson. This'll work.'

She moves away from us. We take the gesture as our signal to leave, and we make our way through the busy streets to Lorna and Lisette's apartment.

Tino's stiffness doesn't relax as we walk.

'I'm getting the impression you have something you want to say,' I venture.

He exhales a large sigh. 'I don't want to be a huge downer. I understand you want some answers, but I don't like this. This whole thing reeks of danger, and the deadly nightshade is just a different drug. One danger for another, only now it's a supernatural one. Aren't you scared?'

Giving the ground my gaze, I say, 'I've been scared for every second, every moment since the day I died. I'm tired of that emotion.'

He glances at me sideways, unreadable.

'What?' I probe.

He turns his face to the heavens, the cool wind ruffling his hair. 'You've been conditioned to believe you're this fragile thing, Lee. But from where I'm standing, you're the strongest person I've ever met.'

I have no idea what to say to that.

He goes on, 'You've been haunted, violated, told you're crazy, and, on top of all of it, you lost your dad. But here you are, pushing forward, trying to remember where you went when you died. I admire you. Trust me, it's a brave endeavour, but perhaps there's a reason why you forgot what happened?'

'Yes, I wonder.' I fiddle with the cuff of my sleeve

before returning my eyes to his. 'But, if you were me, wouldn't you want to find out? Why me? Thousands of people die every day. Why did I come back? Why am *I* haunted?'

He inclines his head, resigned.

THE DEAD ARE ONCE MORE CONSPICUOUS IN THEIR ABSENCE.

If the others hadn't witnessed what happened with my dad, I might have remained convinced that my hauntings have very much been hallucinations these past years. My friends count it as a blessing. It makes me nervous, and, while I don't miss the horror of decaying corpses crawling out of the earth's crust, what I'll never admit out loud is, there's a sick part of me that longs to be cooled by the frosty breath on the back of my neck. Where have my ghosts gone? What are they waiting for?

While I've not partaken in another séance, Marie's informed me that there's been no further contact with my dad. As far as she can tell, he's moved on, leaving Marie with the notion that he lingered with the sole purpose of communicating with me and not because he had other unfinished business on this plane.

That thought causes regret to pool in my stomach. I should have done so much more to reconcile with him while he was alive. Done more to understand my ability instead of numbing myself to it.

Although I haven't felt strong enough to return to the

board, Marie, with my assistance, has dissected my father's apparition in minute detail. How my dad had warned of someone coming for me, giving further credit to Marie's belief that my drowning was no accident. But her enquiries into the spirit world have proved unfruitful, which troubles her. According to Marie, the spirits are too quiet. There are no whispers to be found of me in the veil.

This fact does not surprise me. Why would the spirits have anything to say about me?

The deadly nightshade's frustrating. Like a state-sponsored rehabilitation programme, the doses feel painfully controlled. Marie walks me to that moment in time, trying to hold me at the very second when my world turned to darkness. But the moment is as fluid as the water in my fingers, always slipping out of my grasp. Yet I'm blinded by the certainty that it's there, vibrating, something tangible, millimetres from my grasp. The exasperation of it is painful. I'm in that moment again, suspended, the sea flooding my lungs. Only now, I'm fighting against the panic, trying with every cell in my body to hold on, to witness what happens next. The figures of my parents blur like a mirage.

My last thought was of them.

I will miss them.

I don't want to go.

Blackness.

Then cold and alive on the beach.

'Urgh!' I stomp to the window and throw it wide,

allowing the cedar smoke to escape. The cool breeze is welcome on my face, a relief from the cloying air, while the scent of the lemons that line the window boxes fills my nose. 'Why do you have lemons in winter?' I demand, allowing my frustration to escape me.

Marie shrugs off my stupid question, coming to sit next to me. Her eyes are wide, and she's clearly ready for me to vent. I lean my head against the bottom of the wooden frame.

'Tell me, Marie. The spirits who you speak to—are they on the other side?'

'From my learnings, they're somewhere in between. A transitional realm from this world to the next. Once they've truly crossed over, there's no coming back.'

'So, Carline?'

'She lingers on the fringes of our world. Somewhere in between.'

'Do you believe that's where I went? Not the other side but the in-between?'

'I couldn't tell you.'

A frustrated sigh escapes me.

'Don't be so hard on yourself.' Marie's expression is all soft gentleness, which she exudes in contrast to the angles of her features, all traces of her vibrant aura now vanished. 'You're making progress.'

'If we increased the dose a little. The teeniest amount,' I add in protest, sensing her argument.

'No.' She moves away from me, wringing her hands.

'We need to take a break, some time to let the build-up of nightshade leave your system.'

I'm almost stunned into silence. 'Taking a break is not an option. I'm leaving in two days.'

'Extend your stay. There's more than enough room for you here.'

'I have to work. Marie. Increase the dose.' My voice borders on shrill.

'Lee,' she tries to placate, smoothing her hands along her braids. 'It's not wise.'

'Marie,' I argue.

'No!' Slamming a palm onto the table, she withers me with a glare. 'I said no. Even now, you're vulnerable to possession. The nightshade must leave your system.'

My anger swells in me, an emotion which so rarely sees the light of day, as we stand and glower at each other. If the dose were a fraction higher, I'd punch past that moment where I perish. Marie, however, is unrelenting. So, I leave, stomping a path through the busy street to the apartment, where I find Tino reading by the window when I storm in. Lorna and Lisette must be out.

'How did it go?' he asks as I fly across the room to take a fresh cherry pie from the refrigerator before proceeding to shovel it down my throat with my fingers.

'Awful,' I say through a mouthful.

Tino abandons his book, approaching me with caution.

'It's not working, and we leave in two days. Marie

won't increase the dose.' Pausing to take a few bites, I relish the sweetness of the sticky treat.

He eases his stance, crossing his arms and waiting for me to continue.

'It's beyond frustrating. I'm stuck in this second when the water clogging my throat battles against my cries to shore. The moment is so filled with terror, pushing past it is like staring into a void. Overcoming it is all but impossible. If I had the strength to pierce that dread....' I stop, exasperation pulsing through me.

How does one stop fearing the moment they draw their last breath, even in retrospect? I try to tell myself this is not the case, that I lived. I did not die that day. Yet some innate pull at the centre of me informs me that this breath *was* my last. My madness threatens to spill forth for all to see. It's my *life* that is a lie. The awful reality is, I'm still suspended in the deep blue.

Bringing my gaze to meet Tino's, I drink in his warmth. A perfect juxtaposition to my frozen death. I pant. No words leave his full lips. The sympathy in his stare turns to something else, and the corner of his mouth tilts, delicious and inviting. His fingers trace the borders of my face, his smirk curling in amusement as he wipes a crumb stuck on my cheek.

I am instantly mortified.

I attempt to pull away, but his thumb catches my face. Although I told him not to touch me, that his kindness and sympathy are too much, I reflexively lean into the caress. My eyelids flutter closed as he shifts his hand so his palm cups my face. The depth of my breath increases as my cheek is warmed in his embrace, as if his very touch has released a weight from my chest. I sigh.

When I open my eyes again, his gaze is trained on me, his expression guarded. While he may not be certain, he can, for sure, guess at all the places my body has been, but for one moment, I let myself enjoy something good. I drop my cherry pie onto the nearby counter and then thread my fingers into his, which are still holding my face.

He doesn't retreat. Instead, he inches closer. His chest heaves, the gold in his irises sparking as he winds his free hand into my hair, pulling me closer. Frozen somewhere between horror and desire, my mind wages a war with my body. Maybe, just this once, I'll play pretend and let his sympathy masquerade as affection and allow myself to be held with tenderness. Imagine I deserve it.

But the door opens, bringing Lorna and Lisette in with it. Tino drops his hands, and my hopes fall with them.

My stomach plummets. I was being so stupid, almost letting myself find *that* kind of comfort in my friend, one which would only hurt us both.

Daring not to peek at Tino as I step away, I fix my attention on the half-eaten dessert.

Lorna giggles. 'Another cherry pie bites the dust.'

Embarrassment heats my face.

'Don't feel bad,' Lisette reassures me. 'We bought

more.' She waves the shopping bags in her grasp. 'Are you okay? You're a little pale.'

'I'm fine,' I lie, moving to help them with their bags. 'I'm not having much luck with my memories. Or, even worse, I'm thinking, what if the memories don't exist?' I flap my free arm at my side, easing their shopping onto the counter, still avoiding Tino. 'Maybe there's nothing to tell. I died. I was alive again. Nothing more special than that. Maybe the other side doesn't exist.'

Lisette gapes at me. 'Do you believe what you're saying?'

I avoid her gaze, instead focusing on helping her unpack. 'I may be forced to.' Attempting nonchalance, I shrug. 'I'll be home soon, where I'll return to my old life. The dead seem to have gone back to whatever pit they crawled out of. Aside from my father's cryptic message, maybe all they needed was to be acknowledged. It might be enough.' I offer her what I hope is close to a genuine smile. 'At least I now know I'm not crazy and that my dad has moved on.'

'Right,' Lisette says, though uncertainty wraps around the word.

'Right. Who cares where I went? Or what the dead want?' I say, and it's even less convincing.

Not giving her an opportunity to say anything else, I pick up the last of the pie, ignoring Tino, who's trying to catch my eye, and retreat to the sanctuary of my room.

CHAPTER
TEN

Staring at the high ceiling, determined not to wallow in my own self-pity, I count all the things I'm grateful I came to New Orleans for.

One. At least now I know I'm not crazy. Different, yes. Haunted, maybe. But my madness is something there's no cure for—no worldly one, at least.

Two. There's also comfort in learning my dad has now moved on to the other side. Whatever peace there is in the great beyond, it's something for his understanding alone.

Three. The addicting sensation of Tino's hands on my face, in my hair. To be reflected in his honey-soaked eyes—

No.

Don't think of that.

I squeeze my eyes shut, dispelling those memories in a flash of longing.

Over the past twenty-four hours, I've kept myself close to Lorna or Lisette, managing to avoid being alone with Tino. Soon, however, we'll get on a plane back to England, where I'll return to my elderly residents and, with any luck, find something resembling peace. Once back within the relevant safety of home, I shall put the distance between Tino and me again.

It's for the best, I tell myself. Better off alone. There will be no great love in my life. And in return, no great hurt. The only thing I'm capable of doing for him is bringing a world of pain.

A little less afraid now, I find a certain kind of comfort residing in the fact that I'm not special. Things do indeed go bump in the night. There's a world glimmering beneath our own, a world of unknown things, navigated in the shadows by a select few like Marie. Something bad happened to me once, and now I'm a little closer to that side than this. My situation is as simple as that.

Adjusting to this new reality is something I shall learn to live with. I've no other option.

Easing open my bedroom door, I find Tino eating breakfast with Lorna and Lisette, stacks of fluffy pancakes piled high, bowls of fruit, and, of course, pies filling the table.

'You're awake,' Lisette cries. She crosses the room to take my hands and lead me to the table, where she sits me across from Tino, who gives me a smirk. 'We're so sad you're leaving, but we wanted you to go out with a bang.'

She beams and places herself next to Lorna as I take in the huge feast laid out in front of me. 'You really shouldn't have.' But the rumble in my stomach contests my words, and I force a laugh. 'You do realise, I *will* eat all of this.'

'We thought you'd need your energy for such a long flight.' Lisette wiggles her eyebrows at me.

So, I dig in.

The girls fall into comfortable chatter about how much they have enjoyed having us here and how we should visit again, and how strange it is to have visitors who don't drink alcohol. With all the pancakes finished, I tuck into my favourite—cherry pie. Tino's glances are loaded, and although I'm not great at reading body language, I get the impression that he wants to talk. His gaze flicks from me, then between the two women at our sides before returning to me again. Dread pools in my stomach at what he might want to say. What if he wants to apologise for our almost kiss? Or to let me down gently?

'I was thinking,' I say to Lorna. 'I'd like to go to Marie one last time and buy her some flowers to say thank you for all she did. All she *tried* to do.'

A downpour of embarrassment showers me as I recall that when I was last in Marie's presence, I all but begged her to give me more poison. *Once an addict, always an addict.* It's a good thing I'm going home. Best to attempt to carve something of a normal life for myself. Pretty sure they don't do rehab for deadly nightshade.

'Sure thing.' Lorna smiles. 'She would love that. Only not lilies. She hates those.'

Tino lights up at the notion that he might be able to catch me on my own. Avoiding him forever is impossible, and after all, we have a long plane ride together. However, I would rather put it off for as long as possible. It'll give me time to muster the courage to brush off anything he says is between us. Or not to be devastated when he tells me it was an *almost* mistake.

Nothing even happened, Lovely. You accepted half a second of comfort. That's all.

It only proves to me how dangerous it is to accept even the slightest touch. I give in to a modicum to weakness, and my desire to be loved comes rushing to the surface. Ugly and consuming. I need to be strong with him. His sympathy is not enough, I tell myself. I know in my heart that I don't deserve his goodness, no matter how much I crave it. I would be nothing more than a parasite feeding on his warmth to breathe life into my chilled bones.

'Will you come with me?' I ask Lorna. 'Help me choose something she'll like?'

The flicker in Tino's eyes dies as he becomes enraptured with his coffee, a motion which is not lost on Lorna's keen observations.

'Of course,' she tells me, a hint of strain in her voice.

Winter midday sun shines cool and bright, blinding in its brilliance. The market is crowded with all of life's vibrancy. Shoulders brush against my own, each dragging me with it. The laughter and chatter is jarring in my ears. I'm glad to have Lorna and Lisette's company, as well as their easy manners, to help me navigate the market's winding depths.

'I have to ask,' Lorna starts.

I shield myself from the sunlight's wilting glare as we round on the flower stall.

She stops, frowning at my perpetual squint. 'What's wrong?'

'A little sensitive is all.' I blink in the flowers, their colours coming in as vibrant smudges in my vision as I attempt to shake away the sun's effects.

'The chrysanthemums are lovely.' Lorna brushes the tips of her fingers against delicate orange petals.

'They are,' I agree, but my attention is distracted by Tino barking out a boisterous laugh with Lisette a few stalls away, where they're trying on hats.

Lorna follows my gaze, smiling to herself before turning back to the flowers. 'What's going on with you and him? Your reaction when we suggested you share a room—you would have thought I'd just kicked your puppy. But I've noticed how you look at him.'

'He's my friend.' I give my attention to the chrysanthemums, marvelling at the vividity of their orange hew, attempting not to acknowledge the heat creeping into my skin.

'Yes, he is. And all he does is move protectively around you.'

I sigh, saying quietly, 'I wish I was strong enough to not need it.'

'Nooo,' she says in slow disagreement, admiring some roses. 'It's not a question of being strong, Lee. Life has given you a beating. Plus, it's his way.'

I stare at her for a moment, and she rolls her eyes.

'I'm good at reading people. That's *my* skill.'

I balk as she laughs, high and natural, at the sight of my shock. 'It's nothing supernatural. Just good old-fashioned human intuition.'

Sighing, I chance a half smile. I pull away from the flowers, and my body sags towards her. Maybe dragging information out of people is her superpower.

'He's always wanted to protect me, even when we were kids. In his mind—then, now—I'm his fragile friend. Nothing more.'

'I wouldn't be so sure,' Lorna whispers.

I bat away what she's pushing towards. I can't entertain it. 'The chrysanthemums are perfect.'

The stall owner helps me select some other flowers, bundling them into a beautiful arrangement. Fearing Lorna's all-too-knowing presence, I play it safe by staying close to Lisette as we round on the magic shop.

Marie's perched on her usual stool behind the counter, Ouija board laid out in front of her. She's massaging her brow but then beams when she catches sight of me.

'I'm so glad you came.' She strides towards me.

Rather than taking her hands, I ease the bouquet into her open arms.

'I have so much to thank you for,' I tell her with genuine warmth. 'Though my memories of where I went when I died haven't returned, I'm going home with much more confidence to carry on thanks to your efforts. I'll never forget your kindness.'

Her face is all graceful beauty coupled with comfort, and it's true—she's helped me more than anyone. I'm beyond grateful that she has opened me up to this world.

No matter how painful it might be.

Tino begins to talk. Something's wrong. I don't understand the words. A distant creaking of steel melting strains my senses. Which makes little sense, as I have no idea what the buckling of metal sounds like.

Oh no.

My vision shakes. The world is shifting.

The dead are coming.

Marie stumbles to catch me as my knees give way beneath me, and I careen into the wooden counter.

Raw emotion rolls around my stomach in towering, crashing waves. The old terror rears its ugly head mixed with something new. Marie's powerful aura seeps into my terror, supporting, coaxing.

It's okay to see.

I am not crazy.

Against every defence I have built these past four years, I keep my eyes open to address the dead. When the world splits and spits them out, I'll ask whoever it is what they require of me. Instruct them to impart their message.

In the split second I take to steady myself, become calmer, my instincts tell me something's drastically not right. The others are moving too. This isn't a vision. The world quakes beneath our feet, the belly of the planet rumbling as if starving. Everyone moves to brace against the earthquake's deep tremors, the walls of the shop riding invisible waves.

Yet, when the ground rips, the others don't observe the dreadful scene unfolding before me. They don't hear what fills my head: the colossal grinding of tectonic plates shifting, the earth coming apart at the seams. Before the sound makes my eyes water, I tightly grip my ears with my hands because the noise has never before been so overpowering. Marie's clutching onto me as we shift with the rumbling movement of the ground. As we begin to tumble, my nails tear at the counter, splintering and bloody.

They're here.

Out of the crack in the earth come not one but many. More upon more of the dead crawl like a plague from hell. The dead as I've never witnessed them before. Not wet with drowning but burning. Skin melting and dripping in torturous fiery deaths, they pour out of the ground.

Screaming.

Awful shrieks of the dead reanimated blister through

the shop, haunting tones that reverberate through my soul more than they ring in my ears. Their cries carry no words, only an unspoken language of pain.

Their agony rips at my psyche, the stench of burning skin and harsh chemicals burns my nose, so much so that my veins burst, and I taste the copper of my blood pouring from my nostrils. It cascades over my lips in dripping torrents that I try to catch with now-slick fingers. Marie, as though burned, takes an instinctual step away from me, the tips of her fingers searing, blackened, as if she's the one marred in a chemical death.

Someone is yelling my name, and I can't tell whether the earth is still shaking or if it's my vision. The dead continue to ascend. They pile into the shop, drifting unseen through the others, advancing on me as I cower by the counter. Their screams are unbearable. The nightmare of the skin falling from their faces fills my vision.

With bloody fingers they reach out to me, descending on me, eclipsing the comfort of my friends until I'm in their darkness. When their skin makes contact with my own, I, too, share in the vicious agony with which they were ripped from this life.

Their blazing deaths consume me.

I'm dying again.

Burned alive.

Flashes of blue and gold and fiery torment.

The dead have come. They have come to swallow me whole.

My own screams tear through the air, coming out

like a sonic boom through the small shop, shaking its walls.

Then the earth shudders again.

Hands of the dead pull me to my knees, their pain obliterating, the fire scorching until it feels as though I'm the one who's melting. Their vicelike grip grasps me everywhere. Their eyes are stark, desperate and pleading at the injustice of it all.

When I scream again, the windows shatter, the glass blowing inwards, showering glittering shards over us all. Through the gaps in the limbs of the dead, I see Tino and Marie take cover, crouching, sheltering their heads from the sharp downpour.

The pain ricocheting through my body makes their forms blurry and mirage-like, heat rising from hot tarmac. I hope Lorna and Lisette are safe.

The dead continue. Bloody. Burned. They crawl like locusts out of the crack in the earth's crust and clutch onto my body, every hand a searing brand. There must be a hundred of them, howling. Scrambling over each other to claim their grip on me until it is all too much.

Failing to escape them, my body succumbs, and I crumble into nothing.

CHAPTER
ELEVEN

Dull thudding pounds in my head as I ease my eyes open and peer around, my surroundings coming into soft focus. I'm in a bedroom I've never seen before.

Panic rises in my chest, crashing through me like a tidal wave. I sit up so suddenly, my head gives another definite throb, and though I try to recall the final moments before my body ended up here, I draw a blank.

Throwing back the covers, I find I'm in my own long-sleeve top paired with skinny jeans. I'm pretty sure it's what I was wearing when I passed out. The dull whisper of voices draws my attention to the doorway. I bring my toes to the floor, determined not to make a sound, and creep to the partially open door, grateful the hammering of my heart can't be heard by those on the other side.

'Look at it, Lorna.' Lisette's voice is hushed and harsh as she shoves a newspaper across the table. 'It's him.'

I strain to listen, wishing I could discern what's on that paper.

'We can't be certain. Earthquakes are not uncommon in Russia.'

Incredulity leaves Lisette in a huff as she pulls the paper back across the wood so hard, it scrunches in her fingers. 'The epicentre of the quake was located beneath the power plant, ensuring maximum devastation. Over two thousand people are thought to be dead.'

Peeping around the door as much as I dare, I see Lisette staring hard at Lorna. Lorna, no longer warm and open, appears guarded, borderline devastated, even.

Lisette goes on. 'It's him, my love.' She softens with a sigh. 'At least now you know where he is and what he's doing. In the hands of those witches, chère, it was always going to be this way. This was the reason they wanted him. It's the way of this flawed world. Power breeds greed along with the need for more power.'

Lorna gives a large sniff, and a tinge of guilt passes through me. I've been eavesdropping on a sensitive conversation. Deciding to make my presence known, I ease the door all the way open.

'Everything okay?' I ask.

They jump from their seats, Lorna turning away to hide her tears, Lisette's face becoming a mask of brightness.

'You're awake.' Lisette beams. 'You've been out for three days. Tino will be so annoyed. He's been standing vigil, but he had to give in and admit defeat. He's gone to get some sleep. He's in my old room.' She motions behind her, and for the first time, I realise we're in Marie's familiar flat.

'Three days?' I parrot. 'I missed my flight.'

'Afraid so.' Lisette half smiles.

'I'll get Marie,' Lorna tells us before making a quick getaway.

I stare after her before noticing the expression of concern from her girlfriend that follows.

'I couldn't help but overhear some of what you were saying....' I trail off.

Lisette heaves a weighted sigh. 'It's not my story to tell.' She sits at the kitchen table, her face weary. 'When you lost consciousness, Marie became convinced that you had been overpowered by spirits. She hasn't slept in three days, remaining at the board, not stopping to eat or even drink. Something's going on. The spirits are ill at ease. She's having trouble deciphering what's coming through. So, Lor and I took some more traditional means of research, and I found out that at the exact time of the attack on you, a significant natural disaster was happening elsewhere in the world.'

She slides the scrunched-up newspaper my way. I cross the room to stare at the print coupled with a black-and-white satellite image of a fireball in the sky. I read the headline of devastation. Mass deaths with little event detail other than that it was an earthquake. My insides turn to ice as I recall burning faces on dead bodies, reanimated, reaching out to me with blistering fingers.

'Were you?' Lisette's words bring me back to her. 'Overcome by spirits?'

I chance a glance at her concerned expression and give one nod. 'You think they're the spirits of those who perished?'

She pushes her hands through her hair. 'Maybe. Some of them. I don't believe that earthquake happened by accident.'

I knit my eyebrows, hoping to prompt further explanation, but Lisette gives me a look that tells me she's troubled by her theory and that she's already said too much on the subject.

I open my mouth to talk, but she cuts me off as she rakes her gaze over me. 'Are you okay? It was crazy what happened. All the windows downstairs blew out. Your nose bled for ages. We all panicked, Marie included.'

But I don't get to offer her an answer before Lorna returns, though not with Marie. 'She's fast asleep on the counter,' she chuckles, her face a mask of composure now. 'It seemed a shame to wake her. Maybe I could make you something to eat, Lovely?'

The reaction of sheer joy that must bloom across my face is all the answer she needs.

She chuckles again, approaching me at the table. 'I'm so glad that you're okay,' she says, extending her hand to take my own.

With the brush of her skin against mine comes a

crushing sensation of heartbreak that kicks me straight in the chest. In the millisecond that it takes me to draw a shocked breath, I witness a lifetime of horror.

A temple, covered in crimson. Severed limbs and bloody bodies littering a sacred hall where a blond boy stands weeping in the middle. Lorna's grief and fear rips through me. The vision shimmers before turning to fire, consuming and golden.

Fire turns to water.

Crashing, careening through streets, moving cars, carrying them away along a vast river. Lorna's plea-filled screams perforate my eardrums. Eyes as black as obsidian stare into my own, carrying nothing but destruction.

The water fades to a clearing, bird calls crying overhead, and though I don't witness it, I hear the primal grunts of a massacre, the squelch of metal tearing into flesh. Lorna's nausea and disgust piled on top of terror pumps like adrenaline through my veins.

I snatch my hand away from hers, cradling it within my other and holding it close to my chest as if it's been burned. Lorna's expression turns to confusion at my horror.

'So much death.' My words leave me as a chant. 'How can you bare it?' A tear escapes my eye. I squeeze them tight to try and shake the images of a young girl lying in rubble, of the green of a swamp turned red with bloodshed. 'Who are you?' I ask, retreating from her, knocking over one of the kitchen chairs, its clattering ringing in my sensitive ears.

Lorna holds her palms where I can view them better, alarmed, and approaches me slowly, like I'm a skittish animal. 'What are you talking about? You're confused. We're friends.'

'I saw it.' My voice shakes as I point an accusing finger at her. 'When you touched me, I witnessed it all. I felt it, Lorna. Your heartbreak, your fear. Y-You—' My voice wobbles again as I move towards my room, desiring to be far from her. 'You have seen terrible things.'

Her confusion becomes apparent in every crease in her face. My body trembles as I connect the dots, my world once again crashing in all around me. My hand shakes as I wave it towards the newspaper on the table. More tears roll down my cheeks, dripping onto the floor.

'Your friend, the one you lost. The one you told me is different, *like me.* He committed these atrocities, didn't he? And you compare me to him? You believe me to be a monster?' I swipe at my tears with frantic strokes.

'That's not what I'm saying at all,' Lorna tells me, her voice panic-stricken. 'I don't know what you saw, or think you saw, but it's all out of context. He's made some mistakes, big ones, but he's not a monster.'

'He killed all of those people.' The words bubble on my lips, coming out strangled.

'These things aren't simple,' she utters.

'The apparitions of the dead when they overpowered

me in the shop—they died in fire. Their skin was melting, and the air smelt chemical and metallic.' I turn my gaze on Lisette. 'The power plant in that newspaper. It was those people, wasn't it? Those who died were calling out to me for help. They were in pain, calling to me. I shared their agony while your friend was slaughtering them.'

'Lee...,' Lorna starts, but I don't catch what she says next.

I heave myself into the bedroom, slamming the door behind me before sinking my back against it and sliding down to rest my head on my knees and cry.

I cry for all those lives lost, for the pain they suffered, for the agony I share with them, for the guilt Lorna still carries. For all that horror.

I cry.

At some point I must have retreated to the bed, as when I wake, it's dark outside. Stumbling a little as I approach the window, I observe the vibrant New Orleans night below. So much life. Having been on the outside for so long, I haven't the faintest clue where I fit.

When I first came here, I was so glad there was a slice of this world where I belonged. The unusual. A world of Ouija and deadly nightshade and communion with the other side. A world where I might fit. The revelation of

Lorna's history has thrown this perspective all out of whack.

Maybe not everything here is as dark as Lorna's past. Maybe there's light, too, as she suggests. But all the furthest reaches of my entity are drenched in darkness. I can't surround myself in more. Yet how do I move forward?

A timid knock sounds at the door, followed a moment later by Lorna squeezing around its edge. Her gaze finding me by the window, she gives me a cautious smile. 'Is it okay if I come in?'

'Of course,' I say, more composed now.

She edges in to sit on the bed's corner before fidgeting with the threads of the crochet throw lying on top of it. 'You must understand, before any of the destruction, he was my friend first. There are many reasons why I'll always have love for him, things even you wouldn't believe.' She sniffs before eyeing me with a cautious scrutiny. 'What was it you saw, exactly?'

I wrap my arms around myself and sit on the corner of the bed opposite her. 'A temple, drenched in blood, then a city being torn apart by water, followed by a battle. So much death. If this is what it is to be different, I want no part in it.'

'How is that possible? Tonight wasn't the first time I've touched you.'

I shrug. That thought hadn't crossed my mind—the shock of the vision so terrible, it dulled this new twisted revelation. Has the onslaught of the dead broken some kind of barrier? Pushed me closer to the other side? Or just to being something even more *other*? I shudder.

'Lee,' Lorna continues, 'what you saw were the very worst moments of my life. One of my dearest friends has been at the centre of those moments, but he's so much more than what he appears.'

'Tell me about him,' I probe, leaning in.

A flicker of pain crosses her face. No matter what he's done, his absence hurts her still.

'He was so many things. Gentle and fragile, yet more powerful than anyone you've ever met. Complicated, much like you are, with even more vices. And with so many walls built up around himself, a result of all he'd been through.' Lorna's expression is trained hard on me, the strength in her words pushing on my chest as they land. She moves as if to comfort me before stopping herself. 'If the power plant is him, it's because he's put himself in an impossible situation. Lee, don't make those same mistakes. There's no need to shoulder the burden by yourself. You're not alone.'

I shudder once more, giving her a nod. 'What would you have me do?'

'*Stay*,' she whispers. 'Stay. Let us help you. We're stronger together.'

Toying with the edge of my sleeve, I ask, 'May I speak to Tino before I make my decision?'

'Sure.' She smiles and leaves.

I don't rise, only turn my attention to the window

once more, the artificial light illuminating the room in a dim glow, humming in the air.

The door creaks. Tino, not as cautious as Lorna, leans into the room, deflating as he spots me sitting on the bed. 'Christ, Lee. Talk about scare of my life. You spun the earth off its axis,' he chuckles before casting a cautious glance my way. 'They're saying it was more than one ghost, that you were overpowered by them.'

'Yes.' I stand and cast a furtive glance at the door. Although I'm sure no one would eavesdrop, I motion my friend towards the window. 'So many have never appeared at once before. Truth be told, I've never seen more than one at a time. Perhaps it's to do with the deadly nightshade. But there's something new. When I touched Lorna, something happened. Almost like a premonition but of the past. A lifetime of shit flashed before my eyes. Lorna said they were the worst moments of her life, and in all of them, there was this guy. I'm guessing I'm connected to him somehow. Why else would those memories have come to me?'

Tino stiffens. 'You want to find him?'

'One hundred percent not.' I take a breath. 'But a barrier's been broken. I'm getting closer to... something.'

I gnaw on the edge of my jagged nail while Tino studies me.

'Do you remember anything about the other side yet?'

I shake my head. The precipice is all around me. While I teeter on its edge, I can't decide if I'm too scared to jump off or if something else is holding me back. One more piece of the puzzle.

'I won't be returning to England in the immediate future,' I tell him, resolution ringing in my tone. 'I'm going to remain here and stay the course.'

Tino steps closer, and in that one small step, he commands all my senses. His presence presses against every cell in my body—the scent of freshly laundered clothes, his amber-hazel eyes, the warmth radiating from his skin.

'What are you looking for?' he pushes.

'I want to know it wasn't all for nothing,' I breathe. 'That when I died and came back, it was for a reason. That since I see the dead and if they need me for something, I need to learn how to do this. Running's no longer an option, Tee. I don't want to be afraid all the time.'

Unwelcome desire threatens to swallow me whole, I want him so. I long to be touched, kindly, with yearning, to pretend to be a normal girl whose body is not a possession or a trade. For a moment, I desire all the hurt being held in such a way will bring with it.

But I don't tell him that part.

'You should go home,' I say instead. 'To England and your ma. Stay far away from this.'

His expression darkens, unreadable.

'I'm sorry to have got you involved in the first place,' I add, picking the broken skin at the edge of my chewed nail, and a droplet of blood gathers. Wincing, I suck it between my lips.

'You don't want me here?'

The hurt in his voice takes me by such surprise, I startle, but he doesn't appear hurt but in fact, rather angry, if anything.

'Don't twist my words.'

'You listen to me, Lee Timms. I left you once, terrified by what you were going through.' He steps closer again and is now inches away, his heat warming my marrow. 'Psychosis and addiction. I was terrified for you and *of* you. You were this wild thing, and it broke my heart to watch you get chewed up and spat out over and over again. But I told myself it wasn't in my power to do anything, that you would ask for my help when you were ready. When you disappeared, I didn't look for you because I was scared of what I might find.' He pushes a hand through his hair with a heavy breath. 'Now this? Freaking voodoo and possession. Your world gets crazier by the day, by the hour, and you couldn't drag me away this time.'

Tino's words crash through me, filling me so that, for a second, I forget I'm a broken and discarded thing. The burning in his eyes fills me with hope, a hope I've never dared to entertain—that I might be strong enough to endure this.

'Will you stay with me?' I ask, my request the softest whisper.

His face flickers with confusion, as only moments ago he stated he has no intention of returning to England without me.

So, I clarify, 'Here. Tonight. Stay with me. Please.'

And then something else flits across his face, an emotion I don't have a name for clouding his expression.

As he moves forward, I step away. But he doesn't take offence at my sudden withdrawal, which is not so much a rejection as it is my fear of all the things he might make me feel. While my heart desires his touch, I'm not sure my body is ready. Or perhaps it's my paranoia that if something were to come to pass between us, it would mean more to me than it would to him. After all, I'm sure he's been with many girls, desired them and had them desire him in return. He's not a used creature. He can't possibly understand what it would mean to me to be held in such a way.

He isn't offended, though. Instead, he steps away and slowly moves to the bed, where he lies down on one side on top of the covers, tucking a hand under his head, his eyes never leaving mine. Slowly, I match him move for move. I ease myself onto the mattress, making a mirror image by facing him with my hand tucked under the pillow.

And although we maintain the distance, no parts of our body in connection, it feels like the most intimate moment I've ever shared with another person.

CHAPTER

TWELVE

Waking up to Tino sleeping opposite me is a bliss bordering on dangerous.

Unguarded, his features are soft, reminding me of the boy he once was. Loud and carefree, easily protecting others, always ready for a fight. Somewhere along the line, something changed, and a quiet seriousness now surrounds him. Maybe that's just what growing up is.

Careful not to rouse him, I slip out of bed and creep to the en suite bathroom consisting of a tiny shower cubicle, a toilet, and a sink that's coming apart from its fixture on the wall, looking as if it's been pulled away. Splashing my face with cold water, I attempt to organise my scrambled thoughts. I haven't yet spoken to Marie, but I need her opinion on this strange development.

Without making a sound, I pad back into the room,

grab a cardigan, and leave Tino to his slumber. The flat is quiet, and my nerves about knocking on Marie's bedroom door are unwarranted, as she sits at the kitchen table, coffee in hand.

I sigh with relief. 'I'm glad you're up.'

Marie's mouth twitches, but her serious visage remains. 'Come' is all she says, motioning for me to follow. We make our way out of the flat and into the magic shop below. In the darkness, an eerie aura clings to the four walls containing hanging chicken feet, gleaming crystal balls, and boarded windows. She turns on an old oil lamp, adding to the haunting effect.

'Sorry about that,' I mutter, my fingers indicating the decimated window.

Marie makes a motion with her hand as if to say, *'Don't worry about it,'* then places her battered old Ouija board on the counter. A thrill passes through me at the way she's all business, only guessing at the seriousness of what it may mean.

'Lorna told you?' I press.

'She did.'

'And?'

'And—' She exhales, fingering the edge of the board. '—creature after creature keeps walking right into my shop,' she utters more to herself than to me before giving me her attention, deciding on her course. 'Lovely, this world was once full of magic.'

'Once?' I cock my head, intrigued, moving closer on

some primitive instinct. I've never noticed before how Marie has something about her, a captivating quality that acts as a pull.

'What I, or any other practitioner, or even witch for that matter, have access to are fumes from a time long forgotten. Magic has long been leaving this plane—even the stars are starting to wane. But now, things below the surface, forgotten things, are waking up.'

My skin prickles. I almost feel it. Like the magic is a tangible thing, flaring, giving languid licks, then nipping at the nape of my neck. The icy caress I've come to absurdly miss. Its scent is a dark aroma mixed with the heady smell of the oil burner, as thick and oppressive as long summer nights.

'Why?' I whisper.

She peers into the depths of the board, staring at it as though it should spring to life and bring with it all the answers. 'I believe someone, or *something*, made a mistake, and now everything has been thrown out of equilibrium. People like me are mere chess pieces thrown across the board.'

'Which makes me what?'

She takes her ruby-laden planchette from an inner pocket of her light jacket before running its pointed edge across her lower lip. 'It might just make you a player.'

A shudder of self-importance passes through me. Being a player should fill me with dread, but rather worryingly, the power accompanying the notion fits better than it ought. I recall all the chaos of Lorna's memories and the kind of power wielded there. An image a far cry from poor, terrified Lovely.

For a terrible second, I envy that type of potency.

'Read with me,' Marie pleads, bringing me out of my musings, leaning closer. 'Let us both commune with the spirits. Let us both search the veil—for whispers of *you*.'

I hesitate. 'You already looked before.'

'Not with you here, connected. You might be a powerful pull. The spirits, they seek you out.'

My throat turns to sand, so I don't say anything more. Marie places the planchette on the board, balancing her slender fingers on its rounded edge. Her breath hitches at the contact.

After wiping my clammy hands on my leggings, I follow suit, the metal too cool on my fingertips, the icy sensation jolting in my veins. The sandalwood essence of Carline, ever lingering close to Marie, evanesces in my nose.

Closing my eyes, I enjoy the memories of warm Haitian nights, the calming tide of the ocean lapping at the shore while Marie's words ring in the distance. She's calling my name through the ether, inviting the spirits to her table, to her board. Carline lingers at the shore as Marie chants, 'Lovely, she is here. Is there a message for her? Is someone reaching out to her?'

My palms are slick with sweat.

Carline's magic-filled nights twist, whirled together with the blaring of sirens. Petrol is on the ground, its scent caustic in my nose. But the scene changes again, and the rough texture of rope burns the clammy skin of my wrists as my heart flutters from the bindings' callousness.... Then it transforms once more, and an all-too-familiar metallic tang of metal fills my mouth, but it's fleeting.... Blinding lights, and then... the whoosh of air in my ears... the solid weight of a knife....

Emotions, sensations, and sharp points flash through me, confusing my senses, each coming on strong before leaving me so quickly, I don't have a chance to get a handle on what's happening.

'Eesh.' An unnerving noise escapes Marie, who's removed her fingers from the instrument and flexes them as if they've been under immense strain. Her breathing's heavy, and I'm surprised to find my own coming in gasps. She flexes her fingers once more before sinking her head into her hands.

'What was that?' I ask.

'They were going too fast. I couldn't make out any of it,' she admits.

Casting my gaze to the board, I'm shocked to find the planchette not in its original position. 'I didn't even register it moving,' I tell her. 'I was there, with them. Living every final moment.'

Marie bolts to attention, her fierce expression willing me on. I blink the experience in, trying to recall and give voice to the flashes that held me fleetingly in their clutches. 'I saw lights, blinding.... That one was hit by a car. There was a rope, maybe a kidnap victim. They were scared.' I massage invisible rope marks on my wrist. 'There was also the taste of metal before the vision went blank. I believe that was a gunshot....' I flounder, as the flashes had come thick and fast, but I understand the metallic taste of gunmetal on a tongue. 'You're right,' I confirm. 'There were too many to get a handle on what they wanted. I only caught glimpses.'

Marie, however, is marvelling at me, mouth agape. 'You're incredible.'

Her words are so earnest, my face flushes.

'The glimpses?' she presses.

'Some were smells, others a touch or emotion, a few flickers of images, but nothing concrete.'

Marie massages her temples. 'Impressive,' she says absentmindedly. 'My questions were too vague. There are many spirits attempting to contact you, tell you their tale of woe.'

She rubs her chin, and I can tell her mind is far from here, and she's talking to herself more than me at this point.

'When the emotion isn't strong enough, the dead may communicate to you through an instrument,' she explains. 'However, a strong enough emotion, like the love of a father, or a strong enough desire, and they punch through the veil to where you're able to perceive them in corporeal form. Interesting. But why? You weren't born with sight. Why you? Why now?'

Unsure if she wants an answer or not, I shrug just in case. She pays me no mind, though. She goes on muttering about how she needs better questions, how we'll need to be more specific so the spirits don't jump at the chance to communicate with me all at once.

'We need to go further back to when you drowned. Or before? What came before?'

The question rings from her lips as a soft chant on repeat. The threat of a headache pounds in my temples. I'm not sure if I should be making suggestions rather than sitting here staring at her with a vacant expression on my face.

The first pearls of sunlight peek around the boarded-up windows, and she waves me upstairs to get myself coffee or breakfast, her focus no longer on me but rather some ancient-looking books, thick with dust, from behind her counter.

Upstairs in the kitchen, I pour myself a well-needed cup of coffee. I people-watch the street below as I linger by the window, breathing in the citrus scent from lemons growing in the window boxes. I digest Marie's words in my mind: The spirit world is *dying* to speak to me. To regale me with their stories. Curiosity seeps in. *What might those stories be? What am I to do about it? Why did my dad instruct me to run? Run from whom? Lorna's dangerous friend? An even more dangerous spirit?* Answers dance beyond the tips of my fingers.

The door clicks behind me, and Tino appears in the doorframe of my temporary bedroom with the most glorious case of bedhead, a sleepy smile on his face. God, I want to run my fingers through his ruffled hair. I chastise myself for staring, dragging my attention to the street below once again.

Tino chuckles. When I glance his way, he's shaking his head, then pulls a jumper on.

'What?' I probe, hugging my coffee mug to my chest.

'Nothing.' He busies himself making coffee. 'I've never known anyone as hard to read as you.'

I cluck my tongue, turning my attention to my coffee. Funny that. I always feel like I'm just the opposite, an open book for all to read. But perhaps when you're always scared, instinct finds a way of masking your true emotions.

Tino approaches and leans a shoulder against the frame opposite me, running a delicate finger across the leaf of the strawberry plant nestled next to its lemon neighbour. His gaze shifts to the street below, his expression pensive as my attention turns to his face, my chest constricting a little.

'Do you think me unfair?' I whisper. 'For asking you to stay the night, only to not allow you to put your hands on me?'

A dangerous emotion flashes in his eyes. 'Lee. Of course not.' His voice struggles to remain level. 'You owe no one your affection or your body. I don't—' He grimaces. 'I don't expect payment for staying with you.'

His words elicit a weird mix of relief and rejection. A sick part of me worries that the reason he doesn't want payment is that he finds the idea of being intimate with me repulsive. Knowing he's all too aware of my sordid history, I think he *should* find me repulsive.

Attempting to train my focus on the crowd below, I tell myself I must give up this ridiculous dream of him. If anything were to happen between us, it would be out of sympathy on his part. The free spirit of New Orleans and the easiness of Lorna and Lisette's relationship have compelled me to loosen a closed-off part of myself that is now impossible to lock away once more.

My mind harks back to those moments when I've recoiled. The moments when, in my head, we shared intimacy were just that—in my head. Illusions from being so starved of kindness.

With that sobering notion, a new type of nausea rolls over me. *I'm ridiculous.* I need to get away from him. Now.

'Lee?' he asks, straightening as I twist away, hopeless tears building in my eyes. 'What did I say?'

Forgetting himself, he stretches his fingers out and catches my wrist to pull me to him. In that moment, exploding agony ricochets around my chest. Seeing my pained response, he immediately releases me. The absence of Tino's soft touch takes with it the excruciating pang of crippling fear in my chest that threatened to floor me. Yet the images remain, forcing me to take two steps of retreat from him, my breaths leaving me hard as my mind spirals.

The memory swirls. A younger Tino when he was still full of fight, reclining lazily on his bike handlebars as he observes a heated argument between a friend and someone else. His friend has always had a smart mouth, but Tino enjoys the scuffles. This is nothing unusual. But the argument is escalating. The other guy reaches into his jacket.

The movement is too quick. A sick recognition rises like bile in his veins at the flashing silver of the knife, the sinking sensation at the realisation of what's about to happen coming all too late as the blade finds its mark. Three quick stabs. Then the assailant flees. Tino stumbles off his bike, metal clattering, one of the pedals catching along the skin of his calf and drawing blood as he lunges forward to catch his friend.

The pain is so real, so close to the surface. This is the moment Tino changed. His terror floods through me with the memory of how it was to hold his dying friend in his arms. His friend perished right in front of him, and it happened so fast. I ponder whether the opposite is the case with me. If, from Tino's perspective, witnessing me blunder through life, knocking against death is akin to watching someone die in slow motion.

'You never said,' I breathe.

Tino cocks his head.

'Your friend,' I continue. 'You held him as he died.'

His eyes bulge as he takes a moment. I sense the emotions whirling around him in shades of grey and crimson. Grief rises, saturating the air around us until he can't hold my gaze, and he turns away from me to stalk to a nearby sofa and sink into it.

Resting his head in his open palms, he says, 'It was the worst day of my life. He was there one second, and then—' His pause hangs heavy. '—he was just gone.'

Hedging round the sofa, I then take a seat on the chair near him, cautiously waiting for him to continue.

His face still in his palms, he says, 'When you're young, you feel like you're indestructible, like you're going to live forever. There was never a situation I couldn't fight my way out of. That day—' He shakes his head, finally giving me his gaze. '—everything changed. I realised I was part of the problem. I stood by and did nothing. I thought it was funny to get into fights, to let it slide. All it took was one person I didn't quite have the right read on, and—' He stops, his shoulders hunched, the weight of what he carries heavy on him.

I clear my throat. 'I'm so sorry, Tee. You should have told me. It's not your fault.'

'This guilt is mine. You already have enough.'

'Kind of explains it.' A half chuckle escapes me. 'Why you're so protective of me. You want to save me. Even if it's from myself.'

I attempt a smile, but it doesn't stick. And Tino's eyes are only hard.

'You're not a charity case, Lee. You're not my redemption. That's not how I see you.'

'How *do* you see me?' The uncertainty in my own voice makes me recoil, now wholly wishing I hadn't asked.

Tino's mouth flaps open, but no words come out, and

I wish for once that the ground would open, allowing me to fall down the cracks along with the dead. Much to my dismay, it doesn't. However, Marie does return to the flat, and I'm on my feet in a grateful instant, twirling away from Tino, carrying all my insecurities along with me.

CHAPTER
THIRTEEN

Rather than confront my increasingly complicated feelings about my friend, I immerse myself in Marie. Though this is easier said than done when there's so much that is good about him. The way he pushes his longish hair out of his face, the warmth of those golden eyes, the richness of his skin. I try not to let my gaze linger on him and pretend not to notice his stares fixed on me in return.

I tell myself it's because I'm not used to it. My relationships have for years been transactional, and even though our true estrangement lasted for a mere year, the last time I really knew him, I was deep in my Class A love affair, possessing desire for little else. One addiction gives way for another and then for another. Instead of losing myself to *him*, I get lost in the world of Ouija with Marie. Though even she has an addictive quality—the powers that reside at the tips of her fingers, connecting me to the other side.

There's been no more deadly nightshade, no possession, but I find myself jittery in my eagerness to get to her. Marie being a conduit of sorts has given me a semblance of control, the spirits only making contact when we're both connected to her planchette. Her talent for speaking with the dead has enabled her to stem the flow. No longer are there tides of the deceased clamouring to have their voices heard.

Marie communes with the spirits in words with jumbled, frantic messages, while it's their final moments that assault my senses. The taste of laudanum lingering on my lips, the pressing of fingers bruising my throat. The lone dots we've been able to connect are how they all met violent ends.

Since the onslaught of melting power plant workers, there have been no more dead crawling out of the cracks of the earth. Lorna diligently checks the morning papers and searches the news, paying extra attention to floods, to hurricanes—any natural disaster. I don't ask. Instead, from afar, I seethe at her friend for abandoning her, although from what I gather, he's in some sort of trouble. A question forms in my mind of what it means to be something *other,* if trouble has a way of following you around.

I'm comforted at the board, where the dead are a little less scary. With Marie's fingertips brushing mine, I'm a little less intimidated. Moreover, there's something... else.... Something about experiencing the taste of someone's death that stirs an emotion deep in my core. Not quite anger—something *different*. Its flavour sticks at the back of my throat and conjures a deadly kind of thirst.

The fact that Tino's enduring my silent treatment with so much stoicism jars and bothers me more than it should. But in all honesty, I'm so exhausted from my sessions with Marie that, by the time I return to the girls' flat, I retreat straight to bed.

Tino is sleeping on the sofa again.

Raucous laughter emanates from the apartment, giving me pause before I knock on Lisette and Lorna's door. My gentle taps lost in the blaring drum and bass, I pound my fist until, soon enough, the front door swings open to reveal a rather wobbly Lorna.

A stunning, toothy grin blossoms across her face as she throws the door wide so I may enter the room where Lisette is standing with Tino at the kitchen counter. Lisette's hand rests on his hip as he throws back a shot of tequila before lowering his elbow to her shoulder, shuddering against the alcohol, which elicits a giggle from her. In a wild fit of jealousy, my imagination conjures possibilities of the way Tino has been filling his time in my absence. Which is ridiculous.

Lorna closes the door with a jolt and falls into step beside me.

'We managed almost a month.' Her words are tinged with a tipsy edge. 'Don't get me wrong, the detox has been good. God knows I drink too much.' She accepts a shot from Lisette, along with a sloppy kiss.

I raise my eyebrows at Tino, who gives me a drunken half smirk, his eyes already a little glassy, the effect making him even more appealing.

Lorna peels herself off her girlfriend, turning to blind me with a grin. 'So, we're going out dancing. Your man is coming, and we think you should too.'

Picking up a shot of tequila from the counter, she beckons me towards her. I stare at the amber liquid for a while, considering. I've been feeling a lot stronger of late. I glance at Tino. Lorna called him my man, and he made no effort to correct her. Then again, it might have just been a manner of speaking.

He pushes his hair from his face, tilting his head. 'You don't have to, Lee. I know—totally sober.'

He moves to take the shot from Lorna's fingers, and the sight of his hand caressing her skin sets my blood on fire. Careful not to brush against her, I intercept and accept the drink, downing it in one.

Cheers erupt from Lorna and Lisette, who hastens to pour me another, but a strange expression is cast over Tino's face, like he can't quite figure me out. He said before that I'm a closed book.

The tequila warms my skin as I sink my second shot.

Perhaps appearing to be an enigma is a good thing. How many girls have thrown themselves at him before? Maybe he's not used to figuring anyone out. Or maybe that second tequila really went to my head.

I drink a third anyway.

Somewhat woozy now, I manage to change into a long-sleeved top—which offers relative protection from the skin of strangers rubbing against my own on the off-chance they've witnessed death—then down another shot before we head out, a blurry troupe in the New Orleans night.

This new development since the onslaught defies explanation. Even Marie struggles to explain why my skin has become hypersensitive to death. The spirits who are desperate to talk to me seem more concerned with showing me their deaths, but they reveal no inkling of what they want or what purpose such violent imagery serves. Answers to my predicament are even further from their understanding. Not that they would have any answers for me. They're lost souls. I'm not sure if they even know what they want. Perhaps their motivation is simply to scream about their pain. I can't help but wonder what they'll become, such as they are, unable to find peace, jammed between two worlds, in agony.

By the time we're at the bar, I'm happy to be out of my own head for a change.

'So, what's your story?' I ask Lorna over the music. 'How'd you escape the English countryside and end up in New Orleans?'

Lorna laughs. 'That horror show is a long, *long* story and not something for tonight.' She wraps her arms around Lisette, who's standing a little in front of her. 'Though I'm not complaining, as it brought me to Lisette.'

'Aw, babe.' Lisette pats her arm, enjoying the embrace.

'My life had become this whirlwind of craziness for years. When I met Lis, everything changed. She was something real and someone to stick around for. I'd endure that craziness all over again if it meant keeping her.'

Lorna places a kiss on her neck. I would be jealous of such a notion, but I can't find it in myself. They're too perfect for each other.

'What about you?' I direct at Lisette.

'Me? Not much to tell, chère. I'm from a little place called Avery Island just south of here. It's pretty special, but not much goes on there.'

'How did you get into all of this?' I ask, my gesture a little overzealous in my drunkenness. But she gets the picture.

'Honey, the Deep South is new country, but it's Old Country, if you know what I mean?'

I shake my head, baffled, and she chuckles. 'There's so much open land here. Things are not built on only to be built on again. Ghost towns are left to be haunted. The impression a soul leaves on a place, it lingers longer when the souls are spread thinner. And on a place like

Avery Island, where few come and go, the veil is spread thin.'

The music might be too loud, but I'm sure she's not making sense. 'What are you talking about?' I half laugh.

But she doesn't go on. Instead, she rolls her eyes with a giggle, mock slapping her head.

'Let's dance,' Lorna whispers into her ear, and they whirl off onto the dance floor, leaving me bemused but happy enough in a fuzzy way.

Tino and I watch them dance for a moment in uncomfortable silence, the alcohol in my blood encouraging me to sway on the spot. I'm about to fake an excuse to go to the bathroom when he clears his throat, leaning his arm on the bar to better look at me.

'Are you done avoiding me? I'm impressed that you've managed a few minutes in my presence without running off.'

My smile can only be described as glib. 'Actually, I was just about to pretend to use the bathroom.'

His returning laugh is a deep, warming thing. I seize the opportunity to gaze at him, enjoying the melodic tones of his laughter before his honey eyes return to mine.

'Honestly, Lee, what have I done?'

How to piece the words of a response together when all he's done is be amazing? How to tell him of the safety his very presence brings? How I'm so broken, this safety is as precious as gold to me. Yet he's done it all without meaning to—he's just a decent person.

How do I tell him that the feelings I have for him terrify me?

The words flounder on my tipsy tongue, which feels clumsy and a little swollen. His lips are moving, and I'm having a hard time not staring at his mouth.

'Or is it what I haven't done?' he asks, his voice the barest whisper so I almost don't catch what he's saying over the din of the music.

Unsure of their meaning, I stare into my vodka and Cherry Coke as his body angles into mine. The faintest trace of panic seizes me. I should stop drinking before I say or do something I regret.

'Stop. I didn't mean—' he pleads, then halts. 'Let's dance.'

Despite my protests, he takes my elbow and leads me through the crowd before stopping close to where Lorna and Lisette are writhing, wrapped in each other. Though the song has a high tempo, they dance close. Tino's expression is bright with glee, drinking in the horror in my own mien at being forced to dance. I do an awkward little bop before he cracks up as he advances on me.

His hand resting with butterfly-inducing lightness on my hip, he breathes into my ear, 'You don't want to dance with me?'

The amusement in his voice coupled with the heat and liquored taint of his breath causes my heart to race. 'I don't dance at all,' I tell him, planting my feet.

'It's easy.' He cocks his head, both hands moving my

body in rhythm to the music, his hips gyrating dangerously close to mine.

Slow at first, I let him guide me until our movements become more fluid. His expression is devouring as his eyes graze the curves of my body. His fingers continue to guide me with the gentlest push and pull, dancing along my hips, tracing electrifying lines up my arms—all clothed, safe places. Yet as I match his pace, falling into the liquid movement of the beat, rather than terror, sheer longing aches in my core.

'See? Fun, right?' He grins.

I redden, having been caught hypnotised by his face. My friend has no business being this good-looking. 'You're good at this.'

'It's been said.' His delicious mouth pulls up at the corner in a way that makes my pulse spiral, all too aware that we're now so close, my chest occasionally grazes his.

Feeling a little bold, and very drunk, I let my fingers drag down the hard planes of his abdomen, making a soft gasp escape his lips. 'You should tell me about that.'

He knits his eyebrows. 'About what?'

Pressing a little closer, I whisper, 'Tell me all the ways in which you're good.'

Heat kindles in his eyes, and as his fingers trace the curve of my back, I find I'm now the one who can't catch my breath. How many times have I been touched? Every time I have, I threw up all the barriers in my mind not to feel it. But here, now, with Tino's palms hot through the fabric of my top, I have zero desire to block him out.

He gives me a wicked grin, all gold eyes and goodness. 'It would be easier if I showed you.'

Maybe I nod, but I'm definitely not thinking, because I move into him. My chest flush against his, I meet his wanton stare, heat and lust sparking in the short distance between us. His fingertips, which have been resting in the curve of my back, wind into my hair, forming a fist, causing me to gasp into his lips.

Closing the remaining distance in a heartbeat, he kisses me. Hard and unrelenting. His tongue slides over mine without apology, his free hand clutching my waist and holding me to him.

I'm undone. I close my eyes, losing myself in the ecstasy of his kiss. Warmth spreading through me, my legs tremble.

I deepen our kiss, my fingers digging into his arms a little too hard because now a different sensation is blooming in my chest. Pain spreads down my arms, making me want to cry out as the silver of the knife flashes in my mind while Tino's fear ricochets around me. Unaware, he lets his hands roam my body, his palm cupping under my breast. His kiss is so intoxicating, I never want it to stop; its pure goodness, making me feel like I've never been kissed before. Yet I can taste his terror, sense the ebb of his friend's life as it fades away. It's all rolled into one glorious and destructive sensation.

Managing to peel myself away from him, I realise we're still in the middle of the dance floor. Tino's lips are swollen, his breath heavy.

'Let's get out of here,' I tell him.

CHAPTER
FOURTEEN

After I basically surgically remove myself from Tino, we find Lorna and Lisette jumping about with glee. Rouge heats my cheeks as I ask them for keys to their apartment. They bounce on the spot, arms entangled, their eyelids heavy from the booze, yet I get the picture the night is young for them.

Once we're outside the bar, I falter, the cool air offering me some clarity of mind, though I'm at a total loss as to what to say. This is probably a bad idea. Picking at the edge of my sleeve, paranoia seeps in that Tino is starting to think better of our union too. But when I peek at him through my lashes, the uncertainty in my eyes is met by the unwavering of his.

He catches me by the elbow, spinning me dramatically, my heart fluttering as his palm cups my throat and his mouth finds mine again, chasing away all my doubt. If anything, the freshness of the air has given more fuel to Tino's fire. The force of him has my feet stumbling, his body never leaving mine, like we're magnetised, until my back hits the cool window of a shopfront, his hand still firmly around my neck as his tongue explores my mouth.

My mind tumbles, and I lose control of the murmurs coming from somewhere inside my chest as he pushes himself against the length of my body. My fingers dig into his back as pain crashes against my skin and rolls before receding into my core. His panic, fear, and shock of the past mingle with the desire of our present.

Managing to untangle from our embrace, a smile shakes on my lips. With haste, I pace to the apartment, his fingers locked in mine as he stumbles a little way behind me. I so want this to happen. I want to feel all of him, for his weight to be comforting and something *I* wholly want.

He wears a look of mild bewilderment, as if he can't quite believe this is happening, his lips pursed like he doesn't want to ruin the moment by talking, for which I'm grateful. I don't want him to change his mind, though a spear of guilt passes through me that I'm allowing him to do this when he's drunk enough to not think better of it.

Once we're inside the flat, I head straight to my bedroom, Tino still following a little behind. My heart's pounding so loudly, I wonder if his ears perceive its thundering beats or if I'm wearing my nerves to an embarrassing extent. I switch on the little lamp next to my bed, hoping the dull light will disguise my scars somewhat. My hands shake as I pull my top over my head and discard it on the floor, the tremble making me fumble over my belt buckle.

Tino shifts behind me, his breath ghosting on my shoulder. His hot palms wrap around my waist, putting a stop to my undressing.

'Lee, what are you doing?' he whispers.

'I-I was just... I thought....' *I thought I should take off all my clothes before you think better of this. Not quick enough, Lee.*

He strokes my bare arms with gentle fingers. I lean into the caress a fraction as he turns me to face him, his expression adoring. He sighs, then motions to my hair, which is in a high ponytail on top of my head. 'Can you...?' His words are soft in the stillness of the room.

Without releasing my eyes from his, I work my hair out of the ponytail, allowing it to cascade around my shoulders. His hungry gaze drinks me in, not lingering on my scars but instead exploring the swell of my chest. His tongue runs against his bottom lip before he reaches out and twirls a tendril of my hair.

'You have no idea how long I've wanted this,' he murmurs. 'Even before your accident. I dreamed about you, Lee. Often.'

If his words aren't enough to make my head spin, then his lips on my neck certainly are. He places soft kisses of pure sensation along my throat as his hands roam my skin, pulling me closer to him. Then he's kissing my lips again, and my knees almost give way. All but tearing his T-shirt from his torso, I place kisses of my own along his chest.

Pleasure and fear circling my body, I pull him to me, letting us drop to the bed so I don't fall over. He removes the remainder of my clothes, revealing more skin for him to kiss and lick and bite. Everything's blurred in heat. I'm not in any kind of control as he shows me all he's good at with that tongue of his.

Who knew that, without walls constructed in my mind, intimacy offers an escape similar to any drug? How I'm still present in my body, yet not altogether myself at the same time. The noises coming from my lips are hardly my own, my back arching with every lick of his tongue, though the guilt settling into my bones is entirely Tino's.

His goodness wraps around me, and I let it. I allow those intrusive thoughts of unworthiness to be prised from my fingers that so stubbornly clutch onto them. If I am a leech, feeding my darkness on his light, then so be it.

After several blissful minutes, a begging 'Please' escapes my lips.

He gives a chuckle, climbing on top of me, his eyes dancing across my face.

'I want you,' I tell him. 'Make me yours.'

He bites his lip before biting mine and then kissing me some more. I push his jeans off and then wrap my legs around him, dying for him. All the contact with skin is enough to make me wince, so much so that it's like being there myself, holding his friend in *my* arms as he dies. The blood is so red, yet Tino is so sweet.

Only when he pauses his kisses do I notice I'm crying, tears silently slipping down my face.

The lustful fog in Tino's vision clears somewhat. 'What's wrong?' he asks.

'Nothing. This is just so amazing.' I'm breathless, and it's only a sort of lie, because it *is* amazing. But this time, when he returns his fingers to my skin, he marks my flinch and removes his body from mine in one fluid motion.

'Don't.' I try to pull him back, but to no avail.

The heavy realisation falls like a landslide behind his eyes.

'Oh my God,' he utters, getting off the bed so he can put some distance between us. 'You've never stopped living it, have you? The whole time I've been touching you, kissing you, *going down on you*—you were reliving *that* moment.'

His devastation is almost as strong as his grief and bitter enough to taste, along with my own sour disappointment in myself that I couldn't hold it together long enough to have one blissful moment with him.

'That's only sort of true. Yes, the pain of your past is there, but it's happening alongside everything you're doing right here, right now. Believe me, this is all I want. You're so good. You feel so good. Please don't stop.'

My tone is rich with desperation, though he's unmoved, shaking his head.

'What is it you feel? When you're there.'

'It's the fear and grief and guilt of that moment, but I also feel *you*, your mouth and touch, your desire.' I try to reach out, but he moves a step further away. 'It's all rolled into one, but I want it. I want you. The pain's bearable.'

He remains motionless, staring into me, his expression turning hard, his naked body in relief to the neon lights outside the window. He's like a Greek god.

Until he shakes his head a fraction. 'No.'

As he pulls his jeans on, I scramble to my knees, my voice bordering on shrill. 'No? What do you mean, no? You said you want me, too, that you always have. Was that bullshit?'

He stops at the accusation, pointing at me with his T-shirt in hand. 'I have wanted you. Always. Silently, from afar. It's been unrequited longing for you, Lee. You've always been beyond my reach. But I-I won't....' His voice shakes with emotion as he turns his gaze to the ground. 'I won't be another means for you to hurt yourself.'

He drives the words home before stalking out of the room and slamming the door behind him.

It takes me three minutes to pull myself together. After shrugging my clothes on, I fling myself out of my room to find the apartment empty.

Panic hits me. Tino has left. He wants nothing to do with me.

The pain of his departure washes over me like a wave of withdrawal. I bend at the waist, clutching at my stomach in anguish. The second swell of pain is a deep regret for ever dreaming to go there, for having believed for a fraction of a moment that something so wholly good could happen to me.

Sinking onto the sofa, I lower my head into my hands and weep. Tears seem to be second nature these days. Surely my body has run dry by now.

With the release of my sorrow comes the realisation that the likelihood of Tino deserting me is slim. Retreated to the sanctuary of Marie's is more like it, where he'll avoid sleeping on the sofa and dealing with a hammered Lorna and Lisette when they return. He may forever be repulsed by being with me, but he's too good a person to leave forever without saying goodbye. Unlike me.

As I settle further into the sofa, a hollowness creeps into my insides as I recall what he had said, how he'd always longed for me, before my accident, during my addiction. He was always there, yet I choose the single worst moment of our long friendship to acknowledge that I want him in return.

The front door crashes open, Lorna's back hitting the wood, Lisette clinging to the front of her shirt in a passionate embrace. Hoping I'll blend into the sofa, I pray they don't spot me, but when Lorna lets out a giggle, I peer from beneath my lashes to find they've untangled themselves.

It's Lisette who pauses at the sight of my tear-stained face. 'Chère, what's wrong? Where's your man?'

She takes a seat next to me on the sofa as I huff a huge sigh and say, 'His absence is a sure enough indicator of how much my man he isn't.'

Lisette shoots me a puzzled look.

'He left,' I deadpan.

'What happened?' Lorna eases into the other side of me on the sofa.

'He fled. When he realised the whole time we were... touching, it wasn't only pleasure he induced but also his pain.'

At their confused faces, I recall that I haven't told them about Tino's brush against death, and although it isn't my story to tell, I divulge, 'Tino saw his friend perish. He died in his arms. Murdered.'

'Oh, honey!' Lisette gasps, while Lorna clutches her fingers to her mouth.

I lean forward to cover my face with my hands. 'He told me he wouldn't be a means-for me to harm myself, believing I only want him now because it hurts.'

Lorna's honest eyes swim. 'Is a hug out of the question?'

I shake my head, my own eyes filling in return as my lower lip trembles. She doesn't waste a moment, throwing her arms around me while being extra careful not to make contact with skin. I'm grateful for her care, but at the same time, it breaks my heart that since the onslaught broke through some sort of psychic barrier, this is the life I have to look forward to. The dead may have stopped crawling through the cracks, but now anyone who has brushed death can't come anywhere near me. I'm not sure which is worse.

'I know just what you need,' Lisette announces, and she moves off towards the bathroom, leaving me with her girlfriend.

'You two have it made.' I half smile.

'I'm lucky.' Lorna tucks her luscious hair behind her ears. 'But that doesn't mean we don't argue. She has a temper,' she giggles before turning serious. 'And it's not always easy. There are nights when I wake up screaming, drenched in sweat. I'm a work-in-progress. Lis understands that. She's been touched by darkness too.'

'How do you live with it?'

'Not much choice.' She sighs. 'Listen, Lee, I'm under no illusion. I know I'm not entirely a good person. I'm just doing the best I can, the way you are. But the one thing I do know is, when you love someone, you'd do almost anything for them and pretty much anything not to hurt them. Tino loves you.'

'Don't say that, Lorna. It's not true.'

'Of course he does, silly. All he wants is for you to be okay.' She lightly strokes my hair. 'He just needs to clear his head. Open a chink in your armour. Let him in a little.'

Swallowing the lump in my throat, I nod, my spirit lighter for having talked to her. I wonder if all people have some sort of gift that they bring to this world. If so, Lorna's is the power to soothe. Turbulent souls gravitate towards her to bring themselves a sense of peace and bask in her warm glow.

'Lisette is lucky, too, you know,' I confess to her. 'You have a quality that warms everyone around you. You're like sunlight, and that is something good.'

She lets out a loud giggle as the rosy warmth of a blush spreads across her cheeks.

'I agree,' Lisette calls, beaming from the doorway of the bathroom. She then beckons me with her head.

Curious, I stalk over, only a little unsteady on my feet, and peek into the bathroom.

Lisette has run me a bath full of fragrant bubbles, and there are scented candles around the edge of the tub.

A laugh escapes my lips. They've both done a good job of cheering me up.

'It always helps me de-stress,' she tells me with a wink. 'Enjoy.'

As they leave, I spot the fluffy towel Lisette has left out. I brush my fingers across its velvety fabric. Falling in love with these women would be so easy. Both of them are free and open. Despite past pain, they're unashamedly themselves. If I shuck off enough layers, will I find who I truly am?

After peeling my clothes off, I lower myself into the water, which is just on the right side of hot. It instantly eases my joints, warming me and chasing Tino's sadness away. I can't remember the last time I had a bath. Too scared of water, I stick to showers. I don't even have a tub in my flat. I haven't swum since my accident.

The water soothes my aching muscles. I've been missing out.

Closing my eyes, I sink in further, bubbles popping around my ears. The water is a caress. In its comforting embrace, my mind drifts to Tino and how different it felt to have his hands on me, hot and passionate. The huge relief of truly giving myself to him.

No fight. Or walls.

Only surrender.

To allow myself to be someone's.

The bath is bliss. I sink lower until it rises to my chin. Trailing my fingers across my thighs, I conjure a mental picture of him, of his goodness, his heat, his soft caresses. The safety his clever fingers bring me. In his grasp, I'm safe enough to allow the rushes of pleasure to overcome me. I can let go.

Let go.

Give myself.

What a wonderful thing it is to give myself.

Palms washing over my skin, claiming my own body, I sink further as the water whirls around me, my breath shuddering. All I need to do is let go, give in to it.

'Embrace pure abandon.' An entreaty, strange in its familiarity, for the first time recalling a dream I had on that filthy mattress during my relapse. *'Give yourself. Be free.'*

The water rises, covering my chin, and I sink to my nostrils. A dreamy recognition pulses, a long-held fear of what my return to the water might bring. *Hello, drowning, my old friend.*

'*Just let go. Give in,*' a gentle voice as smooth as silk calls.

It would be so sweet to surrender, so desired am I by the water.

Beneath the water, my heart thumps, vibrating beats in my ears as I submerge myself. Ravishing caresses slide over my skin, so seductive and claiming. My hands slide over Tino's palms sunk into my tender flesh. Starved of oxygen, my heart races, the jolt causing me to catch the edge of the roll-top bath—and in a terrifying instant, it dawns on me that the strokes are not my own.

I thrash against an invisible grip, panic searing my muscles. No longer inviting, the dread of dying overtakes any lingering desire. My eyes flick open. From the shallow depths of the tub, an empty bathroom looms above me. There are no dead holding me under. The grip clutches me from below.

My head becoming light, desperate yells escape me but only succeed in sending a stream of bubbles to the surface. My legs and arms flail against the invisible hands, sending water everywhere, dousing the candles, leaving trails of black smoke evaporating into the air.

The blurry panic-stricken faces of Lorna and Lisette appear before me, framed in violent waters. Their grip is clawlike as they fight against the invisible force to pull me to the surface, the terrified frenzy of their grabbing leaving my skin torn like cat scratches.

The contact of their frantic grasps sears pain through my body. Lorna in the middle of massacres, torn body parts strewn across the ground. Lisette standing next to a girl, her neck at an unnatural angle, but the framing's all wrong, and it takes me a second to discern what I'm viewing. The girl is on the ceiling.

Visions of their pain swirl with my own burning agony of drowning. Black spots cloud my vision.

My screams make me gulp down even more water.

The bath cracks. A tidal wave takes the girls off their feet, sliding over the linoleum floor, leaving me spluttering in a naked heap.

My breaths come in sharp, laboured pants. Lisette's and Lorna's are the same from across the room, their eyes wide at the sight of pieces of porcelain tub floating across the floor like stranded islands in the receding tide.

'What in the name of all that is holy was that?' Lisette stares, her fingers reaching out to skim a nearby piece of the bath.

'Sorry.' Palm fluttering to my chest, a calm settles over me, my pulse regaining its regular beat.

'You're sorry?' Lorna goggles. 'Lee, you were being drowned in the bathtub. Why are you sorry?'

I shrug a naked shoulder, strangely calm. 'It was a nice bath.'

A shaky laugh escapes Lisette as she takes an even shakier knee and rises, grabbing the nearby towel before handing it to me.

'Yeah, it was,' she agrees. 'But we have way bigger concerns here. How were you drowning?'

'It was as if I was locked in someone's grip. How does that make sense?'

'Perhaps it does. We were trying to pull you to the surface with all our strength, but it was as if something was holding you under. Did the dead try to drown you?'

I shake my head a fraction. 'No.' Breathing deeper, I ignore the burn in my chest. 'No one was above me, living or dead. The force was coming from below. One set of hands, pulling me under.'

Lisette and Lorna exchange a look before Lorna shudders, saying, 'That is super creepy.'

I nod, staggering to my feet before wrapping the towel around myself, vaguely aware of the women talking to each other as Lisette helps Lorna to her feet, remarking on what a night it's been and how Marie has missed out on quite the show.

Their words fade into the distance as every tiny hair on my body stands to razor-sharp attention. The cool of a familiar breath tickles the nape of my neck, and I'm certain that when I look, one of the dead will be right behind me. But when I glance over my shoulder, no one is there.

Only the faintest whisper calls to me. *'Lovely.'*

CHAPTER
FIFTEEN

Hot coffee warms my hands as I stare straight ahead at the switched-off television screen, my hair still slightly damp and loose around me where it hangs nearly to my waist. Marie has been called. Her footsteps pound the space in front of me so quickly, she should wear the floor to dust.

They're talking. Lorna and Lisette speak in hushed, hasty tones, relaying to her the events as they happened. Tino returned to the apartment with Marie. He says nothing, though the heat of his eyes burns against my skin.

I feel calm. Too calm.

The voice.

That voice.

It niggles, pulls at the corners of my mind with a hint of familiarity to it, devastatingly inviting.

'I have a plan,' I announce, cutting off whatever they

were babbling about, bringing the attention of the entire room to fix on me. I keep myself still, but my gaze remains locked on Tino.

A minute passes while they wait.

The taste of salt water rises on my tongue, full of anticipation for the words I'm about to voice. The tremors in the power of them, as if all roads led here all along—a final herald before the final answer.

'The only way to get the answers we need—why me, what the dead want, all of it—is if I go back.'

Marie stills. Whatever magic she possesses hangs heavy around her.

'Back where? To England?' Lorna asks.

'No,' I say quietly. 'Back to wherever it was I went for those three minutes when I was seventeen.'

All hell breaks loose.

Everyone's talking all at once—Lisette telling me it's a crazy idea; Lorna reminding me we have no idea where I went; Marie saying God knows what in French, but it sounds like some sort of prayer.

Only Tino maintains his silence as he stares at me.

And I him.

'So,' he eventually starts, his words for my ears alone, hidden within the panicked chatter, 'you *are* looking for a way out. And what then? You communicate the answers to Marie through the board as a spirit? You told me you didn't want to die.' His last sentence comes out loud and harsh.

The others quiet, turning to stare at him while the

silence that thunders in the apartment makes my breath shake.

'I don't want to die,' I repeat, my mantra since being held at gunpoint. My eyes flick to Marie. 'You can return me to life, Marie. You've tried everything to lead me to the brink of my death, to remember. I need to go to that edge. Stay on it long enough to remember.'

'Your plan is a dangerous game,' she warns, her expression stony.

Lisette and Lorna are too shocked to say anything.

'In the bathtub, I was being held under by an invisible force. Then, in the moments after, there was a voice. One I've heard before, I'm certain of it—from the other side. It was so familiar,' I breathe, my brow knitting.

'Was it your father?' Lorna asks.

'No. Not my father. Differently familiar. More like a deeper sort of recognition. It's as if the memory is dancing beneath the surface. It's all distorted, slipping through my grasp like liquid.'

'Do you have any idea whose voice it is?' Marie probes.

Not wanting to reveal the truth for a moment, I keep my line of sight on Tino, whose expression is hard on me, expecting the worst, I presume.

My lips part the barest fraction.

'Who do you think it is, Lee?' His voice is much more coaxing than his expression.

'Death. I believe Death spoke to me.'

Lowering my gaze from Tino to the ripples on the

surface of my coffee cup, the silence saturates the air around us. Until Lorna barks out a laugh.

'Lee, I'm sorry, but you must be mistaken. Death isn't a person.'

But her words fall into silence. I steel myself, rising out of my seat and drawing level with Marie, finding my strength in her otherworldly aura. To admit to myself everything I've ever sought to deny.

'Marie, there was a voice. It was the voice of Death. It called my name, called me to him.'

Stars twinkle in her eyes. It's plain to recognise in the moment that there's a part of her, a part soaked in darkness, that desires this too. To commune with Death himself.

She moistens her lips. 'You're asking me to end your life.'

'I'm asking you to bring me back,' I counter.

She breaks her eye contact with me, giving a glance to Tino. 'It's been one hell of a night.' She shakes her head a little. 'Let us all sleep on it. I'm not agreeing, Lee. I need time, as do you.' Marie rubs her forehead with weary fingers.

As she leaves the apartment, she gives Lorna's shoulder a gentle squeeze. All conversation leaves with Marie. Lorna and Lisette, now completely sober and their appearances beyond exhausted, retreat to their bedroom.

Leaving me with Tino.

'I'm sure there's much you want to say to me,' I murmur.

He drags a palm down his face, shifting his gaze over my shoulder. 'I don't know what to think. Maybe after these last four years of pain, of addiction, it's the thing you crave.'

'Tee, I'm not looking for ways to continue hurting myself.'

'You just asked Marie to straight up kill you.' His voice coming out strong as he stands. 'To return you to wherever you went. You say you don't want to die, that you've been haunted all this time. But I'm beginning to believe that you haven't been running away—you've been running towards it. Only, you didn't want to acknowledge it before, too scared to admit that what you long for, deep inside yourself, is to be there in that place again. With Death.'

Tino giving voice to my most guarded fears serves to spur my anger. 'That's so not fair. You have no idea what it's like to be so scared.'

'You're right, I've never died before or been haunted. I've never been to the other side. But I have seen death. You may be haunted by the dead, but you've never had to watch the light leave someone's eyes. I have. So don't tell me I don't know what it means to be scared, because I do. Death is so much more terrifying for those left behind.'

As if I'm plummeting from a great distance, the air is sucked out of me.

'Tee—' I start, but he isn't done.

'All I've done since we got here is witness you barrel down this road. You've thrown yourself along this path that leads to where? Hell?' He swallows hard. 'From the outside, it seems like you can't wait to get back there, to whomever is waiting for you on the other side.'

I almost choke. 'You mean to Death?'

Taking a solid step forward, he closes the distance between us. 'Death,' he whispers, bowing his head near to my own. 'A Death who has a voice to call your name, who has hands with which to hold you under. Death with a form, the shape of a man, a man who *wants* you. Someone in whose arms you'll feel no pain.'

'Are you jealous of Death?' I say before I think better of it.

'I'm trying to understand why you would do this, why you would run straight into the arms of a being we suspect of drowning you, not once but twice. And now, what? You're giving him what he wants on a silver platter? Lee, what could he possibly tell you that would make any of this better?'

'At least I wouldn't be in the dark anymore. I would know my role.'

'Why do you even want one?'

'I-I—' I choke on my words because the answer is so complicated, even my own mind struggles to untangle its desires. I never chose this, but turning back no longer appeals to me. Barrier after barrier is breaking. I'm now more inclined to allow myself to be propelled forward, wishing more and more to learn what's at the finish line.

'I care about you,' he continues, his hand twitching as if longing to take my face in his fingers before withdrawing as if scorched. 'The deeper we get into this cosmic bullshit, the harder it's going to be to get out.'

I take a deep swallow. 'There is no out. Not for me. Not now.'

The pain flares behind his hazel eyes as his jaw sets, and, running his fingers through his hair, he turns away from me.

'Getting out is still an option for you, though. If you want to go, I'll understand.'

'Wow.' He shakes his head, heading towards the door. 'You're unbelievable.'

And then he is gone, out into the brightening morning of a fresh New Orleans day.

'PLEASE TELL ME YOU KNOW SOMETHING,' I UTTER AT MARIE, pacing round her shop like a wild thing. Did Tino stay here last night? What if he's on a plane heading home? Would he do precisely what I asked him to? Although I didn't ask, not really. I only said he should.

My inability to trust his loyalty prickles against my skin as I question his ability to remain by my side in all this mess and madness, even if it's as my friend and nothing more. No matter how much I want the more.

Would he want more if it didn't hurt me? If I could find a way to block out the visions, would he want me then? Would he ever accept a version of me that didn't want to destroy myself? Does he only want me in order to protect me from the world which has done me so wrong?

My mind is a vicious whirlpool of thoughts crashing in on one another. I'm in no state to make rational decisions. I pace, scratching at my skin, pressing the delicate layers of dermis with my fingernails, breaking it with ease. Beads of ruby appear on the surface. This small pain at least gives me something to focus on. The pain is good. It lets me know I'm still in my body. My eyes dart, frantic, to the door behind Marie, the anticipation of seeing Tino filling me with dread and hope at the same time.

Marie is too still as she heaves a great sigh. 'It hasn't even been twenty-four hours. Time is essential. This isn't an endeavour we should be rushing into. It's serious.'

My shoulders sag. 'I'm aware.' Casting yet another furtive glance at the door, I ask, 'Did Tino stay here last night?'

She follows my gaze before leaning her palms flat against the table as if overcome by weariness. 'Yes, he did. He's hiding. Shall I get him?'

'No. Lord, no,' I'm quick to respond.

'I don't appreciate being in the middle of these things,' Marie quips.

'You would rather be pondering my resurrection?'

'Indefinitely,' she responds with a quirk of an immaculate eyebrow.

Relaxing, I stomp over to the shop counter to toy with some jade beads Marie has in a dish there.

After a while, she softens, a chuckle leaving her lips as she drops her voice so a few customers who are comparing voodoo dolls don't overhear her. 'My expertise is monsters and magic, Lovely. I have no wisdom of the heart to impart.'

I shake my head a fraction, my red hair tumbling over my shoulder. 'Pity. I'm in sore need of it.'

The talk of monsters casts the strange shadows of *other* creatures into my mind. A notion takes root and niggles. I turn my gaze to Marie once more.

'Marie, when the dead overcame me, they changed their form. They were burned. They've never appeared in such a way before. Lisette told me about a friend of Lorna's. She believes we're connected.'

Goose bumps spawn across my arms at the venom entering Marie's glare. Her words drip with pure poison. 'You're nothing like that creature. He cares for naught but himself.'

'What is he?' I ask in a near whisper, taken aback at how my question has elicited this response from her. Surely, she knows him as Lorna does, but why would Lorna want to protect him, whereas Marie does not?

'Don't concern yourself with him,' she advises. 'It's Lisette's theory, but there's no proof. You're connected to the other side, and he relishes sending others there.

That's where the connection ends, my pet. Please, you're nothing alike. Lorna feels a loyalty to him I'll never possess. He doesn't care enough about me to make it so. Your strength is your kindness. I understand that by pushing Tino away, you believe you're protecting him from what's coming because you can't fathom it. But believe me, it's his choice to make. People should always have a choice.'

There's so much pull in Marie's words. I want to believe what I'm doing is noble and is not because I'm terrified. I want to be the person she believes I can be. To accept, somehow, that it's kindness, not fear, that drives me. If I stopped being afraid, would kindness remain in its place? Would I approach the dead as broken soldiers deserving of placation and rest? How would I achieve such a thing?

My troubled thoughts remain as I ascend the stairs.

When I creak open the door, the apartment appears empty at first, until I spy Tino sitting at the kitchen table by the window, observing the blustery weather outside, his hands wrapped around a mug. I take in his cream cable-knit jumper, the perfect contrast to the warm tan of his skin. He looks good, while I present as some sort of animalistic savage with my red tendrils cascading around my shoulders. Frankly, at this point, I'm astonished birds haven't taken residence. I hate wearing it loose, but the urgency of my thoughts makes my fingers tremble, robbing me of my ability to fashion it into a braid.

When I clear my throat, the noise draws his honey eyes across the room in a slow sweep. The air takes on a thick smoky quality, an eternity stretched out between us as vast as the ocean. I hug my arms around my waist as he gives his attention to the life-thronged street below once more.

A swell of emotion rises inside my chest. 'I'm sorry,' I blurt. 'Old habits and all of that. I shouldn't push you away. I shouldn't believe the worst. Not about you. You've been nothing but good—too kind, in fact. I don't know what I would have done without you here. I guess....' I pause, wishing he'd give his attention to me but at the same time acknowledging that it's easier to talk because he isn't. 'I keep wanting to give you an out, but I'm not being fair, because you leaving is the last thing I want. You're my friend, and I need you here. I want you to stay. It might kill me if you left.'

The scrape of his chair against the linoleum startles me, causing me to clutch onto my elbows, unable to avoid his gaze as he crosses the room to stand in front of me.

'Friend?' he states, searching.

I gulp. 'Friend,' I confirm, fighting the treacherous pounding of my heart. His friendship is all he has to give, and I will force myself to grab it with both hands, let myself take it even if I have done so very little to deserve it.

With a careful movement, he grazes the backs of his knuckles against my cheek, and my lips part, releasing a sharp breath, the jagged pain contrasting the warmth of his skin. When he withdraws his fingers, the desire to weep flares strong in my chest.

'You're, at last, going to accept that I'm with you, no agenda or guilt?'

I give a nod as my answer.

An indecipherable smile stretches across his lips as he pulls me into a hug, taking extra care not to make contact with my skin again.

'Friends,' he whispers.

CHAPTER
SIXTEEN

We work with little respite for the next forty-eight hours, poring over Marie's books, a weird calm and methodology to our research. Tino and I rotate around each other like planets in orbit. The sensation that he's observing me follows me around, although the second I glance in his direction, he's involved in something else. I notice how his hair has gotten so much longer now, and I'm fascinated by the action he makes when he pushes it from his face in a smooth, sweeping motion. I'm sure he must have caught me looking and noticed my lip bitten between my teeth when he does.

Our conversation is so polite, it borders on hostile civility. I catch Lorna and Lisette exchanging glances. Sometimes there's a different thickness to the air that entirely belongs to the couple. I imagine it must be a chemical reaction of being so in love. They sometimes forget the presence of others. Like now, when Lorna has her hand resting on the inside of Lisette's leg, her thumb draws a slow circle, causing Lisette's lips to part in a seductive gasp.

The intimacy of the action causes me to blush. I tear my eyes away from this little moment I'm intruding on, and my gaze collides with Tino's, his eyebrow raised at me. My blush deepens, which seems to amuse him, although my mind is in turmoil. An onslaught of senses embraces me. I recall a few nights ago when his lips were on me, when he kissed the shuddering sweet spot of my inner thigh.

I need to stop these thoughts.

I slide off my chair. He turns to watch me go, and I can't drag my eyes from him either. Only when out of the flat, in the quiet safety of the stairwell, do I rest my back against the door, letting out a giant breath.

I wish I knew what was going on between us. We're friends, yet our conversation has all but been out of a Jane Austen novel, the way the past couple of days have transpired. Then in a spark of a moment, his searing stares could melt my clothes right off my body, leaving me as nothing but a puddle on the floor with Tino lapping at my edges.

I shudder.

My steps light, I pace into the shop. Marie's sitting in the glow of her oil lamp, her head poised over a book rather than the board. Thankfully, as I enter the shop, a tall gent wearing a top hat and velvet coat is leaving, the tinkle of the bell chasing him out. Marie's fingers work at her temples, massaging in stress-releasing circles.

I edge closer to her and grip the front desk with my fingertips. 'Too many voices?' I venture.

Rather than answer, she shuffles the book in my direction, revealing a drawing of an ancient-looking tunnel with shallow water stretching across its threshold.

'You found a way,' I exclaim, pulling the book towards me.

'I found a theory.' Her voice comes out dry, her hand resting on her hip.

After scanning the words on the page, I peer at Marie. 'Pluto's Gate. It's in Turkey? We're going to Turkey?'

Marie massages her head again.

I straighten. 'Tell me, Marie. What are you thinking?'

'We're not going to Turkey, Lee.'

I open my mouth to argue, but she cuts me off.

'Your situation has weighed heavy on my mind. You. Death. All of it. I'm trying to make sense of it, how you almost drowned in a bathtub. You and Death both are connected to the water. My understanding is that rivers are what transport souls on to the next life, but when *you* drowned, both when you were seventeen and now, when something was ready to drag you to the door, your soul may not have travelled down a river.'

'I'm lost,' I admit.

'I'm thinking if I get you close enough to a source,

your soul will have less distance to travel. We sneak you in, so to speak. Get in, get answers, get out again.'

I almost blanche, sweat glistening on my palms.

Marie continues, full of trepidation. 'Your soul knows the shape of water. It'll find its way quickest within it.'

'You're saying I should drown again?'

'For moments, close to an entry to the other side. Where your soul doesn't have far to travel.'

Moments of time stretch between us, our breaths the only noise before I glance at the book again.

'You believe this is a gateway?' I run my fingers over the drawing of ancient stone.

'Yes.'

'So, why aren't we going?'

'We might not need to. If I'm correct, there's a gateway much closer. Pluto's Gate is an ancient door to the Underworld, according to Greek lore. But there are other gates across the earth, usually signalled by the presence of water and unusual geological activity.'

'There's such a place close by?'

Her eyes glitter. 'I hardly believed it when it hit me. Lisette lived a haunted childhood—possessions are rife in the South. Her home on Avery Island is a hotbed of spirit activity sitting on a huge dome of salt.'

'Salt?' I quirk an eyebrow.

'If I'm correct, it's right there, all around the bayou of Avery Island. A gateway to the other side. A site that calls souls home.'

There's a part of me that wants to recoil in disgust,

because underneath it all, Marie is something other, too, connected to the other side as she is. I feel it sometimes. The friction of our auras flares against each other, both agents of the dead in our own ways. Marie at her core is a voodooist. And here she is with a willing sacrifice, someone asking to die and to be brought back to life at her hands. The glittering dark power in that is irresistible.

The only problem is, I'm seduced too.

'I trust you,' I whisper.

'You're going to have to.' She half smirks, the beads that adorn her braids glinting in the low light. 'I've been researching ways in which I might call your soul to this world once it departs. There are certain herbs that, when burned, will guide the spirit. As for your physical body, adrenaline will be the best thing to revive it. Lucky for us, it's something easy enough to procure.'

'Please, will you do me a favour, Marie?'

'Sure.'

'Let's not tell the others what we're planning, how my fate is to drown. Again.'

She regards me for a moment before silently consenting with the slightest tilt of her head. 'You'll not die on my watch, Lovely.'

'Only a little,' I quip, a smile tugging at my lips.

She smirks in return. 'A little death, indeed.'

When we venture upstairs, we find the group in quiet contemplation.

'We're leaving,' Marie announces.

The trio cast confused glances at her before she continues.

'I believe I've found a gate, a source where the veil between this world and the next is thinnest, a place where the spirits cross over.'

All faces in front of us drop.

'Where?' The word is a fragile whisper escaping Lorna's lips.

Marie's gaze becomes set on Lisette. 'Avery Island.'

Lisette knits her brow. 'The island? Are you sure?'

In two strides, Marie's hands are clasped around Lisette's, bringing them into her bosom and cradling them close to her heart. 'I know you have ghosts there in more ways than one. It seems I've discovered a root to your hometown's mysteries.'

Lisette takes a hard swallow, only nodding.

When I look at Lorna, it's clear that she is just as perplexed as Tino and me. Yet Lisette closes the distance between them, threading her fingers into Lorna's and resting a head on her shoulder. The private signal between them. This is a story she'll share later. My own heart lurches, hoping this won't be something painful for her.

We all wait for Marie to continue.

'There are several of these entries across the globe. Avery Island is just one. Its unusual geographical makeup and hotbed of supernatural activity reveal its purpose to me now that I know where to look. I'll use this gateway as a means of casting Lovely to the other side. Being so close to the source, her soul will not have far to travel to gain the answers she seeks. Once there, Lee will obtain her answers before I snatch her from the claws of Death.'

'How will you bring her back?' Lorna asks.

'By means both traditional and spiritual. I will take care of the spiritual, but could you acquire the adrenaline, Lorna?'

Lorna gives a faint nod, catching my eye and tapping the side of her nose. 'I know a guy.' My eyes widen, and she chuckles. 'Nothing too nefarious. I have a contact at the hospital who'll help.'

I want to question her further about why someone at the hospital would do such a thing, but Marie cuts off my train of thought.

'Then we should start to prepare. We leave as soon as possible.'

'I'll call my ma,' Lisette says. 'She'll insist we stay with them on the island.'

As we're about to disperse, Tino chimes in, eyes on me though his words are for Marie. 'Hang on. You're missing one vital piece of information here. How are you casting Lee to the other side? I somehow doubt it's as simple as walking through a door.'

Marie doesn't miss a beat. 'Unfortunately for us, no. The finer details must be planned based on our environment. We will face what awaits us there. The adrenaline is a necessary precaution and not something easy to acquire on the island.'

Tino's stare bores holes into Marie as he is for sure reading between the lines of all she's not saying, but he doesn't mention anything else. Though we have established the truce of friendship, he still wants to be my protector, and I suspect that he continues to believe I'll seize any opportunity to hurt myself.

'How long to procure the adrenaline?' Marie directs at Lorna.

'Give me twenty-four hours.'

'In twenty-four hours, we leave. It's not far, a little over a two-hour drive. We need to stay for one night only, Lis. I expect Lee will be somewhat exhausted and unable to make the journey back on the same evening.'

Marie gives Lisette a reassuring look, then spares me a raised eyebrow before leaving us all staring at one another.

Lisette pulls at the frayed edge of her sleeve. 'We need to make a few calls. We'll be back soon.' Lorna gives me a half smile.

Tino and I take our cue to leave them to their private moment. The cool air of the late afternoon refreshes me as soon as we hit the street.

Tino stuffs his hands into his pockets, half turning to me. 'Are you going to tell me the actual plan? Or is the suspense all part of it.'

'Marie told us—'

'I'm well aware of the words she used, just as I am the ones she didn't. There was one important part of said plan missing. The part about you dying.'

'Teeee.' I tease out his name, pulling on the elbow of his jacket with the lightest of touches. 'You have to trust Marie—and me.'

He works his jaw, appearing reluctant to do either of those things. His pause is so long that when he speaks again, it makes me jump.

'What happens after? When she brings you back and you have your answers?'

Pausing, I turn to appraise him better. His hair rustling in the wind, honey eyes radiating with concern, it takes all of me not to lean into him and claim every bit of his warmth.

Instead, I sigh. 'I suppose that depends on what those answers are. Return to England, I guess. I can't stay here forever. Hopefully, I'll return knowing a little more of how to do this, perhaps even help people with this *gift*.'

'That's what you want?'

'I've been selfish for so long. Everything I've ever done. So selfish. I wish it was in my power to take it all back.'

'Lee....'

'No. Let me own this. The decisions I've made have been terrible. I've done horrible things, Tino.' My heart lurches at my admission to him and the truth in the words.

'Yes, you've done horrible things. And every one of them, every single one, has been to yourself.'

He slides a hand to the wall, close to my head so he

may lean in close enough for me to be warmed by his breath. Although my body aches for his, there's only a lingering sadness in his expression.

'When all is said and done, Lee Timms, my hope is that you allow something good to happen to you.'

Without saying anything else, he removes himself from me, then re-enters Lorna's flat.

I close my eyes, wishing he'd allow himself to be that good thing.

CHAPTER
SEVENTEEN

A day later, we're coasting down the freeway in Lisette's ancient Corolla, the white paintwork faded and rusting at the seams. Lorna insisted I take the front passenger seat to save any unnecessary worry about my skin making contact with anyone else's. All but Marie have witnessed death in its worst forms, so it saves me from sharing their pain.

Although winter bites the air, the temperature in the enclosed space of the car is balmy. Tino, Marie, and Lorna are bunched in the back seat together. Tino's forehead is pressed against the steamed window as he watches the world pass us by. A pang of stupid jealousy spears through me as his leg presses against Marie's.

We make it almost halfway before Lorna announces she needs to use the bathroom. Lisette makes a stop at the next gas station, and the three pile out of the rear, needing to stretch their legs.

'You want anything from inside?' Tino asks us as he exits.

'Something sweet,' Lisette calls with a wink.

I give a shake of my head, my gaze following Tino's tall form as he walks inside the service station. Best not to descend the rabbit hole of eating all the car snacks. Strangely, my constant hunger has been somewhat satiated since my decision to return to the other side. Or perhaps its nerves.

Peering up at the Terrebonne Truck Stop sign, I pale, then turn to Lisette.

'We're in a place called Gray?'

'Mmm-hmm.' She nods before scrutinising me more closely. 'Why? Does that mean something to you?'

'No.' I pick at the edges of my nail. 'It's weird is all. That's the name of the man Marie and Tino rescued me from.'

'Shit,' Lisette breathes as we watch Marie pace in front of the car.

'This world seems big, but really, it's so small. You find these things have a habit of happening, kind of like you're born with the threads of who you're attached to already sewn. Somehow, your paths continue to pass as if in orbit. Fate has a way of bringing you to a person or a place, and you repeat it, over and over again.' Something about long car journeys gives my brain extra capacity to give light to lingering ruminations. It's made me philosophical. 'Or it could be a massive coincidence,' I chuckle.

'It's a human desire to find patterns in things,' Lisette remarks. 'It helps us make sense of a chaotic world.'

I side-eye her, but her gaze is set firmly straight ahead, tracking Lorna, who's strolling alongside Tino as they return to the car.

'That is a very logical argument for someone deep in the world of the occult.'

Turning to me, she offers a wry smile. 'What? A pragmatic spiritualist doesn't make sense to you?'

I laugh.

The others clamber in, and Tino passes Lisette a bag of Hershey's Kisses. She snatches it gleefully from his hands, unwraps two, and shoves them into her mouth before throwing the bag at me and continuing to drive.

I regard the bag of shiny Kisses, recalling the flash of an image of when Lisette grabbed me as she was attempting to pull me out of the bath. It happened so quickly, it's hard to make sense of the image, as I had only a glimpse of whoever it was on the ceiling, but Marie did say Avery Island was a hotbed of supernatural activity.

'Who was it you lost?' I ask, unsure how to broach the subject.

She gives the road a frown.

'You don't have to talk about it,' I quickly backtrack.

'It's okay.' She sighs, her brown curls rippling around her shoulders.

A hush falls over the car, everyone taking an expectant collective breath.

'Avery Island has always been a place of the unusual, full of creaking houses and legend.' She chuckles to herself. 'America is filled with real ghost towns, abandoned settlements where the past lingers in the air. Like an imprint a giant thumb pressed on the place that won't shift.

'Anyway, when you're young, you feel infallible. Tiffany and I were fifteen at the time. She was my first girlfriend. We were experimenting—with more than our sexualities. Living in a place like that, where your normal is ghosts rattling door handles, flickering lights, and whispers in the night, you don't fear it. We learned that we should all too late.'

In that moment, the strength of Lisette's memories fills the spaces between us. Thick, balmy nights on the swamp, distressed paint of grand Louisiana houses now starting to crumble, the ripe smell of oil lamps.

'Your childhood sounds far different from mine. This world has been an eye-opener for me. Birmingham is loud, crowded, and ghost free. Well, until it wasn't, for me. I lived near the inner city and never heard of anyone else experiencing rattling door handles.'

She clucks her tongue. 'You'd be surprised. I think it's about perception too. If you don't want to see it, then you won't.' She casts me a glittering glance. 'Plus, you just need to know where to look.'

Something about the sentiment makes me gulp. 'You and Tiffany went looking?'

She nods, caution in the gesture, before becoming entranced with the highway. 'We were bored of the knocking in the walls, the whispers. Would you believe we were sceptical? Our parents talked about the unrestful spirits, how we should treat them with respect, like they were a different species that we simply coexisted with.'

'You didn't believe them?' I ask, incredulous.

'Crazy, right? To not believe what's right in front of you?' She smiles. 'Is that notion not a familiar one, Lee? Didn't you deny your visions for years as madness? How madness is more believable.'

I have nothing to say to that as she continues.

'It's a religious community, and we were teens ready to rebel against anything. It all felt phoney. God and the spirits. But our elders didn't get everything right.' She frowns. 'Or at least not in the right ways. When you deal in the unexplainable, it's like fumbling in the dark. There's no one who's been around long enough to distinguish truth from fiction. You rely on stories, but when they get passed on, they become diluted and embellished. Things get lost.'

'So, what happened?'

'We started using a board.'

Her words are simple, and no further explanation is offered for a time, lost as she is in the echoing hallways of her past. I chance a glance at Marie, taking in that strong aura of magic that surrounds her as someone more connected. I understand, without either of them having to explain, that the use of a board is a dangerous endeavour.

For most people, it would be useless, merely an amusement, with spirits spread thin across the planet and no one to draw them in. But in a place like Avery Island, with its waters rich with souls passing to the other side, calling them to you is a volatile activity.

Lisette breaks me out of my reverie, as if reading my thoughts. 'Of course, we weren't aware of the significance of the geology of Avery Island at the time. At first, we didn't believe the board either. We constantly accused each other of moving the planchette. It was nothing like Marie's, just simple and wooden. It must have been bought in a toy shop in the twenties.'

In the back seat, Marie tsks in my ear. 'As if such things are games.'

'And it was,' Lisette responds. 'A glorious game. After a while, we began to believe. We were communing with those who'd passed, and most wanted to pass on messages. Some clear, most garbled. But we were getting frivolous with our questioning, stupid with our summoning.'

'What do you mean?'

She takes a hard swallow. 'We were fools—young fools. We found it too sad to talk to those reaching out to their loved ones. So, we called out to different kinds of people. Bad people. Murderers.'

The rolling highway becomes flanked by countryside in the amber of the evening, light flickering through the tree branches casting shadows of Lisette's disturbing memories.

The cold in my marrow flickers.

Lisette's grip tightens on the wheel.

'Communing with individuals whose souls are saturated in death caused more commotion. Gusts of wind would appear from nothing, and the messages from the other side were violent. Rock and roll, right?'

There's no humour in her words.

'Before, when I had visions of your past,' I venture, 'they were of Tiffany. She was—'

'Possessed,' Lisette finishes. 'A dark spirit. A murderer who'd been brutally murdered in revenge himself. Such violence leaves a mark on the soul. When we called him to our séance, his soul was consumed with rage. It broke through the planchette and possessed Tiffany. He tried to attack me, but in possession, the spirit is like a puppeteer with no hands. It's a loose and violent type of control. He hurled Tiff at the walls, breaking her bones. With no escape, she screamed for days as the spirit inside her flung her around those walls.'

'Lisette, I'm so sorry.'

'By the time we found a real practitioner with the ability to exorcize the spirit, it was too late. It was more of a relief to release Tiffany from the broken shell she was trapped in. After that, I couldn't stay.'

'And you found Marie?'

'Much later, I'm afraid. After Tiffany, I was determined to never again be so ignorant of the world hidden beneath ours, but it's a difficult environment to navigate. As you can imagine, it's a place filled with fakes. Finding the real deal is hard, and they're few and far between. I was in with a bad crowd for many years, more focused on partying and posturing than the real thing. But it was a way into the occult. It opened the right doorways, and I found my way to Marie. I connected again with the spirits in a safe way and reached out to Tiff, but she had moved on. I've been learning ever since.'

'Learning?'

'About the untold history of the world. The spirits and the creatures we live alongside, in harmony for the most part. The magic that surrounds us. The places in between. The unseen. *Learning*.' She casts a glance to me, her dark eyes sparkling. 'Although, when it comes to meeting something *other*, that's all happened in the space of a few months. Something is happening, Lee. If I've learned anything in all my time, it's this: Everything is connected. Everything.' Her eyes flash at me.

'Lis...,' Marie interrupts, admonishing.

'You've made your feelings clear, Marie, but even you can't deny this is how the universe works. For every darkness, there is light. The universe demands balance. Who is balancing him? We all know he's too powerful for those witches to contain for long.'

'Who are we talking about?' I ask. 'Lorna's friend?'

'Lisette,' Marie states cautiously, 'we cannot be certain. He's not human. We have no reason to believe—'

'It's coincidence, then?" Lisette replies. "Balance is sewn into nature.'

'It's too much to put on her shoulders.'

'Huh?' I interject. 'Who's not human?'

Full of passion, Lisette turns to me. 'I believe you're the light, Lovely. Somehow, it's you who'll bring light to this world.'

'T-The world?' I stammer.

But I don't get any further explanation. The car falls into silence, and even Marie won't offer any further elaboration. We remain that way until Lisette announces our arrival.

CHAPTER
EIGHTEEN

From the close comfort of the car, I'd not noticed the overwhelming, oppressive air that saturates Avery Island.

The houses here creak under the weight of it. It's a place rich in spirits like I've never felt before.

Lisette's parents' house stands a little way from the swamp, a huge building, grand and decaying at the same time. Wind-stripped and faded primrose yellow paint clinging to the woodwork places it in a forgotten time. Trees hang close by, live oaks and weeping willows, as invasive as clawing fingers, marking it as ready to be reclaimed by the earth.

The size of the land they own is gargantuan. Everything is so far apart, there are no neighbours with prying eyes to fret over. I make my way around the side of the house, letting my fingers tangle with the lazily hanging branches of the willow tree. To the rear, there's a huge yard with a jetty out into the swamp. I make my way towards the water's edge.

The bayou is not a gushing stream like one would expect for a place that ferries souls to the other side. Instead, it's stagnant and murky.

Yet...

As I peer at it, the pull of the unseen depths is undeniable, magnetising every cell in my body. From where I stand at its edge, I sense a saturated thickness. The waters are ripe with souls funnelling their way beyond, a diverse melange of people. As I stare, my vision blurs. I catch glimpses of purple and opal sheens in the waters, a vortex of spirits, their faces stretched and contorted as they're drawn in further. Long fingers curl, attempting to grasp onto the watery abyss.

A wayward thought drifts across my mind—*these dead are dying*. I ponder the realisation that there is a second death. There is when you die, and there is when you cross over. A point of no return.

'Lovely....'

The whisper of my name unsettles every hair on my body. The undeniable voice of Death. Glancing over my shoulder, I mark my friends, who are now making their way round the boundary of the old house, none of them perceiving the ghostlike voice. This is my plan, my own —though a trickle of fear seeps in at the seductive tone of the beckoning voice.

I cast my eyes to the water once more, my imaginings now vanished. A second chill passes over my skin at the notion that when I cross, Death will indeed be waiting for me. I only hope he's willing to answer my questions.

'Lee,' Lisette calls, waving her arm. 'You found the bayou, then? Come on, let's get inside before it gets dark.'

I trudge inside, swatting at the midges that hang low in the dying light.

'Shall I show you to your rooms?' Lisette inquires.

Dipping my head, I trundle behind her, now uncertain of myself in this new environment. The others are full of conversation, apparently immune to the oppressive air, but my concentration is as murky as the surrounding swamp, and I'm struggling to remain present, exhaustion creeping in.

On autopilot, I greet Lisette's parents as if viewing the scene from afar. Soon enough I'm alone in a room, perched on the end of a bed and admiring my darkening view of the back yard.

The room is pretty. A ditsy floral, faded-periwinkle wallpaper covers the walls, peeling at the corners, due, I imagine, to the humidity. Black-and-white photographs adorn the walls, hung alongside old paintings of the swampland. I guess this house has been in Lisette's family for generations. Now that we're here, I understand what Lisette meant before. How a place may be old and new at the same time. America is a young country, but its open spaces mean that things remain the same for a long time. The supernatural seeps into unoccupied space where the cracks between our world and the next show signs of wear, as if our reality is merely a frayed garment for whatever lurks beneath.

A knock at the door brings me out of my reverie, my heart skipping a hopeful double beat that it's Tino, then deflating a touch when Marie pokes her head in.

'Are you all right?' she asks.

'Yes,' I sigh. 'There's something about this place that's conducive to exhaustion. Can you believe I'm certain I'll sleep well tonight?'

She chuckles. 'Indeed, the air here is thick. As are the spirits.'

'They commune with you?'

She regards me, thoughtfulness in her gait as she comes to sit on the edge of the bed, mirroring my position.

'In a way. It's their presence saturating the air. It weighs heavy.'

'Exactly.' I nod.

Marie's eyes catch and hold my gaze, the saturated air making me a bit dozy and pliable. The magical aura around her throbs.

'You should know,' she murmurs, 'your skin is glowing.'

I push the edge of my shirtsleeve away from my scarred wrist to observe whatever Marie is talking about, but I find none. Knitting my brows, I shake my head an infinitesimal amount.

'You don't see it?'

'No,' I respond, though Marie's study of me continues, her expression scrutinous, trailing the length of my braided hair. 'What?'

'It must be something to do with the source.' Marie looks at the open window, the dying light casting shadows on her angular beauty. 'Interesting,' she murmurs. 'There's something potent in those waters, in these lands. Something that saturates into our very pores. As mediums ourselves, I would imagine we are more susceptible to it.'

She hasn't quite answered my question, though. 'There's something you're not saying,' I push.

She eases off the bed, then stalks to the window, fiddling with her garnet pendant and bringing it to her lips. 'You seem different. The glow you've acquired close to the waters is just the latest thing. Your confidence has grown in the short time I've known you.'

Though I can't be sure, surprise must cloak my expression.

Before I have chance to respond, she crosses the room without another glance. 'Get some rest, Lee. There's only so long that we'll be able to conceal from Tino our full plan—that you are to drown once more.'

ALTHOUGH I SLEEP WELL, MARIE'S WORDS ARE LINGERING IN my mind in the morning, my imagination fabricating scenarios of Tino's reaction when he finds out the truth of our plan. Will he feel betrayed that I brought him here without revealing the depths I'll go to in order to see this through? His anger is a constant in my imaginings.

Why am I intent on testing the bounds of his friendship? Is there a limit, a point at which he'll say, 'Enough of this madness,' and leave? Is that limit my death, no matter how temporary?

Or does he already suspect my watery fate?

Laden with misgivings, I make my way downstairs, where I find the atmosphere at odds with my internal struggles. Despite living in a haunted place, Lisette's parents are hearty people who have everyone feeling at home, sat around their breakfast table.

I'm pleased to see they dote on Lorna, giving her extra rashers of bacon on her pancakes. They're delighted when I go in for seconds. Lorna and Lisette exchange a glance but don't comment on my bottomless pit of a stomach.

Tino's in good spirits, too, charming Lisette's mother while helping her with the dishes, telling her how his own mother would disown him if he didn't help.

Even I relent and become swept up in the cheery mood and abundance of food. I make the decision that I'm going to tell Tino as soon as possible. Perhaps I might ask him to join me for a stroll by the water.

I'm snapped back to the present as Lorna clears her throat and turns her attention on Marie as soon as Lisette's parents have left. 'We've driven for almost three hours, we're well rested and now well fed, too, so perhaps it's time to share what we're going to do next?'

'Indeed.' Marie nestles her chin on her raised fists. 'Perhaps it is. Now that we're here, I'm certain we're in the right place and that Lee's plan will be successful. The air here is thick with spirits. And though it appears to be in my eyes only, Lovely has taken on a different sheen by these waters. Her skin has a sort of luminescence.'

She pauses as everyone takes a moment to stare at me, and I'm sure that, in this moment, I'm luminous from the burning in my cheeks alone.

'She looks the same to me,' Lorna confirms.

When I glance up, Tino cocks his head as if examining me. Not just examining me but undressing me with his eyes, which makes me blush even harder.

'You're beautiful,' he says in a whisper, leaving me searching for somewhere to fix my attention or some words to say, my skin on fire. He chuckles slightly.

'Either way,' Marie continues, nonplussed, 'we should carry on with the plan as soon as possible. Do you feel up to it, Lee?'

'Yes. We should get it over with.'

Tino hasn't released me from his gaze the whole time. I need to tell him soon. Panic flutters in my blood. This should be a conversation for private, but Marie continues.

'This close to a source, it shouldn't take Lovely's spirit long to cross over to the other side. Judging by what happened in the bathtub, whoever's there may, in fact, be waiting for her. I have no idea how time passes on the other side.' Marie gives her full attention to me now, dragging mine away from my friend. 'But in *our* time, you'll have three minutes before I pull you out. Three minutes is all I'll give you, Lee, so get your answers *fast*.'

All I can do is nod, my throat thick.

Marie continues, giving reassurance. 'You're not the same person you were four years ago. You're going into this endeavour knowing that what you seek is real. When you return, you will be aware of what Death's designs are, the path forward revealed to you. You *will* remember this time.'

'Yes,' I say, although it comes out all rough. In a way, I want Tino to stop staring at me, but my insides feel like they're melting under his gaze. The sensation is not unpleasant.

'What if Death doesn't want to give her up?' Lisette ventures.

'That's where the adrenaline comes in,' Marie counters. 'We have a window before the human body shuts down once the soul has left. There's time. We could stretch to four minutes, but I don't want to take any chances.'

'And what's the point of no return?'

'Seven minutes, I believe. After seven minutes without the soul, the body is truly dead. There will be no return to this world.'

'The seven pounds,' Lisette murmurs.

'Yes,' Marie confirms, 'I believe so. I'm afraid I can't do much more than give my best guesses.'

'What am I missing?' Lorna asks.

'It's the weight of the human soul,' Lisette explains. 'When you die, you lose seven pounds, the weight of your soul. The universe has a nice way of making these little parallels—seven pounds in seven minutes. Poetic.'

'There's one thing you're forgetting.' Tino's rough voice rings over the revelations, his eyes never leaving mine. 'How will you die, Lee?'

A silence falls over us that would be icy if not for the heat in Tino's honey-coloured stare.

'Tee.' His name comes out as a plea, so I change my approach, opting to go direct, much like pulling off a Band-Aid. 'My body recognises death best in the water. It'll be in the bayou. I'm sorry I didn't tell you sooner. I....' But all reasonable excuses fail me. The truth is, I knew he would have had even more reservations, and I wanted him by my side. I tricked him here.

Lisette takes a sharp intake of breath to my left. Tino's expression gives nothing away.

'No,' Lorna exhales, turning on Marie. 'You can't possibly believe this is the best way.'

'Not the ideal way, no. But the best way, yes,' Marie says.

Lorna faces me, fingers sliding across the table to freeze millimetres from my skin. 'Lee, the trauma of drowning. You've lived through that horror once—almost twice—already.'

'I agree with Marie. It's the best way,' I say, feeling admonished somehow.

There's fire in Lorna's eyes as she jabs her finger hard on the table with what must be a painful jolt. 'You mean to tell me Marie is going to walk you out to the bayou and hold you under the water until you die!'

'Babe,' Lisette chides.

Tino maintains his silent stare.

'I will bring her back,' Marie states, as fierce as any witch, voodooist, or witch doctor who came before her. She takes a moment to look at each of us in turn. Determination working at her jaw, we're in no doubt of her resolution. 'Besides, it won't be me alone. I'll need all your help. I don't have the strength to do this by myself.'

'Jesus,' Lorna whispers.

Lisette rubs her brow, glancing towards Tino. Screeching against the linoleum shatters the ominous quiet, and Tino is up and out of the room in two strides.

I close my eyes, deflated, pounding their sockets with the heels of my palms. Although I suppose, of all possible responses, his quiet disapproval was the most I could hope for.

'Are you sure this is what you want?' Lisette's expression of gentle resignation causes discomfort in my stomach. The horrors she's witnessed should be enough to last a person a lifetime, yet here I am, demanding she endure more.

'You don't have to go through with this,' Lorna confirms.

'And how exactly did you two think this was going to

work?' Marie demands. 'That I would stab her? Strangle her?'

'I suspected it would be magically induced,' Lorna counters, exasperation rife in her tone as her palm slams against the table. 'You're drowning her! Again! This crosses a line, Marie.'

'You want to talk about lines crossed, Lorna? What about that soul eater you feel the constant need to protect? He left you and did not look back,' Marie seethes while Lorna's expression turns murderous.

'Hey!' Lisette interjects, a protective hand landing on Lorna's arm.

'Stop.' I hold my hands up at the bickering women. 'Don't fight about me. I've made my decision. This death I have control over.' Giving Lorna my sole attention, I address her imploringly. 'I trust Marie. She'll bring me back. Your girlfriend believes I'm the light. But I need to understand why this is happening to me and what to do next. This is my choice. I appreciate your need to make yours. If you want no part of this, that's fine. I would prefer to have you with me, though.'

Lisette places a reassuring hand over Lorna's. 'Of course, Lee. We'll both be there.'

Giving Marie a shaky smile, I rise from my own chair and leave to find Tino.

CHAPTER NINETEEN

Five minutes are wasted while I flit from room to room in my search for Tino, unsure which one he's been allocated. With every fruitless stop, my anxiety grows as I start to suspect he has left the house.

When I finally find him, I'm breathless with worry. His stance is rigid at the window, though his face is a mask of serenity as he peers out at the cool, sunny morning.

'Those waters will be freezing,' he says.

'Tee...,' I start, edging into the room, only stopping when he swivels in my direction, his mask slipping and his face twisting with anguish.

'Tell me this isn't it, Lee.' He crosses the room in two strides, his chest inhaling so close to my own, though not connecting. 'Tell me Death can't keep you. Tell me you'll come back to me.'

Not expecting this response, I'm floored by his words. I know Tino cares for me, too much, far more than I could ever deserve, but *this*? That his primary concern is for me to come back, no argument, no trying to stop me. He'll support me in *this*. He's so good, I almost can't bear it. 'I'll come back to you.' The words shake as they leave my mouth. Tears begin to form in the corners of my eyes.

His lips part, but he doesn't say anything for a heartbeat. His head tilts, his expression softening. 'How many more times are you going to dance with death?'

'Just this once,' I reply, unflinching. My body pulls me towards him like a magnet to all his rich goodness that I long to feed on, to lose myself to.

'I hate the thought of Death's hands on you, pulling you through worlds. Of the freezing water filling your lungs. How I'm so powerless.'

'I trust Marie.'

He catches his bottom lip in his teeth, thoughtful for a moment. 'I'm not saying you shouldn't, but you don't notice the way she looks at you. The others, they're just here for the ride, their pasts so full of horror that they fail to register the jeopardy you're in. But Marie—she looks at you like she's hit the supernatural jackpot. A diamond-encrusted platinum planchette she wouldn't let be prised from her cold, dead hands.'

A snort leaves me at such a notion.

'You don't see it, do you?' Tino continues. 'She wants you. Death wants you. *I* want you.'

My capacity to breathe evaporates, and I have to take a step away in order to catch it, my shoulders hitting the wall with a dull thud.

Tino closes the distance. 'Before you go, you should know the truth. A truth I'm so terrified to admit because you're going to break my heart into a million pieces. I love you, Lee. Desperately. The kind of love that is destroying me.'

My pulse thunders so hard, I should all but explode. These words are ones I've longed to hear, though part of me rejects the truth of them because how could words imparted with such passion be spoken about me?

He doesn't relent, his eyes drinking in every shaking inch of my body as he continues.

'And every step closer to Death you take, the greater the longing for you that overwhelms me. I love you that bit more with every sun that sets. With each passing moment, I find it harder and harder not to touch you.'

'Then do it.' I tremble. The walls around my heart are beginning to crumble, though I'm somehow still afraid to utter that four-letter word out loud to him in return. 'Touch me. I'm so sick of you *not* touching me.'

The world tilts, and I'm slammed into the wall with the force of his brutal kiss. His lips are a bruise and a balm at the same time. They fill me with heat, setting my chilled blood aflame. A need so crucial mounts in my core, and I know I will die in this moment if I don't have him. All the waves of his pain and grief crash over my skin, tides of desire and guilt making me quiver in every possible way. Wrapping my arms around his neck, I clutch myself flush to him so that my knees don't buckle from the onslaught of emotions.

His hands slide down my back and over my rear before hooking under my thighs to lift me off the floor and wrap me around him. He carries me over to the bed, both of us overcome with need.

He lowers me to the downy surface, then pulls away from kissing me to smooth the tears from my face that I hadn't realised were falling. Pulling my shirt over my head, I don't give him chance to hesitate. He swiftly follows suit with his own as I recline once more, scars laid bare.

Pausing to admire the curves of my body, his gaze holds zero traces of sympathy now, only hot desire. My eyes remain trained on him as he undoes the buckle of my belt, then shucks off my jeans with expert fingers before removing his own.

He eases on top of me, taking my face in his palms. In a slow exhalation, I appreciate the warmth of his skin, his long limbs pressed to mine.

Something changes in the air between us. Softens.

'I don't want to hurt you,' he says.

'Please, don't stop,' I beg, and he kisses me long and hard.

Wrapping my legs around him, I allow my hands to roam his skin, becoming lost to sensation once more. Pleasure grows inside me as I feel Tino hardening against my aching skin. Yet another roll of pain, as if I'm being stabbed myself, echoes through my chest, causing me to shudder and him to pause.

He cups my face before stroking his hand down the length of my throat, then working his way along my chest, kneading, pressing into me, pulling a groan from my lips. Desire pulses through me so richly when he pulls away. I tug him into a kiss before allowing him to rest his lips near my ear, his hot breath sending goose bumps down my legs.

'What does it feel like?' he asks softly.

'Glorious,' I chant, all but rubbing myself against him.

He chuckles, peppering sweet kisses along my neck.

'It feels like accessing every part of you—all of your sadness, all of your desire.' I run my nails firmly along his back, and his skin prickles at my caress.

He stops to regard me for a moment, his honey eyes deep pools of wanting, more alive than I've ever seen them. 'But it hurts?'

'Yes,' I admit. 'It hurts, but in the sweetest way. Because it's you, and right now you're making me feel things I've never felt before.'

'Hmm, like this?' he inquires as he shifts his weight, moving his fingers to my core.

I gasp. 'Yes. Like that.'

'Keep talking, Lee,' he murmurs into my skin as he continues to stroke me.

While coherent thought is lost to me, I'm determined

to do everything in my power to ensure he keeps doing what he's doing with his clever fingers. 'I want it all. Every touch. To live in every moment your hands are on me.'

His low groans against my neck are thoroughly distracting. My body trembles, words escaping my lips without me asking them to. 'Please, don't stop. I can take any pain if it's for you. I will come back for you. I'm yours. Please, Tino. *Please.*'

His pause comes with a sudden shudder, and though it only lasts for a second, I'm disappointed by the absence of his fingers. Then he kisses me hard, moving between my legs, and in one swift movement, he's inside me. The streak of pleasure overtakes every ounce of pain swirling in my body—so much so, I cry out his name.

I'm lost, with no sense of who I am, and so open in spirit that I might as well be him, so merged am I with his sensations.

'Open your eyes,' he commands, and I do.

Locked in his amber gaze, I feel how he has claimed me. My body, my soul, they're marked forever more as his. Maybe this was his plan all along—to give me a reason to fight my way free of the clutches of Death. His fluid motions bring an unfathomable pleasure rising to my surface. Building. Until I shatter and explode like a supernova, closing my eyes as I dig my nails deep into his shoulders. When we come, it's in unison, one glorious blurring of vision and souls.

His head sinks to my shoulder, his breathing deep. The pain curls around me again, yet the euphoria remains.

'I love you, too, Tino,' I tell him, blissful, lost in the sensation of what it means to give myself. To not be taken but to give my body freely. This pleasure can surely only be because of love alone.

He shifts his head, raising his chin to my chest, happiness carved in every relaxed crease of his face.

'I'm sorry it took me so long to see it,' I add. 'I never want to be apart from you again.'

'I adore you. Worship you. Would go to the ends of the earth for you.' He smiles, and my skin tingles, unsure what to do with such devotion in this moment. But I allow it. I want to clutch onto it, to him, and never ever let it go.

He gives me a simple kiss and moves to my side. Although I miss the sensation of his skin against mine, I'm glad of the reprieve from his grief.

We stay this way for a few glorious minutes, savouring the moment. Every now and then, he brushes a strand of hair from my face, and when his fingers make contact with my skin, it shivers with desire and sadness.

Somehow the mixture is more addictive because it's wholly Tino. A sensation he alone, for all his flawed experiences and history, can make.

'Let me come with you,' he says after a while.

'Come? Huh?' I say, dozy.

'To the other side. I don't want to be parted from you either. Let me be by your side when you do this.'

'I can't, Tee.' I smooth my palm over his cheek, unsure if I've ever felt this happy. My blood could be sunshine. 'We have no idea how this works. There's no knowing if our spirits would find their way together. Besides, I need you here on this side. Something glorious to return to. Believe me, I want to come home to this. To you.'

'*Home.*' He smiles, though his expression is resigned as he takes my hand from his face and kisses my wrist before releasing it. 'I can't be there, Lee. I'm not strong enough to hold you under. I've already had one friend die in my arms. It would kill me to witness you dying too.'

I swallow hard. 'I understand.'

Tino's sudden chuckle takes me by surprise. 'It's unbelievably hard not putting my hands on you.'

I half smile. 'Then why aren't you?'

'It's painful. I don't want it to become too much.'

'I can take it.' I shuffle closer.

He frowns. 'How about this—if it gets too much, you let me know, okay? And we'll cool down for a while.'

'That sounds good.' I wrap my arms around him, peppering his neck with kisses.

'Man, I'm so weak.' He exhales, his gentle caresses exploring my body. 'I'm trusting you to stop when you need to, because I'm so done saying no to you.'

With that, I close my mouth over his, and he rolls me on top of him.

A CRY OF SEARING PAIN LEAVES MY LIPS AS I WAKE TO FIND Tino's body wrapped around mine. Shuddering, I wrench myself free without causing him to stir. Panting, I observe his face in the moonlight that is now cascading silver through the open curtains. I drink in his high cheekbones, full lips, and dark hair and allow his presence to pull me, little by little, out of the sizzling agony sleeping with his arms around me has caused. He must have shifted across the bed to hold me as he slept.

My nerves are a little frayed from having him, time after time, not wanting our moment together to end before I must die. No matter how briefly my next death will last, having Tino give himself to me this way has raised the stakes. I don't want what happened today to be our goodbye. As I gaze at him, I falter for the first time since starting this journey. Are the answers worth the risk?

After pulling on my jeans and long-sleeved top, I pad barefoot downstairs to the kitchen to find something to eat, the soft orange glow comforting against the cold of the moonlight. I find a beer in the fridge, then grab a discarded packet of cookies from the counter and methodically crunch my way through them. I try to organise the inner workings of my mind, recalling my questions for Death: Why me? What's the purpose of my gift? What do I do next?

The creak of floorboards interrupts my munching,

but when I peek over my shoulder, it's only Marie. Wrapped in a large crocheted cardigan, she shuffles into the kitchen and gathers the tools to make tea.

'Trouble sleeping?' I ask.

'It's hard for me to sleep in this unrestful place. Even without the board, I sense them lingering close by.'

I nod as an awkward silence stretches out. 'Sorry for delaying,' I offer, picking at the edge of my nails, heat entering my cheeks.

Marie's stare is long and hard, bordering on withering.

Returning her attention to her tea, the steam rising from it giving her an ethereal quality, she releases a low breath. 'I must admit, he's timed it well.' Her eyes flash.

Heat fills my chest, caught somewhere between embarrassment and anger. I grind my teeth while I search for the right words.

She raises a halting palm. 'Lee, he would do anything for you to not go through with this, but you're so close to achieving what you want.'

'He told me he loves me, Marie.'

She scrapes a chair out to sit opposite me, then leans over the table. 'Of course he does. But think of the timing.'

A flare of distrust spikes through me. The room shrinks, the air turning oppressive once more.

Words stick in my throat as I choke on useless tears. 'If not now, when else? He doesn't want me to die, even if it's for a moment. He's given me reason to live, to return to this world.'

'He wants you to stop.' Marie rubs her temples. 'He's threatened by whatever, or whoever, is waiting for you there.'

The accusation that Tino's confession could hold such an agenda stings, and spite boils in my blood. 'What do you get out of this? Why are you pushing this?' I demand.

Her mouth drops. She closes it and opens it a few more times, goldfish-like. '*I'm* not pushing this. You were the one who asked me to carry out this deed.' The heat in her voice rises an octave. 'You came to me lost and broken. My purpose in this life is to guide those who need it—that is *my* calling. If your own has become so unimportant to you because Tino took you to bed, that's no business of mine.'

I recoil as if I've been slapped.

Marie shoves her chair back as she stands and walks away, stopping to linger in the doorway with a large sigh. 'Take tonight to consider what it is you want.'

She walks away without looking back as the tears swell and begin to pour down my face so hard, my breath becomes difficult to catch. I stumble to Tino's room.

By the time I make it there, I'm nearly hysterical. My hyperventilation is so loud, Tino jolts awake. He springs to his feet, seeing that my palms are clutched to my chest. He grips my elbows to draw level with me, releasing them when I wince and taking a pace away. 'Lee. Lee. Breathe, just breathe,' he soothes.

The mistrust rolls through me. Is it Marie who's using me or Tino? Or everyone? No one? Death? Why do I crave Death above all? I almost crumple to the floor, a wheeze leaving my chest.

'Lee.' Abandoning his intention not to touch me, he grasps my face in his palms, locking me within his attention, his hold making my cheeks shudder a little. 'Come back to me, Lee. Come back.'

There's a break in my hyperventilation, and a sob tears itself free. Despite the pain, I sink my head to his bare shoulder.

'I'm... I'm so confused,' I stammer, pulling away to gaze into the depths of his eyes. 'This is something I have to do, Tee. I have to know.'

He nods, stroking my skin, the pain calming somehow. 'I get it. I'll be here, waiting for you. You come back to me, okay?'

I sob again, unable to control them. 'It's not a trick? You really want me? Even when I return, will you still want me? Even though I'm broken?'

'Lee.' He whispers my name with such tenderness, pulling me close to his chest. Grief, bearing no relation to me, judders through my bones. 'I've always wanted you. I love you. That's not going to change when you come back. Once I have you in my arms again, I'm never letting you go.'

My breathing regulates in heavy pants as I cling to him.

'I need you,' I whisper, and he pulls me tighter. My next words come out as a chant, affirmations to myself of a better future with him. 'I wish I didn't have to go. But it's just this once more. Then I'm all yours. *Only* yours.'

He pulls away to give me a fervent last kiss, so desperate it tears me apart. I lose myself to him and all his exquisite pain.

CHAPTER
TWENTY

The sun mocks me with its cheerful glare in the glistening late-winter morning. The air is thick as we approach the bayou. I walk between Lisette and Lorna, following Marie to the water. The aura of magic surrounding Marie flares and glitters this close to the source. My own skin shudders.

Perhaps this is what it felt like to be persecuted as a witch in days past, walking to your demise knowing there's another side awaiting you. The last journey you'll ever make.

Marie holds a bundle of burning herbs, the scent of which has stalked us from the house where I left Tino behind. We didn't say much in the way of goodbye. A goodbye would feel too final. Instead, he kissed me, held me. A memory I plan on clinging to with everything I have.

Staring at my shaking fingers, I attempt to reassure

myself that this plan is going to work. Despite my wobble last night, I do trust Marie. This *is* going to work. I must find my purpose.

As I near the bayou, I betray the slightest trepidation, and on instinct, I seek Marie out, her calm presence a reassurance in my impending death.

Flicking her fingers slightly, she gestures to Lorna. 'You have the adrenaline?'

Lorna wears her worry; it hangs off her every feature like the branches of the willow tree. She offers only a nod, shaking the black leather pouch in her hand. Marie crouches, placing the burning herbs on the ground. Lorna follows suit, settling the pouch near them.

'Shit. I'm shaking.' Her words are as wobbly as she looks.

Lisette rubs her arms in a way that makes me wish Tino were here warming me in the same manner, though I don't blame him for not being able to witness me being held forcibly underwater, much less hold me under too. I would feel the same.

'What next?' I ask.

'Into the water.' Marie motions me forwards.

But when I go to move, Lorna catches my arm, which is covered by my long-sleeved top, the swiftness of the action shocking me with a jolt.

'Last chance to back out,' she reminds me, her expression ferocious and unwavering.

I only hope I appear sure. I give Marie a glance. 'Get in, get answers, get out—that's the plan. I trust Marie to revive me. Three minutes, then I'll be back with as many answers as possible.'

Lorna releases me, and I wade into the shallows. 'I'm not going to be eaten by an alligator, am I?'

'They never come out this far,' Lisette tells me.

I'm not sure whether to be reassured or worried about what that means.

As I lower myself onto my ass, I'm half expecting to be pulled under by unseen hands in an instant. Instead, my breath is stolen by the freezing water, my clothes saturating and carrying the weight of sheets of ice. The other women slosh their way in, shuddering at the drop in temperature. Marie comes to a crouch close by my shoulders with Lorna and Lisette by my waist.

Clouds of fine mist judder from my lips, my teeth chattering so hard, they ought to shatter.

Marie's eyes are stretched wide as if *she's* the deer caught in fatal headlights. 'I won't let you die... for long.'

There's nothing left to do. Taking short gasps, I lower myself further until I'm swallowed, and my world plunges underwater. As I gaze at Marie's familiar face, mirage-like from my watery grave, a sense of peace washes over me. The world is quiet.

Serene.

Marie leans over to place her palms on my shoulders, resting her weight on me.

My chest is tight with a breath that's impossible to catch, but I don't fight it.

Lorna's hands, or what I believe to be Lorna's hands

given her positioning, fall heavy on my ribs, followed by Lisette's grip on my hips. They're strong forces keeping me under as the first flickers of burning enter my chest.

Cortisol floods my blood, and instinct takes over as my arms crash through the surface. My fingers become a vice on Marie's arms, my nails like razors sinking into her flesh as I try to rip her hands from my shoulders. In the panic, I part my lips to cry out, only to swallow more water, while my hips buck against the weight of the girls.

I thrash wildly.

No.

No.

No!

This is such a bad idea—there's no euphoria, no claiming embrace to welcome me home.

Oh shit, this is wrong. So wrong. I'm going to die. Not a little death but oblivion.

Old bile spews itself into my mind. *There is no other side. None of this is real.* The delusions of a traumatised woman, so lost—suicide by murder.

Kicking my legs out, I flail as black spots speckle my vision in disorientating droves.

I'm going to die, and I am never coming back. I have no way of communicating this to my friends.

The black spots increase, my world turning blurry, and my limbs succumb, taking on the weight of anvils—so much so, my attempts at fighting them off flounder and then cease altogether. I could be a rubber doll in the water.

Then a glimmer catches my eye, though the world is fading. A blur of colour blocking out the shining sun that is mocking my death.

Tino.

The darkness shrinks around him.

What is he doing?

Marie is suddenly no longer in front of me.

In the distance, a voice rings like a bell, calling, *'Lovely,'* to me. Seductive and undeniable.

In that second, a fraction of a second, I reach my hand out to my friend.

How sad. To have held love in my grasp for a trifling moment, only for it to slip through my fingers, slide away along with my life. Forever.

His fingers entwine with mine. I fall.

Fall like I've never fallen before. Through time and space.

The jolt in my stomach like I've leaned too far back on my chair lasts for a moment before I'm sailing through water. I plummet through the depths, neither cold nor warm. Gazing at the surface, as if a sailor peering through a porthole, the light of Louisiana fades from view until I'm falling within a blackness so total, I'm unsure if I'm the right way up anymore.

My hair streams around my face, framing my descent or ascent. Whichever it is. I now understand how Alice felt, impatiently waiting for something new to happen in unending free fall.

The waters change as I continue to plummet,

becoming a kaleidoscope of colours, a new spectrum of light I've never witnessed before, their patterns almost musical, dappling the surrounding water. An aurora borealis of vibrant greens, indescribable blues, and incandescent pinks.

No fear fills me now as the lights manifest and play in glowing water bubbles around my body, threading through the strands of my hair. It's as if the water itself is made of life, playful and exuberant in its dancing. When I bring my hand in front of my face, a spectrum of light fractures across my skin. Liquid joy.

I didn't think it would be this way. I didn't think dying would be so beautiful. Is this real? Or my own brain comforting me, protecting me from the horror? Nowhere in the caverns of my memory are fireworks such as these stored.

After an eternity of falling, the endless void is fractured by the faintest glimmer of light. The kaleidoscopic rainbow fading away, becoming lighter and lighter, it dapples until I'm tumbling through a watery sort of daylight. In the distance, a stream of dark bubbles pelts like vicious rain in tandem with me, matching my descent. Though I cannot see, I get an instinctual sense that I'm about to hit the bottom.

With no means of slowing the speed at which I'm travelling, I squeeze my eyes shut and brace for impact.

My landing feels like being thrown into a bed of feathers. When I chance peering at what world I've found myself in and who is awaiting me here, a cloud of black smoke swirls around me, blocking my vision. Panting, I lie here as my fingers slide into the texture of the surface, something between silt and sand, and the smoke evanesces into nothingness.

Sitting up, I find that the world around me has remained underwater. My hair floats in soft tendrils, only I'm not drowning anymore. There's no pain, no burning in my chest.

Another cloud of black smoke ripples nearby, landing like a meteor in the silt. I hurtle towards it, my progress slowed by the non-choking water surrounding me. Without pausing to consider who or what it might be, I throw myself into the smoke, batting it away with my hands in frantic motions as it curls around my fingers like vines.

At last, the phantom smoke clears. 'Oh my God. Tee.' I almost weep as I throw myself into his arms, not giving him a chance to stand.

He doesn't pull away but rather holds me with such ferocity that it might choke me all over again. 'Fuck,' he whispers into my whirling hair, 'I thought I'd lost you.'

We stay in our embrace until I force myself two paces back from him and help him to his feet. 'What happened?'

He casts a glance around at our watery surroundings before his eyes land on me. 'I made the mistake of looking out the window. When I saw you thrashing in the water, I jumped to conclusions about how you must have changed your mind and they weren't letting you come up for air. I panicked.' He rubs the back of his head, guilt plaguing his expression.

'You were right.'

He blanches at my admission.

'I panicked too. I had no way of communicating. You were right, Tee, all along. I've barrelled down this road, and now I've doomed you as well.'

'Lee, I'm with you. This is exactly where I want to be.'

A sharp watery intake of breath shocks even myself, though it doesn't choke me. My brows knit together, the dreadful truth dawning on me. 'Did I tear your soul out of your body and bring you with me?'

'I think so. It was a very disorientating experience.'

Devastation doesn't cover it. 'I killed you,' I squeak.

'Don't worry.' He smirks, rubbing my shoulders. 'Three minutes and Marie brings us back. Simple. Now, where are we? Is this the other side?'

For the first time, I take a moment to peer around.

Nothing.

Just empty, watery nothingness.

Despair creeps in.

'Do you remember this?' Tino asks when I don't respond.

'No.' I try to ignore the worry on his face. 'If I've been here before, I have no memory of it.'

He puts his hands on his hips, his gaze continuing to swing in every direction even though it's an empty vista to behold, as if expecting it to transform in any given moment. 'I thought there would be *something* on the other side. I never expected that when some people said there was no life after death, it meant literally nothing. At least we're together until Marie works her magic.'

Staring around me, I squint into the horizons—which are no horizons at all. Everything is merged grey. 'Something doesn't feel right.'

'Maybe we got it wrong, Lee? There is no other side, no Death. This is it.'

His delivery could be that of a terminal diagnosis. It might be devastating if I believed it.

'It's weird. I was so certain someone, something, would have been waiting for me.'

Tino says nothing to that. This emptiness is perhaps giving more credit to his idea that if there is a Death, he can't, funnily enough, be found on the other side.

Or maybe he's away on business.

Panic rises like bile in my throat. It makes more sense that Death would be found in the land of the living, not the dead. I was so sure the voice belonged to him. I needed to seek him out, and he's not here.

Swallowing my dread, I pace forward. 'We have less than three minutes. Let's explore.'

'Explore what?' he asks, trailing behind me.

'I think I see something over there.' I point in a direction that could be any direction.

The lack of any landmarks is madness inducing, but in one direction, a dark shadow containing the slightest of glimmers echoes in the distance. The one bit of substance I'm able to latch on to.

Our progress is slowed by liquid resistance.

'Urgh,' Tino groans. 'We've been walking a lot longer than three minutes. Do you think we're dead? Like *dead* dead?'

I ignore him and shrug off that notion. Tino's mother would be heartbroken if he didn't come back to her. I remember my uncle when my cousin died. A parent should never have to bury their child. Even in the afterlife, I'm racked with guilt. How perfect.

We walk on. My mind must be playing tricks on me, as sometimes the ghostlike vision of a settlement edges closer, only to become a speck in the distance once more. Sometimes we stop to rest, but for the most part, we walk. I notice the hems of my top are now a tiny bit frayed. Tino squints at the horizon, unable to make out the dull shape I'm aiming for.

My mind is starting to disintegrate. Where is he? Where is Death?

A new guilt settles like a pit in my stomach. Tino made the ultimate sacrifice for me, and here I am, wishing Death's presence before me. I tell myself it's for answers alone. Not to demand why his icy breath on the back of my neck vanished in New Orleans. I try not to examine that feeling of familiarity to which I'd acclimatised over the past four years. Tino is the one who's here. He wants me. Loves me.

We walk.
We walk.
We walk.

'Lee.' Tino's voice sounds rough from misuse. 'I.... We're dead. We've been walking for what, hours? Days? Weeks? Everything's the same here.'

'I know,' I tell him, peering through my lashes and observing the exhaustion painted on my friend's face before picking at a thread of my top. 'The only thing that changes is my clothing. It's becoming more worn.'

We don't say anything for a moment. I stare into the abyss. It doesn't stare back.

There is nothing.

'Lee,' Tino utters again after an age. '*Lee,*' he repeats, more life in his voice than in what seems like years.

He wades over to me and grabs me by the shoulders. Hopeful light twinkles in his eyes, and I slowly turn to follow his line of sight.

There, in the distance, the twisting spires of an underwater city loom.

'You see it?' The elation in my voice borders on hysterical.

'I see it,' he laughs before running.

I follow suit, slow, heavy footfalls beating against the sands of the other side.

We run until our muscles burn towards what appears to be a city of the dead.

CHAPTER
TWENTY-ONE

Ancient spires loom ever closer, an Atlantis long forgotten and haunted looking. Our progress is slow, but we don't tire. The single change on the horizon of what must have been days of walking, the encroaching city appears to be crumbling and, despairingly, abandoned.

I slow my pace as we near the tall walls, peering at the menacing darkened high towers. They could be something out of a Bram Stoker novel. Tino slows, too, putting his hand to his brow to gaze at the structure even though there's no light to protect ourselves from.

He shakes his head. 'We can't be the only ones.' Laughter rattles out of him like old bones. He grasps at his hair. 'I'm losing my damn mind.'

Sliding my hand onto his back, I rub reassuring circles. Descent into madness is a sensation to which I can relate.

A ripple in the water catches my attention, and I glance up to see a ghost of a shadow pass over the high wall of the dead city.

'Look,' I whisper.

Tino follows my gaze, though if anything ever lingered on the wall, it's now vanished. We move on, following the curve of the city's edge, and for the first time in a long time, cold seeps into my bones.

'Do you feel that?' I ask, whipping my head in his direction.

He nods, rubbing his own arms to stimulate warmth. His gaze flits to the heights of the wall in a jerking motion, prompting me to follow suit, and this time, we both witness a shadow pass over the city's border.

'Hey!' Tino shouts before he bolts, running around the outskirts, trying to keep the shadow in view.

I plough after him, although the coldness settles into my marrow and an unsettled sensation crystalises in my stomach. We're being watched. The coolness slows me. Coasting around the curve of the city, I lose sight of Tino, only catching intermittent flashes of his feet. My skin prickles as every hair on my body stands on end.

In the darkness, a voice calls my name. 'Lovely.'

Not the smooth voice of Death, rather a tinkling of magic which ripples the water around me.

I slow to a stop. One footstep. Two footsteps. I strain to listen in the silence. My heart rate gains momentum as I draw the courage to turn around. When I do, my mouth opens to scream, but only bubbles float out in a stream.

Staggering away a few stumbling paces, I clutch my chest as the creature advances on me. The most enormous octopus I've ever seen circles my being, its tentacles catching my waist and spinning me with a certain elegance. Although, on the face of it, it has the appearance of a giant Pacific octopus and is easily four meters across, it's marked as a creature of the other world by its bioluminescence. Colours of violet and cerulean ripple across the surface of its skin as it plays with tendrils of my hair.

The same tinkling voice I heard before disturbs the water around me. 'You are so very late.'

'I-I....'

Stammering is all I have to give the creature before it undulates its long limbs in one fluid motion, pushing from around me to vault over the city walls, leaving me flabbergasted and rooted to the spot.

'Lee?' Tino calls behind me.

When I spin round, the creature is now following him. The sight of it swimming beside my friend doesn't fail to take my breath away again. Although, after a second, I realise this isn't the same creature. This one's skin glows more of a cerise than the other's.

From the expression on Tino's face, he's also facing some sort of shock at being presented with a giant luminescent ghost octopus. As Tino reaches me and comes to a standstill, the creature wraps one of its tentacles around his neck.

'We like your friend.' Their voice is lighter, sweeter than the other. 'He has heart.'

Tino's eyes signal alarm, but I have no time to respond as the first octopus returns over the wall and lands beside us, disturbing the silty ground and throwing up curling clouds of smoke around us that flare the lights of their skin.

The cerulean creature's tentacles curl softly around me once more as I find my voice.

'I'm late?'

'So very late,' they say in musical unison before Cerise continues, 'Although we were not permitted to collect you on this occasion. You cheated.'

There's a slight laugh to its tone. Cerulean clutches my chin in a chiding manner.

'Do I know you?' I ask.

They swim together, perfect mirrors echoing each other. 'Don't you recognise us, Lovely?'

'Dear Lovely.'

'Oh, sweet Lovely.'

'Don't you recognise us?'

They circle me, tentacles running through my hair and across my skin before Cerulean stops their circling and draws closer. 'We thought you might be different. You were so much older when called.' Their tentacles curl around all my limbs, holding me in place with a gentle embrace. 'Though you were such a scared thing. We felt bad for you.'

'So bad.' Cerise comes closer, reassuring. 'We let you go, of course. That is the way. It's time, though.' They smooth a tentacle across my cheek.

'It was you?' My heart sinks through my stomach. 'It was you who drowned me when I was seventeen?' Hurt and accusation floods my voice.

They both recoil, choosing to circle Tino instead.

'Don't be mad.'

'Don't be mad,' Cerulean echoes. 'We came to collect you. It was long overdue—your time. The stars were confused. The fates are sometimes wily. They've slumbered for so long.'

'Hero, hush!' Cerise stills, and the octopus named Hero retreats from me, coy.

'Who are you?' I ask.

'We are the guardians of the beyond,' Hero tells me.

'Collectors of the drowned,' Cerise adds.

'Collectors of the drowned?' I parrot.

They don't answer, though. Instead, they swirl and begin to swim away.

'Follow us,' Hero coaxes. 'Let us go into the city. Your souls were swept so fast, they plummeted far from the borders. We've been waiting. We've been so patient while you've dallied.'

'Dallied? Being lost in the ether is hardly dallying.' The urge to stamp my foot is strong as we follow.

They tsk, and my cheeks flare, but before I get to give them a piece of my mind, Tino hops in front of me.

'Why did we land so far out?'

'Because you cheated.' Cerise swirls around him. 'You took the back door.'

'Most unexpected.' Hero almost chuckles.

'And the city?' I ask.

'A haven,' they chime together before Cerise continues. 'As the guardians, we roam its borders, protecting its endless halls, herding the drowned ones, and serving—well, you'll meet him soon enough, the one who calls you to him.'

'Death,' Tino mutters.

I ignore him. 'You came to claim me when I was seventeen. Why? Why was it my time to die?'

'When the spell was broken, it was time. Though the manner of your calling is most unorthodox,' Hero starts before they're shushed.

'Hero.' Cerise's hackles flare, casting a silver glow as their tentacles wrap around one of my wrists. 'Dear Lovely, these answers you will have from the one we serve.'

I take a moment to admire the pinky luminescence radiating from this creature. 'If they are Hero, what's your name?'

'I am Leander,' the octopus proffers with a sort of bow.

'And you've always been in this place?'

'For many years,' they say but don't elaborate on how long that might be.

They push out in front of us, seeming to be in silent telepathic conversation, bioluminescence tinkling in intricate patterns like a dance. How do I have no recollection of them at all? They were the ones who dragged me to the depths of the Underworld just a few years ago, and yet my memory's blank of them.

My stomach churns at the notion that this is all for nothing. Those memories are lost to me along with all the meaning for which I am searching. I'm grappling for answers in a void. Maybe what Tino said before is right, and I want nothing more than to be swallowed by it.

After walking for an endless time around the walls of the dead city, the horizon changes once more. Tino stops beside me, bringing his hand to cover his mouth.

I take in the view, fresh goose bumps prickling over my skin as we observe a black river flowing under the high gates of the city. I grasp onto Tino's elbow, and we retreat a few paces to admire the towering structures of the passage into the city.

Doors constructed from bones stand at least a hundred feet high, a pale sheen emanating from them while the black water gushes underneath them. Over the top of the gruesome gateway, a high tower peeks, as if winking at us, its roof caving in. Some of the tiling comes away and crumbles into the city below. I gulp down my growing unease.

Tino gives voice to what I'm thinking. 'Is your city supposed to be crumbling?'

The octopuses appear to exchange glances. 'It wasn't always so.'

'What happened?' I ask. 'Do souls live in there?'

'You will see,' they echo.

We don't head to the gates straight away, though. Tino cautiously stalks to the river's edge, staring into its inky blackness that is so slick, it almost looks like oil. Tearing his eyes away, he reaches out and twists a floating tendril of my hair around his fingers.

'Aren't we already underwater?' he asks the guardians.

In turn, Leander twists some of their tentacles around him. 'You're on the plane of the dead, child. The rules of your world are spread thin.'

'But some still hold?' Tino inquires further, returning his attention to the mysterious river that stretches on until it disappears into a murky distance.

They don't answer him, instead advising, 'Don't touch the river.'

'Where does it lead to?' I ask, my focus on that blurry point.

'Why, to your world, of course. The great rivers of the waking world ferry its souls to the next life, where they return to the source. Come.'

They usher us forward until we're staring at the vaulted, towering gateways.

Tino's amber eyes are alight in the pale glow. 'Pearly

gates,' he mutters, giving a low chuckle. 'No one mentioned the pearly gates are made of bone.'

Hero and Leander wrap tentacles around the high bars and ease the gates open in creaking increments.

The sudden pull of Tino's hand sends me a couple of paces in retreat. His chest heaves, the grip of his palm leaving no pain. No desire either. My body is dulled by this place.

'Lee. If we go through those gates, I get the feeling there's no going back. A point of no return.'

The fear in his countenance seeps out, saturating the space between us. I glance to where Hero and Leander are still trying to ease the gates open. A desperation to discover what's beyond them sinks its teeth into me.

I turn to Tino, gripping both of his hands and pulling him to me. 'Tino. We're already dead. There *is* no return. Stay with me. We can be together forever here, like Hero and Leander.' I bring his palm to my lips, placing a kiss there. 'The pain's gone now.'

His eyes search mine, and he releases my fingers to stroke my face. 'You feel this?'

I nod, leaning into his caress. 'No grief.'

Then he kisses me. His arms wrap hard around me, pressing me to him, my hair swimming around us. Suspended in time. While no great sensation overtakes me here in this dead place, perhaps that's for the best. I've spent the past four years assaulted by it, so to feel numb could be a welcome relief. What better way to spend the afterlife than with my friend? To make our home in the Underworld, a place that fits.

He smooths the hair from my face. 'Forever?' he asks, a sparkle glittering across his expression.

'Looks like,' I reply with a grin, threading my fingers into his once more. 'Who would have thought? Together, at peace, in the Underworld.'

As I edge my body towards the gate and our guides, Tino's hand is ripped from my grasp, and he drops to his knees, yelling out as he clutches his heart.

'Tee?' I'm on my knees, too, my palms on either side of his face. 'Tee, what is it?'

But he doesn't have words. He just cries out some more, screaming in agony.

'Hero! Leander! Help me!' I shout as Tino continues to writhe on the ground.

The guides land next to me in a cloud of black smoke, but they make no move to help. They watch Tino's pain with remote observance.

'What's wrong with you?' I yell, pulling him to me. 'Tino. Tino, it's me, Lovely. Your Lovely. Tell me what's wrong. What do I do?'

His breathing shallows, and he stills for a moment, staring at me with panic-stricken eyes. He opens his mouth. But before a single word passes his lips, he's pulled from me. Like a fish caught on a hook, he sails away from me in a stream of bubbles, yanked into a non-existent sky.

I sit staring after him, dumbfounded. 'Wh-What?' I

stammer, brushing away tears that blob and float in the water next to me. Rage surges through me as I get to my feet and turn on Hero. 'What did you do to him?' I demand, beating my fists against their giant body. 'What did you do?'

Leander's tentacles wrap around my wrists, glowing a hot pink from the effort. 'We did nothing to him. My darling, the only place to go from here is back.'

'Back.' I blanch. 'Shit. Marie pulled him out. We've been here so long, I almost forgot. I haven't got any answers. My purpose hasn't been revealed to me. Will I even remember what happened this time?'

My head is a frantic ping-pong ball between them, but they say nothing.

Leander's tentacles still locked around me, I grasp onto them, keening, 'Tell me. You must tell me what my purpose is before Marie yanks me from this world. I'm sorry for cheating, but I need to know. What's my purpose? What do I do now?'

'Lovely,' Hero soothes. 'We cannot. We are mere guardians. *He* is waiting for you.'

'No. I'm out of time. Please help me,' I beg. More tears drip off my face and float nearby.

Hero pops some with their tentacles. 'Let her go, Leander,' they sigh, and Leander releases me from their grip. 'We don't have the answers. But we'll let you go.'

I drop to my knees and weep. After everything, I have failed. Not enough time. A second death. Wasted.

My tears drift around the guardians, who watch me in stoic contemplation until my tears dry up.

I peer at them. Their tentacles hang, suspended in the depths, their rippling bioluminescence the only discernible movement. My hands drop into my lap, and I throw my head back and gaze into the expanse of endless void Tino disappeared into. When I plunge my hand into the silt, a wave of black smoke curls around my fingers.

Time drips on. I gather the courage to speak. 'I'm not going back, am I?'

'We can wait a while longer,' Hero replies.

So, I do. On my knees, I stare into the void and wait until more tears come and float off my face.

Until I gasp for air, throwing my palms to my face, and I scream.

Leander swims over, patting a tentacle on my shoulder like an affectionate mother. 'There, there. It was your time four years ago. You've had four years of borrowed time, but now it's time to come home.'

They both help me to my feet. I brush the tears from my skin and face the half-opened bone gates.

'I'm ready,' I tell them.

They both swim promptly to the high bars, grip them tightly, and yank the gates open in a crunching of bone against bone.

Allowing me to walk into the City of the Dead.

CHAPTER
TWENTY-TWO

The dark shapes of towering buildings dominate the landscape of the city. Vaulted arches topped with spiny pinnacles as if stolen from a grim fairy tale, beautiful and disturbing at the same time. The architecture would be at home in the medieval Romanian countryside. But what takes my breath away as I cross the threshold of the city is the transformation of the river. While still black, with the opening of the gates of the Underworld—now I'm certain this is the true other side—small boats have appeared, sailing down the river and further into the city.

I edge closer, taking my time to examine the vessels while my guides float beside me. Inside the boats are white orbs of light, flickering and stretching. Goose bumps rise on my arms as I realise what I'm looking at.

'Are they...?' I ask quietly, feeling as though I should be respectful in their presence.

Hero smooths their tentacles along my arms, banishing my goose bumps.

'Yes. They are souls travelling on,' they whisper, observing the same level of reverence.

Now when I peer at the gates, the boats are visible, stretching the length of the river, disappearing into the grey vista. I turn to Leander in shock. 'They were there all along?'

'Yes, child. You could not see them until you crossed over the boundaries of the city.'

A weight hangs on their words, something unspoken yet heavy with what they're refraining from telling me. My lips part to urge more information from the guardians, but curiosity wins, and I take a cautious step towards the shimmering onyx river to watch the boats ferry the souls forward.

They're beautiful, shining a pure white. As I stare, I catch glimmers flickering through. The sight makes my breath catch. They are memories.

Holding a baby in their arms.

Dancing in the rain.

I pace along the side of the river, focusing on one boat at a time to relive each soul's experience of some of their favourite memories before passing along.

The view from the top of Machu Picchu.

Lying in the snow, observing aurora borealis lighting up the night sky.

A bright smile behind a veil.

Chasing a chubby toddler through lavender fields.

A different kind of tears well behind my eyes as I glance at the guardians, who have also ventured close to the water, their bioluminescence glowing violently.

When I speak, my voice shakes. 'I never expected it to be so beautiful. Are they...? Do the people these memories belong to.... Are they feeling this?'

'Yes.' Leander wraps a tentacle around my shoulders. 'The waters that bless the river allow it.'

Hero floats close, closing a tentacle around my wrist. 'Only in a life so temporary can this much joy be lived. But best not stay so close to the water.'

I'm entranced with the memories playing out before me like grainy old films. So much happiness, shining bright in this decaying place of death. The best moments in people's lives, projecting as a living movie for them. After a while, I can't help but wonder why I remember my own death with so much terror.

Without realising it, I've walked further into the city. I examine its buildings. Doorways seem abandoned, the windows hollow and barren. Why does the city surround the river? What purpose is there for all this decaying grandeur?

'When I died before, is this how I arrived?'

'No, dear—you're special. It's because of you that your friend arrived retaining his waking appearance.'

I turn to my guides to question this further but am distracted by the sudden movement of a boat floating just past the gates. The soul it's transporting is not shining a brilliant white but is a blackened orb fighting for form, rocking the boat wildly.

Hero and Leander swim above me, forming a barrier of sorts with their long appendages, keen protectors as the orb becomes more violent. It pulses like a demented neutron star, stretching out its limbs. The little boat sways with the effort of containing the spirit within—so much so that it takes in gushes of water.

'The boat,' I yell. 'It's going to capsize!' I move to help somehow, only knowing I want to give aid to this soul in trouble.

'Lovely,' they caution, holding me in place.

As I watch, the glowing black light stretches like a limb, long and crooked, right out of its boat before it clasps onto the bank of the river. Several more arms spike, grasping for the shore, making me take a step in retreat from the sense of menace emanating from its wild actions and desperation to be out of its boat.

'Some souls do not want to pass on,' Hero whispers at my side.

With a final push, the small boat sinks into the black depths of the river, and the shimmering dark soul clambers onto the banks, pulsing and contorting. My guides move protectively in front of me, though morbid curiosity flows through me. I peer around them, marvelling at the light that twists, stretching, beginning to take a form.

With an ear-splitting shriek, the soul contorts, taking

the shape of a huge wolf made of pure shadow. Its hackles shudder as it advances on us, now close enough for me to stare into hollow eyes. Its lips peel back in a final snarl before it turns and flees from us into the winding streets of the city.

I almost collapse into Leander's arms. 'What just happened?'

'Sometimes a soul is marred by a violent demise—so much so, there's little happiness to call upon in the passing. They resist crossing over and become something else in death.'

'A wraith,' Hero clarifies. 'They'll remain here, haunting the city, but they're no true danger.'

I take a moment to process this. 'My friend—Marie—she can communicate with the dead. Is this where they commune with her from?'

They give a sort of nod, as much of a nod as an octopus is able to do, before leading me away from the river into the fringes of the city.

Hero continues, 'Not every soul who leaves their boat is tortured, and some tortured souls do move on. Other times a person's spirit may be compelled to linger.'

'Unfinished business?' I guess.

Hero makes a slight movement of assent. 'All stories come from somewhere.'

A sinking sensation stops me in my tracks. 'My dad. Is he here?'

Their tentacles slide around me in an embrace as

Leander talks. 'He's moved on now, our love. But we did talk to him, yes.'

'Did... did he mention me?.

'He thought of you until the end, during his death and his passing. He loved you so very much. He got out of his boat for you, to speak to you one more time.'

I try to ignore the lead in my heart and ask the questions I need to ask. 'When he saw me, he came with a warning. He told me to run from someone. Who was he talking about?'

They don't answer for a moment but usher me forward, and as they do, I take in more of the city. The beautiful details of wrought iron gates, pearly inlaid archways. Abandoned-looking homes alongside vast buildings resembling cathedrals now greying and falling into disrepair.

'It was unfortunate,' Leander resumes, breaking me from my reverie. 'Most souls never meet him in person, so to speak. It can be an unsettling experience. We've lingered too long. He is waiting.'

The wrongness of the city sinks into my bones, as if the city itself is suffering from an illness. My fingers dance over the rough cracks of a nearby crumbling wall. 'What's happening here?' I ask, my voice quiet.

I proceed along a narrow, abandoned street. The City of the Dead is strangely free of the souls it's supposed to harbour. I plough on, too curious to heed the guardians' protests. Instead, I quicken my pace, walking faster and faster into the depths of the city along winding street after winding street. Not a soul to be seen.

'Where are all the tortured souls?' I ask. 'The ones with unfinished business?' But no answer comes, and when I turn around, Leander and Hero are gone.

'Hero? Leander?' I retrace my steps a little, but they've vanished.

Thinking they may have drifted ahead of me, I pace in the direction I was headed, plunging further into the bowels of the abandoned city, becoming ever more frantic as the streets, filled with broken windows and empty doorways, pass me by, my red hair a flame amongst the greyscale. I break into a run.

I come to a stumbling stop as I stagger out into a large square that is quite magnificent, with tall buildings lining it and an enormous cathedral taking centre stage. Around the chipped pavement of the central square, structures resembling barren trees are dotted, along with long-snuffed-out rusting streetlamps.

I wonder if these streets have ever been bustling with life—wait. *Life* is the wrong word. Bustling with afterlife?

I shake off a nervous giggle and place my hand on the lamp. At my touch, a flame flickers in its glass house and springs to life, prompting all the other streetlights across the square to do the same, casting an eerie watery glow, making sinister shadows of the treelike things. Squinting, I examine their spindly branches, sure that they were holding a different position before.

A low creak emanates from behind me, and I whirl

round to find the double doors of the cathedral easing open unassisted. Swallowing, I brace myself for spirits... who do not descend. Instead, I'm left staring at the open doors, my pulse going rapid fire. With a backwards glance at the strange wet flames flickering in the streetlights, I make my way up the cathedral steps, every nerve singing with caution. For the first time, I take in the gargoyles perched above the arches, bent into grotesque—and some frankly lewd—poses.

I peek inside.

More darkness.

With tentative steps, I pad into the vestibule, allowing my eyes to adjust to the lack of light, my thumping heartbeat the lone noise keeping me company.

Why is my heart beating so loudly when I'm dead?

Making my way into the nave, I run my fingers over the rough texture of the wooden pews sculpted with breathtaking cut-out bleeding hearts in their high backs. Who put so much thought into the architecture of the lost and the damned, this home for wayward souls?

As I walk further in, I break away from my admiration of the craftmanship and give my attention to the front, half expecting to find a looming cross at the altar, for some reason. Instead, a dim glow is cast there, and as I get closer, it becomes clear what it is.

Souls.

Many souls—not in animal forms but flying through the water, pushing at an invisible barrier. Erratic, they pound at a glistening gold wall. As I inch closer, my breath stills as I register what's happening. Every time a soul hits the barrier, it creates a ripple and a shimmer from the other side, and the living side appears.

Sometimes a snatch of a planchette moving across a board. Sometimes a knock through a wall. A flickering light. A smashed teacup. Their work is painfully slow.

After a while spent observing their painstaking messages, it dawns on me—I'm waiting for Marie. For a glimpse of her at her board, waiting for me in return. Head in hands, massaging her temples. This is how the spirits communicate with her—by punching with painstaking commitment at a wall where the veil is thinner.

'Carline?' I shout, my voice coming out shrill.

The spirits pay me no notice. They continue with their mission to communicate.

Tears, always so close to the surface, rise once more, and I push into the throng of souls to bash my fists against the wall between this world and the one I so recently belonged to. With every bash, I send golden ripples through their efforts.

'Marie! Marie! Marie!' I shout, searching the ripples for a trace of her, tears bubbling off my face and mixing with the soft lights of the spirits.

The spirits still.

Becoming more aware of my presence, they begin to push me away from the wall, their pale light stretching into limbs like the tortured soul had, pulling my arms in the air, twisting my hair, prodding at my hips so I'm now within the choir section. Whispered snatches of their past selves echo in my ears and behind my eyes.

'I have to find her.'

A flash of blue eyes.

A feeling of terrible confusion.

'Stop.' I try to bat them away, yet my fingers find no purchase on their glowing forms. Further and further into the nave, they push and pull at me while I gain no traction on them.

Panic rises in my chest. Fighting against the melee, I turn to make my getaway, hopeful that if I clear the cathedral, they'll return to their relentless mission to communicate with the other side. Then, as quickly as it all started, the souls flee, not to the shimmering wall but into the depths of the cathedral's chapels or from the building altogether.

I let my hands fall to my knees while I catch my breath, thankful to be on my own once more. My attention focuses back on the shimmering wall. Perhaps it's possible to get a message to Marie some other way. Through another board. Patience is all I need.

Stalking towards the glint of the veil, I pause only when a deep shudder rumbles through the bowels of the building, making every hair on the back of my neck stand on end. Fighting every ounce of terror pounding in my veins, I force myself to turn.

I'm met with the snarling muzzle of the behemoth shadow wolf.

I take two slow steps in retreat, as my instincts tell

me running would be a bad idea. Its nature would be to chase.

I ease backwards, palms raised and extended in supplication as it advances with snapping, frothing jaws and cold, shining eyes.

As my feet hit the steps of the choir section, it occurs to me that this beast, with shadows dripping from its lips, is not here for me. Some spirits cannot let go. It's here for the wall, to rage against the veil.

Instead of ascending the steps, I twist, turning into the transept while continuing to back away. It tracks me in its sights while advancing through the nave. My heart plummets through the floor when it follows my path rather than continuing to the veil.

Shit.

My retreat becomes more urgent as its barks become more vicious. The only positive now is that I have a clear run to the doors. When I bolt, it must be perfectly timed if I want to escape. I pray that, free of the cathedral, it will give up or Hero and Leander will come to find me.

With a snap of its jaws, the shadow wolf pounces. Turning my back on the creature, I flee, hurtling towards the doors with its stagnant breath hot on my neck.

From five paces away, dismay sinks through me in a fleeting spurt. The doors are closed, and I'll have no time to yank them open with the wolf snapping at my heels. Instead, I make a sharp turn to the right, returning to the nave.

At the suddenness of the turn, the paws of the

monster behind me slide on stone, a thunderous crunch signalling it's careened into the wall. Stones crumble into the seating, smashing some of the painstaking work of the carpenter. For the first time, I glance towards the heavens, sweat streaming down my back—sweating underwater is a bizarre sensation—and notice that there's a vaulted gallery. Taking a sharp left turn, I push my limbs through the opposite transept and throw myself up the stairs.

More crunching wood tells me the wolf has ploughed through some of the wooden pews to close the distance. It slows as it mounts the stairs, sensing its prey is cornered. I maintain my pace, running to the end of the gallery, where I grasp onto some of the wooden beams to bring myself to the ledge and peep over the gallery edge to the carnage below while the wolf maintains its snarling advance.

The rules of this place are a mystery. I'm surrounded by water that doesn't suffocate. Is it possible that if I jump, I'll float down to the floor?

So much for the wraiths not hurting me.

'What do you want?' I plead out of sheer desperation, toes teetering on the brink, scrunching the soles of my shoes.

Its answer is a growl.

Choosing broken bones over being mauled, I jump.

Something between falling and floating happens, though I hit the wood of the pews hard, splintering the bones of my arm, which I then clutch in agony. I instantly realise my mistake as the wolf, seeing that it's relatively safe to jump, follows suit. Its descent is far heavier, and it crashes through the remaining pews, sending debris spewing everywhere.

Seizing the opportunity, I gather every bit of my will and fly towards the front door, then heave the heavy wood open inch by tortuous inch and slip through the gap as soon as I'm able to fit.

Out in the still-lit square, I scream for Hero and Leander as I propel myself forward, certain that once I'm lost in the narrow lanes of the city, an illusion of safety will comfort me. My chest burns from the exertion.

'Not far, Lee,' I whisper to myself.

Heavy paws land like talons on my shoulder blades, sending me hurtling forward. My face scrapes the silty ground as I slide, tasting ash. As I pull myself up to sitting, the shadow beast advances over me.

This close, the echo of its ghost speaks to me, repeating one word alone.

'Consume. Consume. *Consume.*'

Pathetically, my response is a whimpering 'No.'

The wraith lunges, grasping my wrist with its razor-sharp jaws and clamping down onto my broken arm.

The ear-splitting shrieks of my agony snuff out the lights of all the streetlamps. With its teeth deep in my arm, I see it all—the horror of this creature's death as he's cut into pieces.

I relive his death as he feasts on my flesh.

CHAPTER
TWENTY-THREE

Past methods of protection crash into the barriers of my mind like waves against a cliff face, my brain urging itself to switch off the pain. To disassociate from the ripping of skin from my forearm, wet and searing hot.

I'm not here. Don't think about words like flayed *or* meat. *It's not my arm being consumed.*

But putting the distance between myself and my agony only puts me more in tune with the wraith's. Images flash through my vision as devastating as lightning bolts—a saw grinding through bone, pints of blood saturating taupe shagpile carpet. His murderer fancied himself a surgeon but was in truth an amateur who made up for his inexperience with zeal.

Unsure which pain is more terrible, I scream again and force myself into my body, landing a solid kick into the ribs of the shadow creature, which earns me a yelp and a moment of respite from the attack. Attempting to shrink away, I fold in on myself, dragging my body weight with my one good arm.

A low whistle cuts through the snarls, and the entire square plunges into darkness. An enormous shadow scales the cathedral and spills onto the ground in front of us. The wolf whines and cowers from it. I curse my bad luck that another wretched creature has come to devour me.

The mass of shadow looms above me as the wolf snarls as if to protect its kill from the thing taking shape in front of us. It takes on something resembling a male form in a billowing cloak, its head an elongated skull akin to that of a bull but with four antlers which grow menacingly long.

It makes no movement to attack the wolf, which has settled onto its haunches and is giving intermittent growls towards this new predator. I get the impression of its invisible intent trained solely on me. After a time of quivering, I realise the skull is not its own but more of a crown as I focus on two ice-blue neon eyes penetrating me from the depths of its hood, luminous and otherworldly, the only defining feature in the mass of shadow writhing underneath the skull crown.

Death.

I must be glaring into the cold stare of Death himself.

My heart goes crazy as he reaches out a hand to my mauled arm. Too terrified to do anything else, I stare, unblinking, as he lowers himself to where I lie. Though it is human in shape, his hand is not made of skeletal bone. Shadows cascade around it like water running off a smooth surface.

His fingers disappear into the cavern of his hood, then re-emerge with a black oozing substance on their tips. I fight the urge to flinch away, revulsion rising like bile, but as his fingertips trace that unknown substance over the bloody remains of my wrist, all the pain is gone, and with the gentle strokes, my muscle and bone are restored to how they were before the mauling—covered in scars. If only he could fix those monstrosities. Death traces their patterns with delicate fingers, shadows trembling across the fresh skin, evoking a feeling so very far from terror or revulsion. I shudder at the betrayal of my own body.

Death's gaze is swirling pools of ice, his stare stealing my breath. The barest tips of his fingers continue to trace the ridges of scars adorning my arm, sending cool electric currents along my skin.

Death's voice is a low rumble that seeps into my pores. 'You've been playing my tune for a long time, Lovely.' *That* familiar voice. A sound like belonging.

He takes my other hand and helps me to my feet, releasing it as soon as I'm standing. Shimmers of a face are visible within the blackness of his cloak. An impression of a face. There but not there, as if he is wholly insubstantial. The desire to figure out the planes of his face rises in me. Shadows writhe around him, then catch the contours of my body, twisting into the ends of my hair.

'Forgive Kane.' He approaches the snarling wolf. 'He's new, and as you probably already know, he suffered so horribly in the final moments of his life.'

He gives the gargantuan wolf—Kane—a sort of bow, and the wraith returns the gesture of respect. As Kane stoops his head, he brushes against the hood and crown, though not revealing the face beneath it.

The wolf takes a shuddering step backwards, and only the faintest of growls rumbles in his chest, rattling my own soul within me.

'Rest now,' Death soothes. 'You're in no danger here.'

Kane rears up and canters away from us into the bowels of the city, leaving me staring once again at Death. He inches closer. I take a nervous swallow, gripped by a sudden need to flee.

'Y-You're Death,' I stammer, needing to break the tension in the air.

He chuckles, though the sound holds no mirth, causing some of the buildings around us to shudder. 'Forgive me, no. I'm not Death, for death comes to all and is no one being. I am The Ferryman, Shepherd of Souls, Master of Boats, Ruler of the Underworld.'

'You're not Death? We.... I...,' I falter.

I was wrong.

Our plans, we had them all wrong.

His shadows flicker in the air as if they have an agenda of their own, licking at my edges before retreating. 'You have many questions. I have the answers. Walk with me.'

He extends his hand, so big it would make my own look like a child's if I took it. He's gesturing for me to lead the way, yet a perverse instinct to slip my hand into his flits through me. Though the incessant stream of shadows that ripples across his skin gives the impression that if I were to grasp him, I'd be devoured. Instead, I fall into step beside him, and he leads me away from the square into a nearby lane that is just as abandoned as the rest of the city.

'Where are Hero and Leander?' I demand. I need to get a grip of myself and not be so easily seduced. Death or not, this creature wants me dead.

Wanted. I suppose I am dead.

'Ah yes. They were sorry for having to abandon you, but as guardians, they're only permitted so far into the city. Their role is on the borders and to protect the river. They're waiting for you.'

'Where?'

'My house.'

Falling into silence, images of how his home might look spool through my imagination. A grand castle, perhaps? Spires looming, hundreds of empty rooms with high ceilings and beds made from bone. Or rather an expansive underground cave spanning the entire city, dank, with stalagmites to hang his cloak on?

'Am I to call you *The* Ferryman, or just Ferryman?' I ask, casting off thoughts of The Ferryman's bedchambers and fighting a blush as I wonder what form he takes beneath the cloak, what kind of face frames neon eyes.

What is wrong with me?

'Whichever you wish.'

'Ferryman,' I mouth quietly, testing the shape of it on my lips.

He glances at me sideways. 'Yes, Lovely,' he returns, voice wry.

'It sounds a little weird calling you Ferryman.'

'It is what I am.'

'Exactly,' I say as we approach the river again, the glowing souls shining a little brighter with him nearby. 'The Ferryman is *what* you are, not *who* you are. Haven't you got a name?'

'Many, through the eons.'

'Which was your favourite?'

He stops to regard me. The shadows lingering at the fringes of his being reach out, wrapping around one of my wrists and circling into my hair. An inextricable urge to throw myself at his feet swims through me again.

Lord, I really do have a death wish. Perhaps being the King of the Dead has that effect on a person.

'You wish to know me by a name?'

'I do.' I inch closer.

'Charon. That was my favourite name. I've not been called it in many years.'

'Charon,' I whisper. His name tastes like a sweet secret on my lips.

His shadows pull me closer, wrapping around my

waist, forcing me to arch my back to look up at him at his full height. My fingers coax the small stretch of water between us, desperate as they are to discover what kind of beast he is. They never find their mark. He withdraws and continues along the river, the softest tendrils of shadow urging me along with him. I swallow my disappointment.

'Why did Kane attack me? Hero and Leander said I'd be safe from the wraiths.' My brain is not able to find a better question at this moment. While I came with many, now they pale into insignificance around him.

'Kane's soul is marred by his violent death. Ravaged by rage. Souls like his can do much damage on the living world if they don't move on. Kane's did, but only so far. Often a soul like his will fight the passing.'

'Why? What does he want?'

'Revenge. His soul will find no peace. Souls such as his will transform to wraiths the moment they clamber from their boat. He will haunt the Underworld for an eternity. I'm his protector now, for he will never agree to move on.'

I peer at the lights drifting on the river. Serene. 'Where do they go when they pass?'

His affection as he contemplates the passing souls is that of a shepherd guarding his flock. 'Back to where they came from. The source. The infinite chaos of the universe.' He glances at my bemused expression, his low chuckle gently rocking the nearby boats. 'They will be recycled, become souls once more. And the universe goes on.'

'Huh,' I breathe, watching them pass. 'That's....'

'Beautiful,' he finishes for me, his gaze fixed on mine. 'As it should be.'

He walks on while I follow, marvelling at the secret I've been let in on. Where do we go when we die? We pass through our favourite memories, under the watchful gaze of The Ferryman, before we go on to become shining souls once more and live a thousand lifetimes through different eyes. Eternal.

'We're all made out of the same elements, Lovely,' he says, drawing to my side and catching on his palm some of the tears I hadn't realised were floating from my face. They remain glistening orbs lost in blackest night in the storm of shadows covering his hand. He eyes them before knocking a couple together like marbles and popping them with a long finger. They fracture like tiny spheres of sunlight.

'You didn't answer my question, you know. About why Kane attacked me,' I say to his back as he walks on.

'Clever' is all he says for a while before halting and turning to face me.

The action is so sudden, I stumble into a nearby dilapidated building wall, my palm at my throat. His shadows bloom behind him, snapping like *Nepenthes rajah*, ready to eat me, barely restraining themselves from tangling in my limbs.

'You represent to him that which he wants most—a way back to the land of the living.'

'I'm not dead?' I gasp, not sure which is more of a revelation, that I mean something to the shadow beast or that I might yet be able to live.

'The answer is complicated.' He moves on, pulling his shadows with him while I deflate against the wall. 'We're close.'

His pace quickening, I half jog to keep up. In amongst my swirling renumerations, a question that I've been plagued with finally returns to me and floats to the surface.

'Charon.'

He stills for a moment before walking on, though going a little slower now.

'Charon, why am I here?'

Instinct takes over, and without thinking of the potential consequences, I plunge my fingers into the depths of his cloak, finding purchase on his arm—a human-seeming arm—slowing him to a stop. The contact of his skin sends my every cell ringing with life. Or death. *Something* that makes my body sing. A gasp frees itself from my parted lips.

He tears out of my grasp, only to be on me in a second, my body immediately swimming in shadow. He's standing so close, my toes teeter on the floor as his presence dominates every free space around me.

His fingertips ghost the lines of my jaw, the suggestion of them setting my skin shuddering with a crazed sort of anticipation.

'Something is happening on the earth's surface,' he finally states. His eyes brighten as his hand brushes the faint curve of my right hip. 'You have a choice to make.'

'Choice?'

'Whether you'll stay or whether you'll move on.'

He retreats once more, giving me room to breathe, seeming to take in a steadying exhale himself. Then turns his gaze to the silhouette of his city. 'You must have noticed there's something wrong with my kingdom.'

I nod, looking at the decaying buildings.

'It was not always so,' he continues. 'For eons my city has thrived without threat, a sanctuary for souls while I and the guardians watch over the river. The world is changing, however. And now fewer souls are passing through these gates, while magic is being bred in the living world.'

He returns to the souls passing peacefully.

'Fewer people are dying?' I ask, coming to his side.

'There are many factors. The world was once full of magic and its people with it. Then the population boomed, and the magic was stretched thin across so many living souls as more and more people were born. Now something else is happening in the waking world. With this new magic there that is at odds with the waning of this world, there's an imbalance. Something stopping the souls from travelling on as they should. It's not been seen in a long time.'

'I don't understand. What does that have to do with me?'

He remains thoughtful, staring at the river. 'Lifetimes have drifted by,' Charon murmurs, distracted. 'Your gift has opened your eyes to the plight, and now it's for you to decide what you'll do with it. Whether you'll embrace your power or renounce it.'

'My gift? Plight?' Blood drains from my head, my vision starting to swim. My words come out all breathless. 'I want to know what it all means, Charon. What's my purpose in this?'

He tilts his head. 'You're drawn to this place by the souls that demand your attention. *They* call for your assistance.'

'You mean the dead? I've been haunted all this time. It's been terrifying—years of gory, drowned bodies appearing before me. I thought I was crazy, and you *sent* them to me?'

Charon stalks closer, the shadows enveloping me. His glittering eyes, cold and alive, dance over my face, his fingers entwining in my hair. 'The dead demand their vengeance. Count yourself lucky. Most of The Drowned pierce the veil so young, they spend their entire lives haunted until they answer the call.' A sick sort of humour sparkles in his rough voice. 'Though you avoided the water so thoroughly, I resorted to peculiar means.'

'The bath?' I breathe, remembering, before fury sets my blood on fire. 'You tried to murder me.'

A small gasp escapes his lips as if my anger at my attempted murder shocks him. It's a moment before he answers. 'You *called.*'

Moments pass. I knit my eyebrows, unable to decipher the meaning of the simple words but wanting to protest. I never asked to drown. "You have plagued me. Tortured me."

He takes a step closer, his head tilting, a predator assessing prey. 'You desire to accuse me? When, in the end, you came so willingly.'

Gulping down my fear, I attempt to square my shoulders. 'I came for answers.'

As he gives a slight tug of his fingers still in my hair, his words could be fire against my skin. 'You came home.'

'Home? This place is not my home,' I argue as my neck arches into Charon's grip.

'Those scars on your arms say otherwise,' he snarls. 'It's been millennia since the Furies stalked the planet. You want to understand your purpose? Fine, this is it: Take up their mantel. Become my right hand on Earth, tear down those in retribution of souls marred by violent deaths, send their souls to the Underworld. Bring balance to my world once more.'

I try to speak, but I choke on non-existent air. I'm swallowed whole by his will.

'Be my Fury.'

His fingers tingle along the skin of my jaw, his touch like ice as his grip firms around my throat. It's a type of freezing I have no words for, frosting over my skin and settling into every cell until I think it should turn me into an immovable sculpture held in his grasp.

'Leave fear behind you.' The cold urgency in his voice makes my heart tumble. 'Your touch will mean madness for every murderer. Those who've wrought terror in others will tremble in your presence. You will be reforged in fire.'

I shake and I shake and I shake.

He withdraws from me.

I crumple, unable to control my body any longer. My knees crash to the floor, my bones continuing to vibrate long after impact. I claw at my chest, trying for air that will not relieve me of this incessant trembling, ice and cold flooding my veins.

'Forgive me,' he says quietly from a distance.

I'm unable to stop my trembling. My words leave me in teeth-crunching jitters. 'What's happening to me?'

'I shouldn't be touching you in your mortal form. It's unsettling for your soul. My embrace usually used to urge a spirit on.'

My sorrow is an animal cry direct from my chest as my mind tumbles. Every weak desire I've had is the devastating truth and then some. I long to die, to drown in death. Consumed by Charon's touch.

I sob and I shake, the juddering a relentless cold unshifting from my blood.

He continues to peer at me crying on the ground, his massive form made even bigger from my lowly perspective, cowering like a wounded animal.

'I'll go retrieve Hero and Leander. Please don't move.'

As if I could move anywhere.

He echoes his earlier sentiment. 'Forgive me.'

Curling into a ball, I will the shaking to stop.

It doesn't. Until some minutes later when soft tentacles wrap around my limbs, and with slow rocking motions, the guardians help me to my feet and ease my shaking.

'There, there child,' Hero coos.

One on either side of me, they ease me forward along the river, wrapped in their suckered limbs.

CHAPTER

TWENTY-FOUR

The river winds a little around the outskirts of the city as the guardians lead me gently on. After a time, my shivering stops, and my teeth no longer chatter like rapid gunfire. When I glance behind me, Charon has gone. Deflating, I'm only disappointed in myself for being unable to resist his presence.

'Don't dismay,' Leander says, as if reading my mind. They give soft chuckles. 'It's The Ferryman who's at fault. Because of your calling, it's natural that you're drawn to him. After all, he is ruler of everything and everyone here.'

'He's excited you've come,' Hero titters at my other side.

'I'm so confused.' I rub my forehead, exhaustion threatening to overpower me.

'It'll be easier when you transform,' Hero assures me

as we approach a small chapel on the outskirts of the city.

The chapel is modest in comparison to the cathedral and has a circular window in its peak. It's not quite as decayed as the rest of the city, nor as grand, although its single room is large enough that when the two octopuses enter, there's room for them to float around with relative ease, as its ceiling is tall due to exposed beams. The far wall is consumed by a window overlooking the river as it journeys on further, skating around the city.

The room is sparse, containing a large armchair facing the vast window, a small table to its right, and another high-backed wooden chair that resembles the pews of the cathedral on the other side of the table. On it sits a chess set in play. I lightly drag my finger over the crown of the black queen, glancing at Hero.

'He wins every time,' Hero chuckles. 'You would think after all this time, he'd let us win just once.'

I smooth my fingers over the deep grooves and ridges of the tall chair. 'It looks like the ones in the cathedral.'

'Of course.' Leander eases me forward and into the armchair. 'The Ferryman crafted this entire city.'

'What is he?'

'He is The Ferryman,' they both chime.

'No, I mean, how did he get here?'

With their soft laughter, bubbles flitter around them like liquid magic, bioluminescence splattering across their skin. 'Your question might be a little beyond us. He has always been. As long as there have been humans, there has been The Ferryman to shepherd their souls through to the other side.'

Leander settles into the grand chair, and I register how odd it is to see a giant octopus sitting down. I stifle a laugh, tearing my eyes from the sight, and glance around the room once more. My cheeks redden a little at my next question. 'Where does he sleep?'

Hero speaks from behind me. 'He does not sleep.'

I do a double-take, shocked, only to be met with more laughter.

'Have you slept since you arrived here, Lovely?'

My mouth opens and shuts like a fish's for a couple of silent flaps, a few bubbles escaping my lips. My fingers tease at the edge of the sleeve that remains intact after Kane's ravaging.

'What is a Fury?' I ask in a whisper so fragile, it might shatter.

Hero swims up next to Leander, chest puffing. 'The Furies were the emissaries of the Underworld on Earth. At a time when the world was savage, the Furies took retribution on those who had committed horrendous acts and slain others.'

I gulp. 'Charon wants me to be a Fury? He wants me to kill people?'

'Your wrath will be reserved for those who are evil,' Hero assures me, wrapping my hands with their tentacles. 'Your gift will show you the way.'

'By gift, do you mean the hauntings, or the searing agony when someone brushes my skin?' I ask dryly.

Either they're oblivious to my sarcasm, or they choose to ignore it, as Leander continues.

'Your gifts will manifest in full when you transform. Those who've committed great evil will turn mad at your touch. Hauntings won't be necessary, as the dead will talk to you face to face in the kingdom of the Underworld. You'll be their vengeance on Earth.'

My heart skips. 'On Earth? I'll go back? Be alive again?'

'You will be Fury,' Hero answers.

'Would I be able to see my friends again?' It's almost too much to hope—to see Marie and tell her of the other side. Tino. To hold him once more. For him to take me in his arms and tell me that everything will be okay.

'You'd be visible to human eyes, yes. But your home would be the Underworld.'

'With Charon?'

'As his right hand,' Leander states.

'Your human form is confused by his presence,' Hero picks up. 'A push and pull, if you will. A part of your soul that wishes to carry on to the source—it fights against your self-preservation.'

I don't interrupt to inform them how my self-preservation around The Ferryman has vanished, and I would happily cast myself into oblivion to have his hands on me. That despite all my protestations in the waking world, my will to live isn't strong enough.

'When you are Fury, his embrace will not chill you

so,' Hero adds after a moment of hesitation. 'Nor will you welcome it.'

'Why me?'

'Many reasons.'

'Such as?' I press.

'Born under a shooting star,' Hero utters.

'Drowned one,' Leander sings. 'In the shadow of a god.'

Hero picks up the melody. 'Aren't you tired, Lovely? Sweet Lee. Tired of being so scared and weak and alone? What if you had the power to fight back against everyone who ever used you or hurt you? Fight for everyone who is like you?'

'They deserve a champion,' Leander finishes.

'I'm no killer,' I whisper, although I can't deny the heat growing in my heart as I stare at the old cuts marring my skin. Recalling every shitty memory I've seen through brushing against the skin of those who've witnessed death. Kane's violent demise. The burning skin of the power plant workers.

The unjustness of it all.

Sensing my wavering, Hero continues, 'When you're Fury, you'll be strong. Powerful. You will be the defender of the defenceless. Your work will restore the sanctuary of the Underworld.'

Their eyes are shining black holes, stretched, glittering pools.

'Why aren't the souls passing through here? What's happening to them?' I ask.

'They aren't our concern. Only maintaining balance and providing a home to the wraiths and wayward souls. As a newly called Fury, you will urge more souls through the gates.'

Leander interjects, 'We're running out of time. The Underworld is dying. Perhaps with more souls moving towards the source, this would no longer be the case.'

Avenge lives taken too soon. Save the Underworld. Not to mention return to Tino. That's a lot of responsibility.

But my heart yearns for this.

Not to be weak or broken but a champion.

The light.

Sleep may not bless those of us who reside on the other side, but a calmness settles over me. Watching the souls float along the river in an ambient steady flow is like marvelling at a thousand sunsets. A relief close to sleep washes through my muscles, releasing the tension held there. Unable to measure the ticking of a clock, I count my steady breaths right up to two hundred, emptying my mind of all else.

The weight of the secret I've been made privy to settles into the furthest reaches of my bones, chasing the impossible cold away. As I sit and marvel at the miracle of the passing, I become less weary and surer of what I must do.

I contemplate the incredible responsibility that could be mine as watcher of souls, protector of innocents.

Avenger.

Easing out of the chair, I find Hero and Leander are now elsewhere. I wrap my arms around myself, fighting off the invisible chill that has now returned, or perhaps it's the weight of what I'm about to do making me shake. Raking my fingers across the softness of the armchair and pushing a strand of my floating hair aside, I take in Charon's humble home once more. The place where he chooses to dwell rather than within the grandness of the cathedral, or some other opulent dwelling he's created for the lost souls. His home.

They deserve a home. The souls lost, unmoored in eternity.

I deserve a home. As much as I hate to admit it, I'm not at odds with this place. Something about the Underworld fits. The guardians have the aura of long-lost relatives. And Charon, well... *comfort* might not be the right word to describe how I feel around him. I'm in awe of Charon, though from what the guardians say, my relationship with him will be more like a business arrangement following the transformation. Could it be I've found my place in this world? Straddling one world and the next? Could such a feat be possible?

Tino is my most compelling pull to return to the land of the living. Right now, I'm dead. If I don't act soon, I'll never again enjoy the warmth of his love. I'll never bask in the light of all his goodness and imagine myself healed. I chew on my lip, thinking. Is it worth it? Killing the guilty so I might stare into Tino's honey-coloured eyes?

If I become Fury, my brain wouldn't be so muddled around Charon. I'd no longer wish to be ensnared by his shadows. My home would be in the Underworld, but my heart would remain in the living one.

Huffing a large sigh, I make my way outside to find Hero and Leander haven't strayed far. They glide over the river in rippling bioluminescence, strange and gorgeous. Hero spots me and wafts over, their tentacles dipping near to the river, giving the boats a gentle motion that reminds me of tinkling bells.

'You were lost in thought,' they hum.

'Big decision.' I smile, my fingers digging into my elbows. 'Hero, tell me the truth. If I become Fury, is it possible for me to have a relationship with Tino? How much time has passed? Is he alive?'

A tentacle wraps gently around my wrist. 'We're bound by the laws of this place, and there are certain answers we're not permitted to give. Though I can tell you, his soul has not passed through the gates, so we would assume he lives.'

My heart lurches as I give a nod. I told him I would go back to him. I promised.

'Lovely,' Hero says, interrupting my musings. 'Love isn't the reason you should make this decision. You'll no longer be mortal. Your life with Tino would be temporary. Your life with The Ferryman will not be.'

I digest that information. It would be enough, though. One lifetime of bliss with Tino, followed by an eternity of guarding souls, avenging them. Sounds like a fair trade.

'Do it for you,' Hero quietly encourages.

We dawdle along the river, catching up to Leander, the soles of my feet scuffing silt and sending tiny clouds of blackness in our wake. 'I've never wanted to hurt anyone else. But I understand how it feels to be lost. Alone. A victim. I'm trying to think of it more as being a protector. I'll prevent more people from getting hurt. Now, I'll be the one with the power.'

Hero stills, Leander drawing level flaring full fuchsia. 'You will answer the call?'

Swallowing, the words stick in my throat, I only nod. 'Will it hurt?'

'Yes,' they chime in unison, so cheerful I think they might have misunderstood.

'I'll fetch our master,' Hero says as they float away in the direction of the gates.

Leander glides through the boats, sometimes pausing to observe a particular memory, their bioluminescence glinting in swirls of cerise, or swaying a boat a little by tapping its side, or dipping a tentacle into the black water, as if dipping a nib into ink.

'Why do you do that?' I ask.

Leander abandons their playing with the river and the souls floating on it to drift over and settle beside me in quiet contemplation. 'The ripple in the water sends echoes through the memories. It inspires a sense of euphoria in their spirits.' If an octopus could smile, Leander's face would be bright with it.

'What happened to the Furies who came before me?' I continue.

'They journeyed on to the source when the gods died.'

Everything in Leander's tone is nonchalant, yet it leaves my mind reeling. So much to unpack in one small sentence.

'What gods died?' I ask, baffled.

They chuckle a little. 'This was long ago, when man measured time by the height of the sun. Back when I was still alive and human. In days when Poseidon's trident scorched the earth. When men still held Athena's favour. A different Earth.'

All coherent words tumble out of my head as I stare. 'You were once human?'

'It's a long story. But yes, though I have little memory of it now.'

'What happened?'

'I died.' Leander settles a tentacle onto my hip, their melodic sigh tinkling through the water between us. 'As did Hero. Drowned too. You see, though only one river flows to this place, The Ferryman is connected to all waters. But we couldn't let go of each other, bound as we were. When two souls are so entwined, it's rare, but interesting things sometimes happen. So, we made a deal with The Ferryman.'

'And now you're this.' I stroke my palm across their luminous skin.

'He was very generous.' Their words are a whisper.

I wrap myself in their limbs, resting my head against them in something resembling a hug, and release a huge exhale. It's been so very long since I've been held.

'Am I doing the right thing, Leander?'

'Yes.' They continue to hold me tight. 'Besides, Hero and I have got quite used to you. We would be awfully sad if you chose to go on.'

I smile.

A shadow stretches over the river, clambering close to us, with Hero swimming by its side in genteel silence. I steel myself as Charon materialises in front of me, huge and looming. The same antlered skull hangs high above me as I stare into the vibrant blue of his eyes buried deep within his cloak. As always, his shadows twitch with the apparent need to encircle me.

He doesn't say anything. I, on the other hand, have forgotten how to breathe.

'It was important that you decided this for yourself, free of my influence.'

I nod.

He inches closer, a shadow catching my cheek. A heat burns in my chest. I close my eyes. This is not for him, I tell myself. It's for Tino. It's to protect others. In fact, when the transformation is done, I won't be overwhelmed with the desire to abandon myself in him. To drown in the unfathomable depths of his darkness.

'What is it you want?' he coaxes, his voice slick and silvery.

'Surrender.' My answer came quick, a shock to myself, the words like a sugared secret on my lips. 'Unadulterated surrender.' My body and brain caught in a fight-or-flight response to him, I'll be relieved when I can organise my thoughts in his presence.

His shadows whip out and curve around the planes of my body, drawing me to him. This close, I see the flickering of his face, still only silvery skull-type outlines. Not Death indeed. His grim reaper stare is alive with shards of ice as he gazes down at me.

My bones shake. 'Charon, make me your Fury,' I get out while I'm still able to form words.

Elegant fingers appear from within his cloak to trace the line of my clavicle, sending goose bumps over my body. When I shudder, he pulls away, leaving me both hot and cold at the same time as he turns to the guardians.

'We must prepare,' he commands before moving inside.

CHAPTER
TWENTY-FIVE

Charon leaves a smallish package on the table inside the chapel, which I swear he wasn't holding before, then moves the chess set aside before turning to Hero, Leander, and me, who have just entered. Despite the high vaulted ceiling, Charon fills the space. I find myself standing in the middle of the room, staring up at him. I'm quite tall myself, yet he towers over me. Without a word, he exits, and I take a breath again.

'Is he avoiding me?' I sulk, moving to gaze out the large window at the rear of the chapel.

'Honestly? I believe he's nervous.' Hero wraps their tentacles around my arms, turning me to face the room once more. 'Plus, he wants to give you some privacy while we prepare.'

Together they unfurl the package to reveal a bolt of black silk. It ripples, ghostlike, in the water.

Leander approaches. 'May I?' They tug a little at the bottom of my top.

Shuddering at being so exposed, I nod in consent, allowing them to remove my top and then the rest of my clothes piece by piece with a certain ceremonial reverence.

'You will be reborn.' Hero's voice rings with affection as they drape the cold silk tightly beneath my arms. They crisscross in balletic movements through the depths, tying the fabric around me in a toga-like fashion, leaving my arms and most of my back exposed.

Tracing my fingers along the scars that adorn my arms, my eyes glisten with tears once more. 'I did these to myself,' I confess.

'We know,' they say in harmony, soft and understanding.

'Like the phoenix rising from the ashes.' Leander nudges my chin with one of their limbs, their chest swelling as if they're filled with pride from the notion of their first Fury in thousands of years.

An excited anticipation circulates through me. I can do this—make a difference in the world. Maybe Lisette was right. I am the cure.

Looking down, I barely believe it's my body wrapped tight in the shimmering black silk. It leaves little to the imagination. Now the guardians take a small amphora, which I hadn't noticed on the table, and begin to rub oil into the exposed skin of my back, suckers clicking against my shoulder blades, then moving to my arms, not shying away from the rough, abused skin.

Hero moves on to my hair, which never stops swirling around my head, working more oil through the ends, although there's no apparent purpose to the pampering.

'Why the oil?' I ask.

'It'll ease the transition.' Leander smooths some more of the substance onto my cheeks and under my eyes. 'Lessen some of the pain.'

My heart doing a double beat at the notion, I have nothing to respond with. Tino had once accused me of being addicted to pain, that I didn't know any other way. *'How many more times are you going to dance with Death?'* he'd asked. *'Just once,'* I'd told him. This final time—emphasis on final. I need to become Fury and fight my death so I might return to him. Perhaps doing some good in the process.

Yet Charon's presence, or lack of it, itches under the surface of my skin. I'll be glad to be rid of the sensation.

HERO HOVERS BESIDE ME WHERE I STAND BY THE RIVER, watching the souls journey on, my stare intense as my heart threatens to jump out of my chest. Waiting for Charon seems to have stretched for an eternity, fraying my nerves. What if he's had second thoughts about me?

Maybe I'm not cut out to be Fury. Or he suspects part of my intention is to return to the man I love. What then?

'Where's the source?' I ask for no other reason than to fill the silence.

'In the centre of the city. The river circles the city, then passes out of sight underground,' answers Leander, who is a short distance on my other side, still carrying the amphora clutched in their tentacles, their cerise skin flaring from the strength of holding it, though it's not huge. Perhaps, though it looks innocuous, it's laden with a magic that the octopus reacts to.

'Under the Underworld,' I titter, a shaky smile playing on my lips. 'You aren't permitted near it?'

Leander shakes their head. 'The Ferryman is the sole guardian of the source. Only he has sight of the final point of passage.'

'Why?'

'It is as it has always been.'

I tilt my head in the direction of the city in time to witness an elegant shadow passing over the spire tops, a mass circling their turrets and slinking past.

Charon.

My treacherous pulse thunders, and I tell myself it's nerves.

He materialises in front of me, antlers rising on top of endless shadow before the penetrating gaze, as cold as ice, holds me in its grasp. Tendrils of shadow work themselves into the tips of my swirling, oiled hair and skim the bare skin of my shoulder, eliciting an audible gasp. The shards of ice in his eyes melt and burn at the sound.

I'm unsure if he's in control of it or not, but his shadows pull me closer, and my brain begins to lose its grip on composure. Being close to him is a dangerous intoxication, a new addiction to feast on. The broken pieces of myself falling away bit by bit, I could forget every inch of myself in his arms.

When his eyes flick down to examine my tightly bound body, I'm hypnotised by the brief outline of a face, edges sharp as if he's a living hologram. The need to figure out what he is infuriates me. Everything about him is black on black except for the cool shock captured in his irises.

His existence would be impossible in the living world. It's easy to see where tales of the grim reaper originated. In that fraction of a moment as I linger close to him, I realise this is part of his tragedy. Unendingly alone as ruler of the Underworld, shepherd of souls, seeing them on. Where he remains. Always alone.

'Charon.' To whisper his name is a new type of drug. There's a certain magic in speaking a name believed long forgotten. It means something. Ancient. Private. Delicious. Unthinking, I let the barest tips of my fingers sweep inside his hood, grazing a faint outline of a sharp jaw. My simple touch draws his unflinching, undying attention.

Shadows suck me in further so the hard planes of his

body glide against my own, the bones of him seeming entirely human, although exaggerated. And although I can't see his true form, he seems to be suspended in a sort of shaking fury, hinged on its last thread of restraint. I'm so close in his embrace, my feet leave the floor. I must be near his mouth, because in the whisper of a distance, I can taste the saline flavour of his breath against my lips. Like the sea air the first time I died.

I know I am going to drown again.

In a flurry of water, all my senses become confused by the tentacles wrapping around Charon's arms and body. I'm flung out of his grip. Cries of protest from Hero and Leander had fallen on deaf ears, so consumed were we in that moment as I was seduced and Charon slipped. The Ferryman snaps sharp-sounding teeth, snarling like the wolf Kane, trying to get to me as I wiggle free of the remaining shadows.

'No!' they chime, alarm ringing high in their cries, which become more soothing as he comes to his senses. 'We need her. She is your Fury. If you embrace her now, she would go on.'

Embrace is a nice word for it. *Devour* would be a closer description.

'Master.'

'Master.'

'Master.'

They sing the word as a litany, as if reminding him of his station, until he goes slack in their arms before turning his back on me, reaching into the depths of his cloak. Although the guardians remain poised, ready to restrain him should he lunge again, his shadows are now militant in their control.

My chest heaves, and smoothing myself down, I remember I'm wearing a ridiculous dress-type thing, which he was already admiring before I decided to utter his name like some kind of spell and lay my hands on a being who probably hasn't been touched in lifetimes. Understanding now dawns that if he'd kissed me, I would have truly perished in that instant. His touch, let alone his kiss, is death to the dead, and I all but threw myself at him.

Stupid Lovely.

Stupid death wish.

'I'm sorry' is all I have to offer as I attempt to find an edge to fiddle with on the silk toga. It shouldn't be possible to sweat underwater. Yet here I am, sweaty palms and all.

'Your predecessors were not quite so willing to throw themselves at my mercy.'

His words bite, and I'm sure I blush. Though in the same moment, it occurs to me that while I'd almost kissed him, he'd also desired it in return.

Satisfied that The Ferryman is in control, Leander swims to the river and dips the amphora into its waters before passing it to Charon. 'It's time.'

Although his shadows are restrained, everything

about Charon screams of a simmering fury as he approaches me, and my tremble now has everything to do with fear.

The King of the Dead is so mad with me.

'Open your mouth,' he commands in a growl.

The guardians linger nearby in case he pounces again. I have no time to consider him, a creature with wants and desires. For a brief moment, he wanted me in a very human way.

Instead, I part my lips. The twitching shadows betray that he's fighting an internal battle at my nearness. Whether it is a pleasure or a pain to him, I know not, and I panic that he'll change his mind, so I step into his orbit.

A certain confidence swirls in my stomach as I notice that as soon as I do, his shadows ease and thread around me once more. I affect him as he affects me. The pull is on both ends. Magnets of light and dark.

His movements are guarded as he reaches to tilt my chin, my mouth still open.

'This will hurt,' he says, his icy gaze on my lips.

I resist the urge to lick them. A different sort of anticipation fills me, something hot and desperate in my core as he brings the amphora to my lips, tipping its contents into my mouth. His hand now steadies the base of my throat as I drink, trying not to think about how it tastes —like decay and rotting things.

His gaze drifts, becoming fixed on my throat and the languid glugging motions as I attempt to swallow the waters of the dead river. Sluggish tears escape, and I fight to keep my vision trained on the slithers of ice in his devouring look, churning like a galaxy. Celestial.

The liquid is rancid. When I nearly splutter, he clutches tighter, not spilling a drop as he forces it down while I fight against him. Cold seeps into my bones. A jittering freeze quelling the heat in my core, tearing at my flesh.

I want to scream. I choke the last of the foul stuff in large gulps so I may give voice to the pain. But when I finally gasp at the watery air, senses in tumult, Charon's lips are on mine, stealing that very breath. My vision swims, and I clamp my eyes closed. This time no guardians come to my rescue.

My world turns dark, enveloped within the depths of his black cloak. Even when I open my eyes, I do not see.

Ice dances its way into my blood as my lips slide over pointed teeth. His hands roam the silk-covered curves of my body, clawing me to him. Claiming. The cold sinks in deeper and deeper, his kiss the sole bit of substance I'm clinging onto; otherwise, I would slip into blissful oblivion.

His kiss is so desperate, it could last forever and it would never be enough.

What is air? Breathing? Who needs life when you have this.

Only when he draws away am I free to witness the universes that live in his eyes, so close, their luminosity blinds me, and I crumple in agony at his feet.

No longer ice, I am fire.

I scream.

Tear at my skin as it scorches my flesh, yet it will not yield. It rages from my toes, consuming my body in a flame. Sinking so my nose hits the ground, I take a gasped breath to scream again as the flesh of my back splits along the curves of my shoulder blades, my bones jutting and coming loose.

The heat rises, blistering, needing escape. The red of my hair, ever swirling around me in this place, flickers before catching fire. Sparks fly until there is nothing left of my hair—instead, it is a simmering flame in the water. The burning eases out of my body, allowing me to breathe once more, a dull ache lingering in my shoulder blades.

Yet I remain panting at Charon's feet, my brain still singed with the pain of being burned alive. A distant memory of burning men flits and vanishes. There's something important I need to remember. All I can focus on is the way every nerve fizzes with the remnants of agony.

I glance up at The Ferryman and imagine him smiling down at me with the dazzling mien of a wolf, fangs and all. He offers me a hand. 'Rise, Daughter of Darkness. Drowned One. Fury.'

The words echo in my mind with a deeper kind of recognition, like my deathly visions in the land of the living. Memories of Furies past, connected now. Free from the ties of humanity, I see it all. The terrible truth. The awful destruction rained in fire on the earth by my

Fury sisters before me. The river filled with souls of the Furies' awful revenge, bloody, and all at The Ferryman's command.

I stare at my trembling hands. We had it so wrong. I'm not the light. Only darkness resides in me now.

The pain of my past lifts from my chest, a dead weight I'd become so used to carrying. The sudden lightness steals my thundering heartbeats, which slow and stutter to a final stop. Clutching my breast, the understanding shatters all around me—I have condemned my soul to a legacy of bloodshed.

Leander lingers a little beyond Charon. Waiting. I launch myself at the guardian.

'You're a liar!' I beat my fists against their body. 'You tricked me. I don't want this.'

Hero is on me then, restraining me from their eternal partner as I continue to rail.

'Their memories are now my memories. The Furies before were monsters. They were no champions.'

'They were justice,' Hero attempts to soothe, successfully stopping me beating Leander.

I shrug free of their grasp, looking wildly around, the gravity of the Furies' executions and sentences of madness crushing down on me. 'No. I don't want this.'

Charon is still—too still—his shadows restrained under his antler crown.

'Take it back.'

'You answered the call,' he says, as cold as the ice in his eyes.

Turning to flee, I trip and stumble, and for the first time, I glance behind me, realising why my back is aching so much. Two huge batlike wings protrude from my shoulder blades.

My screams fill the Underworld once more.

CHAPTER
TWENTY-SIX

Stumbling through the narrow, winding alleys of the city, I catch my shoulder on the wall of a decaying building, breaking away brickwork, and tumble to my knees. In my panic as I rise, the wings attached to me beat as if by instinct, lifting me into the air. I make it about ten feet before I collide with a building and careen to the ground with what should be a bone-breaking thud. Yet I'm unharmed.

My escape continues on foot. Escape to where? I've no clue. All I know is, I must be away from Charon and the guardians. While Charon was a mystery to me, I'd come to view Hero and Leander as friends. The urge to cry wells inside, but no tears fall.

Memories from Furies past ricochet around my mind like pieces of bloody shrapnel, as beautiful as they were deadly, walking vengeance. Most of their victims were driven to madness and suicide, although in exceptional cases, they partook in the ruin of others. There was no gentle passing on of souls. A retribution so bloody hardly seems like justice. They were no simple avengers—their names were feared to be spoken.

A shadow darkens the water above. Seeking the shelter of a nearby building, I fling my back to the wall, hitting brick with a crunch. Much to my surprise, the endless grey sky is free of accosting guardians. Panting, the inception of a plan stitches itself together in my brain. Fury now, escape from this place is within my grasp. Escape to my friends, to Tino, though I have no idea how many days have passed. Maybe months, even—but I must find him to explain that I didn't abandon hope. I kept my promise and returned to him. If he's found someone else, I'll be happy for him. I'll find Marie, explain what I've learned. Tell her of my calling. She'll help me to channel it into something good.

I will not kill.

Taking a life makes me just as bad as every awful creature who stalks the planet. There must be a way to use this form to protect human life, not destroy it.

The rough texture of the building scrapes at the tender skin of my new wings. Taking a step forward, I arch them before me, running my fingers over their length.

Wings.

I can fly.

Once I've breached the city limits, flight will be my path home. When Tino and I first came here, we landed too far from the city to be collected, heading straight through a gateway. We travelled along no river. We didn't come by boat. There's a finite distance the guardians may follow.

My mind swims, ancient knowledge seeping through the ether. Attempting to grasp it is like clutching smoke—there but not there. I press the heel of my palm to my eye to ease the strain.

When I carry on, I do so with more purpose, taking myself towards the river while remaining in the cover of the city. As I walk now, I spot more souls. They are shining white orbs moving towards the river, searching for The Ferryman, I suppose. I feel another searing pain in the rear of my eye at the awareness coming to me in my Fury form.

Other souls, ones who have remained in the city for longer, their lights stretch and pulse as if clamouring to take on their previous form but failing to grasp onto who they once were. Why don't they pass on?

They reside in the dilapidated buildings. I peek through a grimy window. One dances before me in a grand hall, a shade of who they were before, simply a glowing orb with long limbs of light twirling against the paintings of the city that adorn the walls. I press my ear to the window. A sweet melody plays as the spirit pirouettes. I stare at the intricate gramophone that sits in the corner. Charon must have made it for this soul. A slight tug at my centre eases me away from the window, leaving the soul to their private dancing.

Bringing my palm to my chest, the cavern where my heart once pounded now houses an invisible yet somehow luminous thread urging me to the feet of the Underworld's ruler.

'You idiot,' I whisper to myself, pushing the sensation away.

Continuing forward is my sole option. My mind continues shedding its fog, the truth turning crystal clear. Charon may not be Death per se, at least not the way we envisioned it, but he's the closest thing to it. The master executioner of the Furies. I refuse to be his tool on Earth. As their memories collide with mine, I see it—they were slaves.

I turn a corner that I believe will lead me onto the river, but instead, it brings me to a dead end and a sight that chills my blood all over again. A wraith stands before me, a colossal caribou, moss and rot dripping from its antlers. The edges of my flame-filled hair hiss in its presence, and I take an instinctual step away as it stamps its front hooves, hollow eyes staring into me.

It's ready to tear me apart.

It gives chase the moment I turn to flee. I heave my way forward, feeling its rancid breath hot on my neck. My wings clamour for purchase in the water, beating against the battered stone housing. Breaking free from the narrow streets into the expanse of the square, my wings finally find the freedom to stretch, and in three swift beats, I'm airborne. With a snap of its jaws, the caribou just misses my heel.

My heart soars with the liberation of flying. Up I go, higher over the city. My arms expand to embrace the watery abyss, the thrill of flight dancing on my skin. Up. Up. Up. The desperation for the fresh taste of freedom, which the surface will bring, tantalises my lips.

Suddenly, four strong tentacles wrap around me from behind, securing my ankles and wrists.

'No!' I cry, kicking and thrashing, beating my wings against their protests. The weight of the guardians attached to my body is too much, and I'm dragged down to the city's skyline, scratching at building tops with clawlike fingers. 'No.'

Finally, I fall limp in their grasp, my wings hanging listless over them. 'How could you do this to me?' I continue to whimper in their grip.

They move along, floating above the turrets but not in the direction of the river. Instead, they skirt around the city limits in a direction I've never travelled before.

'We didn't betray you,' Leander says at last. 'You're Fury now. You need time. The Knowledge is as disorientating as the transformation.'

They're attempting to placate me, but there's a tension in their words that knots my stomach.

'What's wrong?' I ask. My question goes ignored. Turning my attention to Hero, I attempt to decipher the expression of an octopus. My endeavours are fruitless. 'Where are you taking me?'

'Somewhere for you to rest while you adapt to your

new form,' Hero tells me as we're propelled forward, beginning a slight descent towards a long, low building.

'Is Charon in there?' The tug at my centre tightens.

'No' comes the harsh answer from Leander.

'He shouldn't have been so hard on you,' Hero whispers. 'The transformation is enough. Millennia of information being forced on you, your mortal form torn. It is enough.'

'Hero,' Leander shushes.

'What are you talking about?' I press. 'How was he hard on me?'

They continue on without a word, closer now to the building, which is simpler than the rest of the city, reminding me of a rudimentary barn.

'Are we not friends?' I demand.

They still at the query. Leander sighs, easing their grip a little. 'It is not for us to question The Ferryman's actions. We serve him, as you will. All will be well.'

During the pause, I inch towards Leander, pleading, 'Please tell me, Leander. How was he hard on me? Did I displease him?' The last question slips out before I know I'm going to ask it. Surely a result of this thread which now connects me to him.

When the answer comes, it's Hero who gives it.

'The water of the dead river flows with the blood of The Ferryman. The Furies are transformed by being twice drowned and ingesting the blood of the river. *Nothing* more.'

My jaw snaps into place. The kiss that consumed me

like life and death rolled into one sensation was a moment of pure weakness in him. 'I assumed it was part of the transformation.'

They fall into silence, Leander pushing me forward. I don't resist. The kiss had seemed so vital, Charon pouring part of himself into me, in harmony with the river, the river itself full of Charon's blood. All Furies are forged in his blood. Yet, for some reason, he chose to kiss me during the transformation, knowing that the transformation kept me from moving on.

'Is he okay?' I ask before I can stop myself.

'We find it's best for him to keep a distance while you adapt,' Hero tells me.

That tug in my core aches. A wave of sympathy rises through me for Charon, for how lonely his years have been. The Furies have been his companions in more ways than one before, although those specific memories don't come to me, for which I'm grateful. I may be bound to him as a Fury, but I'm glad that, when I'm next in his presence, my mind won't swim too much or, if he touches me, my bones won't rattle.

My feet touch silty ground, and I allow myself to be ushered into the building, which, despite how low it is, is still high ceilinged, though empty. At the bottom of the long structure, a large window sits, framing the river that glows in the distance. I walk its length, pressing my fingertips to the pane to hold vigil for the low glowing orbs that bob like ceremonial lanterns along the black river. The steady stream of souls.

The sonorous clinking of a metal mechanism slams behind me. When I turn, the entire width of half the building has been cut off with wrought iron bars, trapping me. The guardians remain on the other side, observant, as I rail against my prison, attempting and failing to shake the trappings.

'I'm a prisoner now?' I shriek.

'For your own safety. You need time to acclimatise. To absorb the memories of Furies who came before you. To accept what you are now. It's not easy to change form,' Hero says before Leander interjects.

'In time, you will accept your sacred duty. There is an honour in retribution, Lovely, should you be strong enough to endure it. Bear in mind, this is what you chose.'

'I didn't have all the information. This is wrong! The madness of my touch will drive others to suicide.'

'Only the unworthy,' Leander counters. 'Those guilty of the most heinous crimes.'

Grasping the bars, I grit my teeth. 'This isn't what I want.'

'You need time,' Hero advises in another attempt to pacify.

As they turn to leave, I become frantic. 'Charon. I want Charon! Bring him to me.'

They continue their retreat.

'I need to see him. Please. Please. Just let me see him.'

They leave me there.

Charon does not come.

Days are long in the Underworld.

At least I think they are. From where I sit on the stone floor of my prison, I let my gaze linger on the hue of souls travelling along the river and the unchanging grey-blue of the vista around it. It's best not to dwell on the infinite nothingness surrounding the city's borders. Is it day or night here? Does it matter? Will I spend an eternity behind these bars before I cave and serve as executioner? How much time has passed?

Every day I spend here is another day I don't return to Tino. The notion of returning, if only to make him aware I didn't give up, that it was his memory I clung to, keeps me from the madness of isolation. Without sleep or hunger as a guide, it's impossible to gauge the passage of time.

Somewhat annoyingly, the guardians were right. In my solitude, it's been easier to sift through the memories of my predecessors. When I'm still, the sudden burst of a new download, so to speak, is less painful. The memories are less a haze of blood-filled images. Now the threads of individual lifetimes spool before me as if I was there.

All of them beautiful and devastating, with hair of flame and wings of night.

Alecto's memories come clearest, as they're the most powerful, driven as they are by an unrelenting rage. Entire cities burned if found unworthy, guilty of harbouring criminals. Tisiphone favoured inducing madness on those guilty of murdering their own families. Her cold stare masked the acidic flavour of insanity she savoured on her tongue as her victims claimed their own lives, relishing the light leaving their eyes. Megaera took a certain delight in inflicting generational curses, a reminder of the evil of ancestors, whole families cursed to disease.

Though their victims were guilty in some respect, nothing seems to be just about the gory enjoyment of their calling. Because during their reign, they were both worshipped and feared amongst men.

Through their long-forgotten perspective, the Underworld is a thriving kingdom, the river's slow current a gushing tide, while wraiths roam the city under the Furies' watchful gaze. When not reaping justice on Earth, they kept peace within the Underworld's high walls, wraiths more or less their pets. A giant shadow lion pads through the meandering streets, seeking out its Fury's company. I almost feel its coarse fur through Tisiphone's shimmering memory as the beast rubs against her like a giant cat.

Most maddening is their memories of Charon. Unchanged by the ages. Experiencing Alecto's pleasure as his fingers skim the skin of her jaw. His voice telling her, 'Good girl,' rumbles in my memory as if he'd spoken the words to me. I see him through the eyes of Megaera while she kneels at his feet, hands raised in supplication. He is always hooded and just beyond reach, his gaze devouring as if it were me, reverent, before him.

The memory heats my skin. Perhaps the reason behind the kiss is not such a mystery. He misses his Furies. Their weariness must have been a loss when they chose to move on rather than continue to serve him.

The door eases open behind me, and Hero drifts in. I rise from where I sit on the floor and move to rest my forehead on the cool metal of a bar of my cage.

'I thought you might like some company,' Hero says, cautious.

Loath as I am to admit it, I'm so very glad for it. 'Where's Charon?' I demand, desperation lacing my plea.

'Lovely.' Hero rests a tentacle on my hand wrapped around the bar. 'You need more time. Becoming Fury—it takes a while to accept. As does your bond to The Ferryman. He'll keep his distance until you're ready.'

'Hero.' I close my eyes as I plead. 'You don't understand. These memories I'm experiencing of him... it's like they're my own. Not seeing him is killing me.'

Hero withdraws, cocking their head as if confused by my statement. 'You're not angry?'

'I have no fight left in me.'

Hero's hesitation permeates the air.

'The Furies loved him,' I settle on saying—anything to bring him to me. To negotiate the terms of my release. 'Which makes it difficult to remain angry with him.'

The cerulean bioluminescence glitters around Hero's body. 'The Furies didn't love The Ferryman, child. They were his servants. His hands in the land of the living. Their power was an extension of his.' Hero comes closer again, running the tip of their tentacle along my chin. 'The Ferryman does not love—he is *just*. His concern is the maintenance of his kingdom, the balance between life and death. He shouldn't have kissed you. Don't mistake longing for love.'

Retreating from Hero, their caress now as welcome as a slap, I try to shake the Furies' memories out of my head. They're all lies. Or perhaps I'm searching for scraps of humanity buried deep within the Furies and Charon both. The cool blue of his irises, the rareness of his touch. Their craving for it. How they admired him, longed for his approval. Of that much I'm certain. Separating my desires from theirs will take practice.

Relenting, I withdraw from the bars of my cell and turn from them. 'Am I to be kept here?'

'For the time being. Please, allow me to bring you something.'

'May I have a bed?'

Again, I'm met with confusion. 'A bed? But sleep does not visit this place.'

Stalking to the giant window, I huff. Hypnotised by the passing once more, I give my attention to the souls alone, done with the guardian's presence. 'That may be, Hero. But in case you didn't notice, I'm being held prisoner, so I would prefer somewhere comfortable to wallow.'

Hero misses my sarcasm entirely, telling me they'll try their best.

Something must be broken inside me. I want nothing

more than to return to Tino, yet Charon's continued absence chills me. In my mind, I sift through the Furies' memories of him, lingering on each brush of his fingers, every word of praise for a job well done. I cling to the flickering comfort of being close to him and curse my contrary heart.

Hero must be right—it's the confusion of the transformation clinging to me. Charon wasn't playing by the rules when he kissed me. It's disjointed everything.

I'm to be his servant, nothing more.

I lower myself to the floor and curl into a ball, allowing my wings to stretch out behind me, filling the expanse of my cell, and wish sleep would take me.

CHAPTER
TWENTY-SEVEN

'If you attempt to escape, we'll only catch you again.'

The musical lilt of Leander's voice brings me back to my body, where I remain in a ball on the floor. I ease to my feet, my muscles sore from lack of use.

Hero flanks their partner, encumbered by a grand bed they both struggle to accommodate in their grip. With their free tentacles, Leander springs a mechanism to my bars, and they slide the bed inside my cell. I make no motion to flee, trusting their threat. I'm too unused to my wings to resist them, and I'm without any weapon to fight them. The Furies' powers work on the surface of the earth alone, not in this halfway place.

The bed clunks to the solid floor of the cell, and I inch closer to inspect it, running my fingers over the intricate filagree carvings of the headboard.

'Charon made this.' I half smile.

'He makes all,' Leander says before turning slightly to me. 'How are you feeling? You've been lying on the floor for an awfully long time. We came to check on you, curious if you'd change your request. You've been unresponsive.'

'Sorry. I didn't notice.' My fingers splay over the soft mattress, exploring the decadence woven into it. 'What's this made from?'

'Silk, I believe,' Leander responds, and I ponder where silk is harvested in the Underworld.

The bed is so comfortable, I could die all over again and be happy about it. They help me position the monstrosity so I have a good view of the river. Then I throw myself into the downy embrace of the mattress, snuggling into what feels like the height of luxury after my stint on the floor.

'Lovely,' Hero sings, 'is there anything else we may get you? To pass the time? An instrument, maybe? Or paint? Needles for sewing?'

The needles are a brief consideration so I might stab them with it, though I'm sure they would take measures against this. I almost remark how ridiculous it is for them to suggest paint when we live underwater, but the joke is unlikely to land.

Hero smooths a limb along my flaming hair and remains unburned.

'I want to see Charon' is my answer.

Deflating somewhat, they leave, their tentacles swimming out of my peripheral vision.

Wrapping my arms around my body as far as they will go, I cuddle myself, closing my eyes to pretend to sleep. Pretend I'm not in the Underworld but alive still. Pretend not to notice that my heart no longer beats in my chest. Pretend the arms embracing me are Tino's and not my own.

Not bothering to turn when the door creaks open behind me, used to its familiar complaint, I continue in my campaign of ignoring the guardians, training my gaze on the horizon.

'You've been asking for me.'

Charon's low grumble brings me out of my despondence. I sit up in a hurry before throwing myself at the bars of my prison. He stands nearer the door, filling the space as the tips of his antlers scrape the ceiling, fringes of shadows curling around the prison bars. I'm tempted to reach out to them, though I worry he'll withdraw.

Composing myself, I take a step in retreat. 'I'd like to negotiate the terms of my release.'

His humourless chuckle causes the bars to tremble. 'I'm impressed. Your predecessors were still far too angry to communicate with me at such an early stage. The guardians were worried you were slipping into a state of paralysis. Though I've never been demanded in such a fashion. I'm flattered.' He cocks his head, his last phrase dripping with curiosity.

I try not to let it rattle me and place my hands on my hips. 'You mean the previous Furies were mad that you tricked them too?'

'The gravity of your calling may only truly be understood once you transform. It offers clarity when you are free of your mortal form.'

'I will not kill.' My wings twitch behind me.

'It is the sole condition to free you of these bars. When you take up the mantle, you must submit to my will. Your Fury form is my extension in the waking world. I will facilitate your executions. They will be sanctioned by me alone. Other than that, you'll be free to walk the mortal world as you see fit. However, when I call, you will come.'

Megaera's memory swims before me, one of her on her knees. The rest are swathed in darkness just out of my grasp. My jaw twitches as he observes my internal struggle with rapt attention. Something tells me if I submit, the action will be binding and not something it'll be possible to lie my way through in order to return to the surface.

'I'm no dog,' I sneer.

'Time,' he continues, wolfish amusement rife in his tone, 'is all it takes. I'm very patient, though I look forward to your submission in particular.'

I shudder, though it doesn't escape my attention how his shadows grip tighter to the bars. Something of my own power fizzes in my blood.

'Thank you.' Tilting my body, letting my hand hang

loose, I run lazy fingers along the soft mattress. 'For the bed.'

His head inclines once more. 'A most curious request.' He inches closer, a movement so tiny, it would be easy to miss if it were not the tell I was praying for. This is the key to my escape. The Ferryman's loneliness. He misses his Furies.

The corner of my mouth quirks, and I shrug. 'Comfier than the floor.'

'The others asked for more practical things to fill their time.'

'And the others, they stayed mad with you for a long time? For what you turned them into? Even though they agreed, just as I did.'

'A few hundred years.'

I stumble at that, pacing round the bed a little before sinking onto the mattress in front of him in a pouf of silk. 'Hero said time was of the essence.'

'These things are relative. Worse than what is happening on the surface would be a renegade Fury on the loose.'

The notion brings a grin. 'I've never been called renegade before.'

'What things have you been called?' His words come quick and urgent. He's now at the bars of my cell, his stare so intent, the entirety of the Underworld could melt away.

A tingle of power sizzles on my skin. I stretch my arms back, leaning on my hands, and, arching my spine, allow my wings to give a lazy flex. 'Must I speak to you through bars?'

'I told you, there's one way out of there.'

'True. Can't you come in here? Or am I a danger to you?'

The shards of ice in his irises churn at the challenge, though I fail to conceal my shock when he steps straight through the bars like an apparition.

'You seem surprised.' He advances on me, shadows cascading along the floor in my direction. 'Yet I am the master of all in this place.'

'But not me.' I arch my back further to gaze up at him fully.

'Yet.'

'Yet,' I echo in a whisper.

His eyes devour me, curious and penetrating. But, without a beating heart, nerves do not rattle me.

He leans over me, his height and shadows consuming until we're illuminated solely by the crimson, licking flames of my hair. 'What game is this?' His deft fingers graze my cheek, upturning my chin and causing me to arch even further, the coolness of his breath frosting my lips.

'Is it one you feel like playing?' I counter.

Taking his time, he draws his thumb across my lower lip, snagging it to part my mouth. 'Submit to my will.' His quiet command is a tempting invocation, sounding as if *he* is the one appealing to the gods.

My every cell trembles with life underneath him. I'm

glad my Fury form allows me a clear mind. I pause, drawing so close, our lips are almost grazing before I give a firm 'No.'

We remain locked in a staring contest of fire and ice before he finally withdraws to the other side of the bars.

'Until then,' he croons, then turns to make towards the door in a swirl of shadow.

I'm on my feet, hands on the cool iron bars. 'Come back to me,' I command.

He slows but continues without returning a glance.

Smiling to myself for my devious plan, I slink back to bed.

IT'S ONLY HERO AND LEANDER WHO COME AND GO, OFFERING me conversation that I engage in with my back to them, my attention on the river alone from where I languish in bed. Despair threatens to seep in, exposing my plan as a foolish one if I can't tempt Charon to visit me in my cell.

The audacity of my plan to seduce the ruler of the Underworld—its creator—is enough to make me want to descend into hysterics. I'm hoping it's a plan so stupid it might just work. Resist submission. Make him desire my companionship. Strike a different bargain.

With Hero and Leander floating about as my sole source of company, my new mission is to glean as much information as possible about the Furies. Their earliest memories of the cell have not returned to me.

'Why did the Furies stay mad for so long?' I ask Hero one day, if it can be defined as a day.

'You're called Furies for a reason,' they chuckle.

'Why is that rage a stranger to me?' I'm particularly melancholy today. 'Why doesn't he come to me?'

'Are you ready to submit?'

'Never,' I say, though there's zero effort behind it.

'Then he will not come.'

A standoff, I think, as Hero continues, 'Lovely, the submission is not what you fear it to be. It's nothing untoward. Its purpose is to keep your powers in check. After all, you're The Ferryman extended on Earth, and such power requires a bridle.'

'I'd be nothing more than his slave.'

Hero tsks. 'He already shows you far more favour than he did the others. The submission is not about your body but your will. He will not take advantage of you.'

A wave of panic washes over me. 'Will he create another Fury instead? Send me on?'

'After such little time? He's more patient than you suppose. Besides, you occupy our only cell.'

This piques my interest, although I make no move to show it. 'The Furies were made one at a time?'

'Yes. Alecto was the first I knew.'

Alecto. Her memories are, for sure, the fieriest, though her skin would still prickle under his embrace, the sensation maddening.

'You must understand, she served under him for thousands of years. Such devotion comes over time. He is just and fair. He'll not treat you unkindly in your duties. You'll have praise, freedom to roam the city. Time to walk the living world....'

They leave that last sentence lingering in the air, a seduction of their own. Another trick.

'Hero,' I whisper. Calculating. 'I want something else.'

'Yes,' they chirp.

This is a good sign for them, a pattern similar to the Furies before. My rebirth may have been different, demanding Charon rather than rejecting him. But now I'm on a path they recognise: a need to fill my time.

A wicked smile stretches across my face. 'A bath.'

Their astonishment is deafening. They don't acknowledge the request; instead, they leave and don't return for a long time.

I remain in bed, now and then stretching my limbs to keep atrophy at bay and yawning for dramatic effect, hoping that my lazy dissonance annoys everyone.

Until the clattering of the door one day brings with it Hero and Leander carrying a huge ivory bath. I can't believe he did it. I was praying he would storm my cell, demanding that I explain the reason for such a ridiculous request—after all, we're surrounded by water. Now that it's here in front of me, inescapably delightful and beyond absurd, the sight prises me from my bed with a disbelieving laugh.

The guardians don't bother with their warning against escape as they plonk it along one of the walls so as not to obstruct my view of the river from the bed. The thing is ridiculously extravagant, and it dawns on me that part of the reason I demand these gifts is the knowledge that Charon has crafted them. I make a mental note not to ask for anything else. It's impossible not to have admiration for his exquisite work.

'What's this?' I grab a small object that shimmers like a pearl where it's held in a divot on the bath's rolling lip. When I glance at the guardians, it's obvious from their shuffling that they don't approve of the gift.

After a loaded pause, Leander answers, 'It's something of his imagining, for your... enjoyment.'

Frowning, I pull the pearl across the palm of my hand, and a slathering of soapy bubbles coats my skin before they float away, dancing across my cell. A laugh escapes my lips. How delightful.

With the glee of a child, I shed the toga I've worn since the moment I was turned, then climb into the ridiculous tub before running the pearl over my exposed skin. It's a little tricky, as I have to remain leaning forward to accommodate my wings. I'm unable to conceal my childlike exuberance at the results as glistening orbs soon fill the bath, covering me and floating around the cell and out, popping in the space between Hero and Leander, who appear to be quite frozen.

In the bath I remain, giggling, until every last one of the bubbles pops or floats away or breaks against my skin. I trace my fingers over the scars on my arm.

Remnants of a life long lost. Attempting to piece that girl together again, I find it harder to recall who I once was.

I get out of the tub and retreat to bed, unsure when it was that Hero and Leander left.

IF I LIE WITH MY WINGS FOLDED BENEATH ME AND CURLED around my ass, reclining in the tub is possible. The pearl lies unused since my little display of excess. I've taken to ignoring the guardians altogether, although my anger is with myself for finding a moment of happiness at Charon's hands.

I'm sure he views it as quite the victory.

So, I sulk.

Fully clothed and slumped so low in my ridiculous tub, my view of the river is obscured, leaving me to scowl at my toes.

Charon's deep voice fills my cell. 'You enjoyed the pearl, I'm told.'

Sitting up, I turn to find him with his fingers resting on the bars, a long nail clicking against its metal.

His shadows lick like flames crawling across the floor and receding against the bath. Now that he's here, I have no idea what to say, managing only to maintain his stare. In the time he's not been here—it could be days or weeks —I'd almost forgotten the neon glow of his stare.

With a quirk of an eyebrow flitting in and out of a holographic face, he turns to leave. This is a game he's used to playing. Anger. Silent treatment. The usual pathways of the Furies. His curiosity satiated, he's relented first. The guardians informed on me after he facilitated my unusual request. He received an account of my even stranger jubilant reaction. This realisation comes to me almost too late.

Almost losing my footing as I hop out of the bath, I let whatever comes to my brain tumble out of my mouth. 'Does it bring back memories?'

When he turns, his icelike eyes trained on me, I gesture at the tub. 'It was when I first heard you call me to you. Felt your hands claiming me, holding me under…. Or was it the guardians caressing my body in that bathtub?' I tease.

Pretending his gaze is not hot on me, I trace my fingers along the silk fabric of my makeshift dress. I have his attention—now I need to keep it. Pleased that my fingers don't tremble, I loosen the knots of my toga and let it sweep to the floor in a silky pool, exposing every inch of my pale skin. A blackness fills the building as we're plunged into shadow, and though he maintains his distance from me, his presence envelops the room.

Stepping into the tub once more, I pick up the pearl and rub it across my skin, leaving a wake of glistening bubbles from my collarbone right to my navel, intending to put on quite the show. Before I have chance to lower myself into the tub, he is across the room and on me, his behemoth hand around my wrist sending the pearl clattering to the floor.

I don't fight. It's he who battles a ferocity barely contained in the most fragile of cages. Angry he's here. Angry he's tempted.

'Care to join me?' I ask, tipping my face to his, managing to keep my voice level. Only seeing his eyes, I'm desperate to raise my other hand to push back his hood and discover what lies beneath. A grotesque curiosity to unveil whatever beastly form he hides beneath his shadows.

'Stop this madness, Fury.'

Though his words are rough and demanding, attempting to demean me by refusing my name, his shadows betray him, greedily caressing my bare skin. Their faint brushes, like ghosts passing over me, are cool and goose bump inducing. My own body reacts to his proximity, dropping by degrees, all my edges extra sensitive to the writhing shadows—though my mind is clear, all hesitation gone.

No wonder the Furies lost themselves.

'Maybe I'm lonely,' I purr, pressing myself to him.

Something in Charon breaks. He releases my wrist, and his hands, firm and demanding, explore my body. As if he wants to commit every inch of me to memory, he traces each curve until I'm trembling in his grasp. His stroke is death, an icy intoxication, his fingers like glacial fragments against my hot skin.

Not succumbing to the safety of love but rather the danger of desire, I sink my head to his shoulder, my breath coming short. Catching his fingers, I guide them to skim my sensitive skin beginning from the swell of my breasts, then trailing lower. He emits a low growl of pleasure and pain. *Just give yourself to me,* I silently beg. A heady scent of opium fills my nose, radiating from him. I'm not prepared for the electrifying shock of his cool fingers grazing my core in the faintest of traces.

At my soft gasp, he snatches his fingers away. 'This will not come to pass.' His voice is rough, quivering with barely held restraint as he removes his embrace from my shivering body, leaving me engulfed in fire, desiring nothing but his ice in this moment.

At the retreat of his touch, his shadows following suit, I'm left bare, the flames of my hair crackling against his looming antler crown our sole remaining contact.

Balling my fists into the depths of his cloak, I bring my eyes to meet his. 'Stay,' I demand.

'Submit,' he counters.

I don't answer straight away, lost in the moment, in his freezing depths, perceiving the flickering of a face that is there, then not. I contemplate the impossibility of his demand.

He grasps my face, the tips of his fingers bruising. 'Submit,' he says again, a plea, a litany, a bargain.

'I can't,' I whisper, undone but ready to give myself in the one way I can.

I close the distance to kiss him. My lips swipe air.

He's gone.

CHAPTER
TWENTY-EIGHT

Cursing myself, I rewrap the black silk around my curves without any of the grace of the guardians. I'm a fool. I've played my hand too hard too soon, seduced by my own seduction.

Heaving a sigh, I collapse onto the luxury bed. Charon will not return—I'm certain of that much. What I'm unsure of now is what happens next. How long will it take before I break? As the memory of his touch reverberates around my skin, I can't deny how much I relished it.

My desperation at having any opportunity at all caused me to be too eager, and now I will be left here to rot until my mind snaps. Though if what Charon said is right and it took my predecessors hundreds of years to cave, my chances of returning to Tino die by the minute.

And yet submission is impossible. Something in my soul rebels against the notion of not being my own master. I spent so much of my human life afraid. I don't want to spend my next life in fear of another's command, even if it means I live a life in jail.

A grief settles over me. For my mortal relationships. For Tino.

I will myself to cry tears that will not come.

THE DOOR CREAKS OPEN BEHIND ME, AND, EXPECTING HERO and Leander's tittering, I don't bother to turn around. They're quite used to me ignoring them.

'Are you so despondent that your schemes didn't work on your first try?'

Charon's deep voice drips with amusement as I fly up, sitting bolt upright to face him. My face betrays the surprise that consumes me at the sight of him, his fingers resting, languid, on the bars of my cell.

'I must admit,' he continues, 'my guardians are a little hurt by your continued silence.' He waits a beat. 'And now it seems I am subject to it also. A new game?' His eyes glitter.

'No game.' I rise and close the distance in two strides, stopping short of the bars.

'You will submit?'

'Never.'

He cocks his head as I pace.

'I've renounced my schemes. They're futile.'

He matches my steps, mirroring me. 'Shame. I was most looking forward to their coming to fruition.'

'You hold all the cards, Charon.' I place my hands on my hips, drawing to a halt, aiming to get some kind of read on him.

He's markedly in control now, his shadows caught firmly on his side of the cell.

'Don't toy with me,' I say, narrowing my eyes at him, unsure of his angle.

'Yet you almost succeeded.'

My mouth drops open, though I recover quickly. 'I bet you say that to all the Furies.'

His chuckle rumbles in the water, and for the first time, it's a sound that has a little humour in it. 'A Fury has never attempted to seduce me. I was caught off-guard.'

'Another trick,' I scoff. 'You forget, I have their memories.'

'On the contrary, I'm aware of that. Though your perspective on them is interesting. We were bonded, for sure. Over many lifetimes, that bond evolves.' He chuckles, that flat tone returning. 'They were human once, and humans have... needs. But most would recoil in my presence.'

'Why?'

'Because I signal the end, which is why I allow the souls who reside here their own space. I pass through the city sparingly.'

Turning from him, I gaze out at the river. 'Sounds lonely.'

'It's as it always has been.' His shadows coil around

the bars, straining as though, if their inky tendrils didn't clamp onto the iron, they would be compelled to seek me out instead. 'The Furies were of a different time. This place may appear unchanging, but it, too, evolves, and all of us with it.'

'So, why make a new Fury now?' I inch closer, intrigued by this new willingness to share information.

'The city has been crumbling for a long time. Fewer wraiths, fewer souls wanting to make contact with the other side. The ever-growing population of the living world means souls are stretched thin. The time of the kingdom was waning.'

Joining him at the bars, I clench my hands around them, exposing the whites of my knuckles. 'What changed?'

'Something unpredicted,' he replies, that wolfish tone returning to his voice. 'The stars aligned. A new magic was released on the earth. At that moment of its unravelling, I felt your pull in the water. *Drowned one,*' he whispers, reverent.

'You drowned them all? The previous Furies?' So close are we now, the thread that binds me to him wraps around us, its effect like stardust in this place of grey. The scent of opium fogs my thoughts.

'Twice.' His voice contains a malevolent grin as he continues, 'Once to become haunted, and a second time to join me once more. They were mad for a reason, you understand. They were drowned young and haunted long. It would appear that the effect of your haunting is rather... singular.'

As he begins to drift away, the urge to shoot my fingers out and catch his arm coils within me, though I maintain my restraint. Best not to test him again so soon.

'Pity you've given up on your schemes so easily.'

'Will you come back to visit me?' My voice, steeped in desperation, is sticky in my throat.

'Your wish is my command,' he whispers, irony rich in his tone. With a slight bow of his head, he disappears again, leaving me reeling in confusion.

FEELING GUILTY, I'M TALKING TO THE GUARDIANS AGAIN, WHICH they're joyous about. They drift about and make happy conversation with me, though I sense a lingering reservation from Leander. I can tell that they're on the cusp of saying something, but then they withdraw.

Charon visits often. Never straying from his side of the bars, he talks about the happenings of the Underworld and answers my questions about the previous Furies and the inventive number of curses they reserved for him. Their cutting words make me chuckle, and he tells of their insults with fondness.

On one visit, I sit listening to him with my hands wrapped around the bars as he talks from a distance about Megaera's distaste for him and how for the first two hundred years, she would spit when the guardians said his name.

In fact, I look forward to his visits more than anything. He urges me to make more demands for gifts, though I refuse. My afterlife has become a routine of lying in bed, sitting with my head resting against the window, pacing my cell and counting the steps, or reclining in the tub while the pearl lies unused.

I'M LOLLING IN THE TUB, LEANDER FLOATING AROUND BEHIND me. Charon has been gone for a while.

'Where does he go?' I ask, breaking the silence. 'How does he fill his time?'

'Maintaining the city, of course. Building or creating, ferrying on the lost souls who are ready.'

There's a pause, and I turn round to attempt to discern the reason for the octopus's hesitation.

They finally tell me, 'There's been an increase in wraiths. They take managing.'

'Oh.'

I can only imagine what kind of mayhem they're causing. A small portion of the city is visible to me, though from my vantage point on the outskirts, it's nothing but peaceful.

Leander's silence is palpable. So much so that I'm compelled to break it.

'Do you have something to say, Leander?'

They draw closer, their pink luminescence illuminating my cell in a cherry-toned glow. 'It's not usual for The Ferryman to visit the Furies before they submit.'

Frowning, I rise and make my way to the bars. 'Then why does he visit?'

They avoid my question. 'Lovely, it would be better for all involved if you submit soon.'

'Better for you maybe.'

'For all.' They wrap their tentacle around my wrist. 'You will never be out of this cage until you do.' There's a pause while they collect their thoughts. 'There must be something wrong, for him to visit. It must be an attempt to encourage you to submit sooner. Things must be more dire on the surface than anticipated. Whatever it is you believe you might gain from him, trust me, you do not want it.'

'I want my freedom alone.'

'He'll never allow it. The Underworld will crumble before he allows it. You're his creature now. The sooner you accept it the better.'

It would be so easy to give in. Yet there is a part of me that fights against it, this urge to relinquish all my new power and simply be his servant.

Backing away, I move to the window and press my forehead to it, savouring its cool, and give my unused wings a stretch. 'There's something else I want. Chalk. I'd like some chalk.'

Leander sighs and leaves.

From my spot leaning against the huge window, I continue my vigil over the souls sailing on to their next life. I try to picture where they've been, where they're going, and hope there's some sort of symmetry in it.

The door creaks open.

'Chalk?' Charon's brusque voice makes my head swivel as he approaches the bars.

I get to my feet and amble over, maintaining the accustomed distance between us.

He produces a thick stem of brilliant white chalk from the depths of his cloak. Clutching it between his fingers, he passes it into my own as he tells me, 'It'll never wear down.'

I, too, handle the gift, turning it over while he savours each tiny reaction I give. But my reactions are dull today.

'All my family and friends are going to die while I'm in this cell, aren't they?' I demand.

'Fury.' His voice is soothing, though his refusal of my name stings.

'Let me go. Please let me go home to the people I love. I'm Fury now. I'll come back. I'll take whatever vow to promise that to you. Just one lifetime with him, with them, and then I'm yours.'

His eyes devour me at the sentiment. 'That's not how this works.'

'Please.'

He drifts through the bars, chest grazing mine. 'Submit to me now, and you'll be released.'

His paces send me into retreat, the mixture of ice fighting fire filling my limbs.

'New magic is running rampant on the earth, tipping the scales. An unchecked Fury is the last thing the waking world needs.' He runs a finger along my chin, tilting my head and arching my back. 'Although hearing you beg is a sweet melody.'

'Please,' I say again. Breathless. Starved of everything.

His head tilts, and he considers my lips. 'Why don't you recoil from me?' he asks, the perplexity in his tone genuine.

'I've been having an affair with the end for a while now. Remember?'

'Hmm,' he muses, his palm exploring the curve of my neck. 'Submit to me.'

I hold his stare while pretending to contemplate, enjoying the shards of ice forming in my veins that his presence evokes. Slow and cautious, I reach out. When he doesn't withdraw, my fingers find the hard planes of his chest, and leaning into him, I whisper, 'And how would you have me, if you were my master?'

His fingers dig into my flesh, the fire of my hair casting the looming antlers into relief on the walls of my cell. When he replies, his words are steeped in shadow. 'I would have you down on all fours.'

My lips fall into the shadow of his hood, the ice in my

blood contrasting with the fire in my belly at his impossible nearness, yet he is still so far from me. How absurd it is to be filled with hunger for Death, a creature whose face is completely unknown to me.

'Is that how you like your Furies?'

'No,' he whispers. 'It is a desire reserved for you.'

Goose bumps sparkle along my skin. To imagine all the depraved ways in which I might serve him on my knees makes me shake. Yet that's all I would ever be. When now, in this form, with Charon's eyes level with mine, hungry and demanding, I crave so much more.

'I don't believe you,' I bite. I have their memories. I know how Tisiphone crawled across darkened halls to him. I know how he liked them.

Then I'm moving, my feet sliding backwards to match his advance until my wings hit glass and stretch across the expanse to accommodate his pressure.

'Submit,' he growls, now furious. 'You'll lose everyone while you wait. What then? Your loss will serve to add fire to the fury you will rain down upon the living lands when you finally give in. You'll have nothing. There will be no *him*, only me. And I will delight so very much in your scraping when you're on your knees before me.'

My chest heaves against his, his antlers tearing into the tips of my wings. My teeth grind against the sensation, but I am unwilling to let my discomfort show.

'Call me by my name," I grit out.

'You're nothing more than a thing to me, *Fury*,' he snarls. 'The sooner you accept it the better.'

'I'll never be your servant. My heart will never be yours. It's something that'll always be his. Something you cannot take.'

He grumbles a low mocking laugh, glancing down, pressing harder into me. It takes all my restraint not to tilt my hip and allow room for him despite his savagery.

'It was only your body you were so willing to offer me.'

Defiant, I hold his stare. I clench my teeth. 'It's a price I'm familiar with paying.'

His hold on my neck eases, though he stays locked against me for moments longer before he retreats and leaves without a word.

I crumple to the floor, resting my head on my knees, and wonder who will submit first.

Though I have no idea what it would mean if he submitted to me.

Then I retrieve my chalk.

From my place at the window, I focus on the glowing river and count a hundred souls. On my hundredth, I stand and finish the tally I've marked on the wall, signifying my five hundredth soul counted. Feet clapping against the solid floor, I return, businesslike, to my watch.

When the door creaks open, I don't bother turning to register who it is. The betrayal of my body is enough to tell me it's Charon. A fleeting fear passes through me that it'll be me who gives in first.

I've lost my current count of souls somewhere in the sixties, giving my attention to the black waters and shrugging away the notion of Charon's blood flowing through them. Curling my toes, I resume my counting.

'Forgive me. For my behaviour before.'

'You're death personified,' I spit. 'I'm a whore. Let's not pretend we don't play our roles perfectly.'

He's silent at that, passing through the bars and into my cell, pausing to observe my tally of souls.

'To mark the passage of time?' he asks.

I nod, attempting to resume my counting, though his presence is distracting. An errant shadow closes the distance and wraps around my bare ankle.

Charon comes to crouch in front of where I'm leaning, his long fingers resting on the floor. His antlers still loom over me. He reaches up, gripping his crown. It shifts on his hood and comes away in his grip, and as he rests the skull on the floor next to him, my lips part in a gasp. His hands plunge into the depths of his cloak near his neck, and after a few seconds, it shimmers as it falls off him into a pool on the floor that looks more like a black hole than a discarded garment.

The chalk falls from my grasp. Revealed before me, he could almost pass for human. Almost. His blue eyes are fluorescent in their brightness, his olive skin so smooth, it could be carved from stone. He has high cheekbones and a jaw so sharp it could slice through bone. His black hair swirls around us, its ends melting into shadows, shimmering both short and long. His parted lips reveal fanged teeth, and although he's crouched, his height still betrays him.

'What?' I fumble, having no idea what I'm going to say next, and my words die on my lips.

With tentative fingers, I reach out to touch his face. He flinches back, then allows me to run my fingertips over his cheek, closing his eyes.

'You look... human.'

He shrugs a shoulder. 'So do you.' His eyes flick to the fire of my hair, the expanse of my wings. 'Relatively.'

The corner of his lips tilts into a sad sort of half smile, and I think I might faint. The bond that ties me to him simmers in my chest. This is so not fair—for him to be here, to expose himself like this. To look like a person and not a beast. I wanted him as a beast, and now.... Now I don't even know how I feel or what it means for him to do this.

'Your coming here gives me hope.' I peer at him through my lashes. 'That's somewhat unfair.'

'I know,' he murmurs, dropping languid fingers to run them across my scars.

'Then why?'

'Because I'm tempted.'

The flames of my hair flicker and flare, and the shadows that cling to him weave their way into its depths.

'So? We're to be locked in a battle of wills?'

'Or—' He smiles a wolfish smile that almost has me submitting right there. '—you could submit to me now.'

'Never.' I grin.

'For now, I must be content being caught in your schemes.' He glances at the chalk discarded on the ground. 'I look forward to your next request.'

He eases out of his crouch to tower over me. Battle lines drawn, of sorts, I match his action. Although tall myself, I only reach his chest.

'Have you ever lain in a bed?' I ask.

'I have not.'

I make my way around him and gesture to the grand bed. Amused, he takes up the challenge and lies on the soft mattress, though he's forced to curl on his side to fit on it, shadows dripping off the edge.

Once crammed onto it, he brings his gaze level with mine. 'And now?'

'Now you rest.'

I manage to squeeze into the space opposite him, wrapping my wings around myself. Lying in bed with him, not touching, transports me to a night spent with Tino. Our first in the same bed. A wave of guilt washes over me to be sharing this intimate moment with someone else.

'I miss sleep,' I tell him to distract myself, giving a half smile. 'And eating. When I was alive, I ate like a horse. I would eat ten burgers or a family-sized pie and still not be full.' He chuckles.

I frown. 'Was that your doing?'

'For what purpose would I do that? Everything I do, Fury, is for a reason. Even keeping you prisoner.' He catches a flame of my hair, twiddling it between his elegant fingers, errant shadows still sliding over his skin like dappled water, though not as much now that he's discarded his cloak.

'And this?' I take his hand in my own, the ice of it a balm I have no name for, and fix my eyes on him. 'What purpose does this serve?'

'A selfish one,' he replies without hesitation. 'You. I find myself wanting your company. It seems a pleasure I can't deny myself.' He frowns, thinking something he does not voice.

Seeing the emotions play over his face, the line of skin pucker between his eyebrows, and a fang dent his lip causes a tumult of emotions to crash inside me—mostly terror.

'My heart belongs to another,' I whisper so quietly, it's almost a bargain with myself. A promise I must keep.

'This will do. For now.'

He stays by my side. I close my eyes and pretend to sleep.

CHARON VISITS SO OFTEN THAT THE GUARDIANS HAVE LESS cause to frequent my prison than before.

Every visit, he requests I submit, and every visit, I tell him no. We say it so much, it's now more like a formality we must get past before we go on living our lives. Or afterlives. Mine, at least. Charon has never lived.

Then we lie together. Sometimes I tell him of my living memories. Sometimes he talks about the activities of the wraiths.

Other times we're silent.

I continue to tally the passing souls.

CHAPTER
TWENTY-NINE

In the dim glow of the Underworld, the walls of my cell glitter white from their coverings of chalk tallies. I've long run out of space to mark the passing of souls and have let go of my grip on the passage of time.

My human life is long past, a different life embraced. Though not one of submission. Charon lies next to me, eyes closed. Pretending to sleep—a habit he has learned from me. The antlered skull crown of The Ferryman lies on a nearby table, his cloak discarded on the floor. His shadows wrap around my limbs, though they don't sink deep into my skin, while he keeps his hands to himself. Always to himself. The cold clutches of dying haven't found me in a long time. My pining for it has become an emotion I'm so familiar with, I can't remember feeling anything else. While he seeks my company, the guardians were right—he doesn't desire my body.

Doesn't desire me. We're two beings wrapped in loneliness.

Though I've never made any more requests for gifts, things have arrived: a table, a grand high-backed chair large enough to accommodate my wings, and a chess set. Charon has taught me how to play, and I occasionally play with Hero. Leander, I fear, has gone off me.

When he's not tending to the city, Charon returns to my cell, where he all but lives. His request that I submit is made each time he leaves, though it's more out of habit. I always give a gentle no before reminding him to come back to me.

Which he does.

I know it's this stasis that Leander does not approve of. As the lifetimes stretch on, it's Charon who's submitting. Every time he returns to my bed, my no is a little more certain. His shadows wrap a little deeper, though the line he'll never cross is to kiss me again. He never touches me beyond skimming my face with slender, wintry fingers. He stares into the depths of my eyes with such a cool intensity that I, in turn, become lost in the universe in his and wonder if it's possible that all the world is his imagining, that the land of the living exists only in his being.

'You're all I have left,' I admit to him. *You're my home* are the words I'll never bring myself to utter aloud. For that's something he can never be. He desires me to be his slave, and I desire him because of our bond. This is a truth we never give voice to.

His shadows cling to the curves of my waist. His edges are tinged with the scent of opium. I breathe him in like air. I'm not his servant but his companion, and he mine. Neither of us is alone in this expanse of eternity. With no one to return to, I've stopped trying to negotiate my release.

On occasion, Charon vanishes for so long that I slip into despondence, and the guardians remind me that The Ferryman does not love. That I should submit.

I FEAR MY QUEEN MAY BE TRAPPED. STARING AT THE chessboard, I try to figure out my next move. Chess is a game I rarely win, and the times I do, I have a strong suspicion it's because Charon lets me. Chuckling at the notion, I realise that it's a fitting analogy for our relationship. By his residing with me in my cell, he's let me believe I have won.

I bat that thought away. While I *am* in prison, I have not submitted. Neither of us wins. We're at an eternal stalemate.

Something growls beyond the front door. The unfamiliar menace brings me to my feet the second before the whole door is ripped off, revealing the huge form of a wraith wolf. Kane. He has to stoop to enter the building, disturbing some of the brickwork, fangs dripping with shadow.

Retreating, I slam my back to the window, feeling a

crunch in my left wing. Reeling in pain, I drop to my knees, clutching my wounded appendage.

The wolf huffs. 'Do you know how long I have searched for you?' His voice creaks like a dead thing, half creature, half human. He advances on my cage, stopping to observe the bars.

'You can't be here, wraith. Charon will….' I falter because what Charon would do if he found Kane here is a mystery to me.

'Ah yes, what would your Ferryman do? You've been denied to us long enough, Fury. I have waited an eternity.'

His muzzle presses into the bars, testing their durability. I clutch my wing, hoping that the shriek swelling inside me will call Charon to me, or at least the guardians.

'Do not scream, stupid creature,' the wolf chastises in a hush. 'I'm not here to eat you. I'm here to set you free.'

The wail that was about to burst free from my mouth dies in my throat. 'Why would you want to free me?'

'There's a price.'

'Of course,' I deadpan. Though he continues regardless.

'Once free, you'll enact my vengeance on the one who did this to me. The one who tore my soul. One human life for your freedom.'

A bitter laugh escapes me. 'In case you haven't noticed, I've been trapped here for God knows how many human lifetimes. Your murderer is long dead.'

He snarls, 'Any living descendant will do. Do your duty, Fury. Just once. Then you're free to raise any kind of hell on Earth you so please.'

I all but roll my eyes. 'I don't want to raise any kind of hell.'

'How dull.'

Collecting my thoughts, I consider Kane in all his awful glory. 'Why would I trust you?' I ask.

'Who says anything about trust?' His hackles rise. 'You may be willing to fade away with this crumbling city under the wrath of the wraiths, but I'd rather see my vengeance done. If it means freeing you, so be it.'

'I don't understand.'

'The city is being torn apart by the wraiths,' he growls, pressing himself to the bars again. 'The time of The Ferryman is ending. The river will roll on. The age of the wraith is here. Do you want to be here to bear witness? Or do you wish to return to the living world.'

My mind reels. I knew Charon had to manage the wraiths, not that the situation was so dire. Then again, Kane may be exaggerating.

'One soul. That is all I require, Fury.'

'I can't break the city limits. The guardians will catch me and return me to my jail.'

His fangs snarl into something resembling a grin. 'You will not be going up but through.'

My treacherous heart aches at the idea of betraying Charon. Spending every day with someone for eternities forces one to grow rather fond of them. It's not love, not on his part, the more rational side of my brain acknowledges. He merely wants me for his servant. If I were to submit, I would be his slave. Charon doesn't hold me as his equal. I'm more like an amusing pet. And I have become so happily domesticated. It's all an illusion, his submission. Perhaps I needn't say the words. There will come a time when they're redundant. My submission will be so total, they need not be spoken aloud.

'I'll do it,' I announce. Freedom once meant everything to me. Maybe it could again.

'Come here.'

He beckons me to smooth my hands through his rotting fur. As I do, the revulsion leaves me. Memory unfurls of Furies past and their pet wraiths, trickling along my skin as my fingertips press into Kane's matted shoulder. At the contact of his fur and my flesh, the horrific memories of Kane's agony-filled death spill into my own being. I consume his pain, the fire of my hair turning a dangerous red. I cry out as something primitive lashes me to this beast. The images of his murderer come before my eyes, revealing him to be in a cage of his own. His pain, now my pain also.

I release Kane, falling back. The bargain is done. Our touch has passed a bond, a tiny glimmering thread my assurance that his vengeance will be carried out when I break through to the living world. How I will find his living descendant is a puzzle for a later time.

'Stand in the corner. Once I break you free, we'll not have much time.'

I back into the corner. Kane rears, then, at full speed, crashes through the bars of the cell with an ear-splitting howl. The jagged broken bars catch on his flesh and spill shadow across the floor, where chess pieces lie scattered.

For a moment, I think he might eat me.

Instead, he howls, his wounds healing in a terrible tear of yelps and shadow. The scent of decay fills my broken cell.

'Come,' he beckons, and for the first time in lifetimes, I spill out into the streets of the city.

In the vast openness of the space, I panic, and my wings flap on instinct, taking me a few feet into the air.

Kane takes the same wrist he once mauled gently in his jaws, pulling me to him. 'No. You must stay hidden. Follow me.'

He barrels forward along winding street after winding street, expertly treading the path. I manage to stay at his heels a little more easily now as he slows. With his lessening pace, I observe the damage done to the city. Buildings collapsed or with their roofs caved in, the signs of destruction are everywhere.

Opening my mouth to ask the question, it dies on my lips, replaced by a scream as the side of a nearby building explodes, knocking me backwards in a crunch. There, between Kane and me, is a wraith the size of a car in the form of a tarantula.

'Fury,' it bellows as it looms, its pincers oozing shadow that drips along my exposed legs in a sludge.

Kane turns with a roar and pounces onto its huge

body, causing them to crash and take out another building. The arachnid screeches in horror as Kane rips off one of its legs and tosses it aside like a chicken bone.

'Quick,' Kane shouts, and I flee, running further into the city and leaving him to deal with the spider.

Within twenty paces, Kane is at my side once more before he cuts me off, throwing my body into a nearby wall that has not yet crumbled. I don't have time to cry out in pain before the weight of Kane's body is pressed against me, consuming me. He stills, peering around the corner.

He shifts his weight, letting me breathe. 'The cathedral is close. The veil is thin there. You'll be able to break through.'

'That's your plan!' I shriek, noticing a huge eagle of a wraith perched on top of the cathedral as I, too, peek round the corner. 'I've been there before. The souls can't pass through, only send messages.'

'Hush. You're Fury. You'll pass through,' he insists. 'It's only your soul trapped here, not your body.'

'Kane.' My voice tremors. 'The wraiths?'

He bares his fangs at the presence of the eagle. 'Yes, they all want you, Fury. You're a beacon to us. Our revenge. The City of the Dead is doomed.' He turns to me. 'Go now while it's still possible. I will distract the bird.'

'Kane!' I call, but he's gone, pelting across the square.

He coils, springs, and flies through the air, his enormous paws landing heavy on the front of the building, startling the eagle. It flies, surprised, emitting a squawk so terrible, I must crouch to cover my ears. Then it flies after Kane, who disappears into the winding alleys of the city.

Seizing my chance, I make a run for it towards the cathedral. Its nave is now in darkness, no longer illuminated by the battering souls. Where have they gone to? Terrorized by the wraiths maybe? No longer dancing in halls to gramophones crafted by The Ferryman himself.

The city is dying. *His* city is dying.

And I'm abandoning him.

Before I talk myself into staying and submitting to Charon to save his kingdom, I throw myself at the glistening veil between this world and the next.

Hitting the brick wall with such force, I stagger and fall, crumpling onto my wings in a heap. Frantic, I look around, still in the land of the dead.

I get to my feet, and as I pound the barrier, flashes of the living world appear.

'No,' I cry. It didn't work. Through the veil, the planchette shuffles, spelling the word *No*.

'Shit.' As I pummel the wall anew, I witness S-H-I-T being spelled across the board in spiky jerks.

Withdrawing from my onslaught, I realise Kane was wrong. And now I stand in the enemies' den, every one of these wraiths ready to charge me with their missions to wreak hell on Earth. I must get out, call Charon before it's too late.

Marching towards the entrance, I halt in my tracks as Kane enters the grand space, again advancing on me in his predator state. His hackles rise with his growl. 'Where are you going?'

'It didn't work. I can't pass through.' My eyes dart furiously, attempting to calculate a way around him. *Charon, I need you,* I think.

'You have to want it, Fury.'

His continued advance sends me in retreat.

'Have you been prisoner so long, you don't know how to be anything else?'

'No,' I whisper.

He snarls. 'I will have my vengeance. You will give it to me.'

My wings hit the barrier of the veil, shimmering gold around their edges. When he lunges, I duck, and he slams with full force into the veil, shaking the foundations of the building. The ceiling above him crumbles bit by bit until it caves over the wolf. I dart forward, escaping the falling brickwork in a flurry of wings and flying out into the exposure of the square, where I have seconds to recover from the short exhilaration of flight.

The eagle has returned, perched on the top of a building with his keen stare trained on the prey that is me.

Well, shit.

I make to run into the bowels of the city with one purpose in mind—get to the river and the guardians.

A gargantuan shadow passes, blocking out the dim light of the city. Then a thundering presence collapses into the square, causing the eagle to rear up and give a battle cry.

Kane frees himself of the rubble, growling at the form manifesting between the two wraiths. Black shadows cover every recess of the city. The form reveals icelike eyes surrounded by simmering rage. A fury so unbridled, even Kane slowly withdraws, cowering. However, the anger is not trained on him, nor the eagle, who also makes his retreat.

The Ferryman is here, and his fury consumes me.

CHAPTER
THIRTY
TINO

The harsh light of Louisiana assaults me in a cacophony of colour and agony. Clawing at my chest, I sit, spewing swamp water onto the ground between my knees.

Clutching my head, I try to come to terms with the confusing sights and sounds coming into focus, including soft brown eyes flowing with tears.

'Holy fuck. You're okay. Are you okay?' Lorna's words are garbled. She doesn't give me a chance to answer, just throws her arms around my neck.

'What happened?' I ask, not expecting it when she slaps my arm with full force.

'What the fuck did you think you were doing? You've been dead for a full minute. We don't even know how that happened.'

I've been dead for a minute? My brain tries to grasp at murky memories that aren't coming easily.

When I peer down, an empty needle lies discarded on the floor beside me. 'You brought me back?'

Lorna nods. 'It was chaos. One minute you were in the water, throwing Marie off, and the next you were face down. Somehow when Lee died, she took you with her.'

Lee. I'd come out to stop them drowning her, and somehow I'd died too. We'd been somewhere, but that isn't important right now.

I stagger to my feet, blinking in the bright afternoon sun. I stumble at the sight of Lee's lifeless body, which has been dragged further up the bank by Marie and Lisette.

I run over, crashing to her side, unsure why they're both observing her with such calm detachment. I knock Marie aside, sending her flying off balance, and bring my palms to Lee's chest, ready to give compressions.

'What are you waiting for? She's dead. Bring her back.' Tears cloud my vision.

'Tino.' Marie shoves me off Lee. 'Don't be a fool. She has more than a minute left. These three minutes are hers.'

My brain scrambles, trying to sort through the confusion of being so violently returned to life. 'You gave *me* the adrenaline?' I seethe.

'We have two more.' From her vigil by Lee's side, Lisette holds two needles aloft for me to see.

Nodding slightly, I try to calm my nerves. Three minutes—that was how long she had to collect answers on the other side. Lorna rubs my arm, warming me up some while Lisette checks the timer on her phone and Marie returns to her spot on the other side of Lee.

I blink the tears away at the sight of Lee dead on the ground and no one doing anything about it. This was the plan. This was always the plan.

'Do you remember anything?' Lorna asks.

Rubbing my forehead, I ache, soaked and clutching at straws of memories that barely seem to be mine and are already fading into blackness. 'It's like walking through mud.'

'Give yourself a little time,' Lorna soothes.

'We were *somewhere*.' I attempt to pull the images together.

Marie glances my direction.

'There were gates made of bone. Gah!' I shake my head at the pain of trying to recall my death.

'Gates of bone?' Marie quirks an eyebrow.

I rub my head again, pacing. 'Something was wrong, though. No one was waiting for us on the other side.'

'Hmm.' Marie turns to Lee, smoothing her red hair away from her face. Her lips are now turning blue.

Lisette passes Marie a needle. 'Ten seconds.'

My heart has never beat so loudly as Lisette commences the countdown. Lorna clutches onto my hand with such force, it should break my fingers, but I'm glad of the distraction. Both Lisette and Marie are poised at Lee's sides, ready to administer the adrenaline.

Lisette counts out 'One,' and they each slide their

needle into opposing arms, Lee's scars open to the elements. The adrenaline administered, Lisette starts compressions while Marie burns the herbs again, talking to Lee, instructing her to follow her voice though the ether. To wake.

Wake up, I pray.

Lorna's grip on my fingers increases as the pair continue their work, an aura of panic settling over Lisette.

'Marie. Four minutes. Something's wrong.'

'Keep going,' Marie demands, then speaks louder to Lee. 'Lee! Come back to this plane. Follow my voice.' She blows some of the smoke into her face.

Lisette continues her compressions, the force cracking some of her ribs.

'Lis,' I yell, trying to move towards her, but Lorna holds me in place.

'I'm sorry.' A tear trickles down Lisette's face. 'Marie, five minutes.'

'Shit!' Marie stands, her gaze flitting across Lee's body, her mask of composure slipping.

'Marie, she's not coming back. There was always a chance this would happen. That Death would keep her.' Lisette's tears drop onto Lee's arm, and though her words are hopeless, she doesn't stop her compressions. More ribs crack.

Marie appears as paralysed as I do.

Lisette sobs again, glancing at her phone. 'Six minutes.'

She stops her compressions, leaning back on her heels and covering her face with her hands as she begins to weep. The weight of Lorna's head rests on my shoulder. I only stare at Lee's lifeless body.

A rage floods inside me at Marie and her willingness to send the woman I love to her death.

'No,' Marie yells, kneeling once more. 'You will not die today, Lee.' She settles her palms on Lee's chest, though not to resume compressions. She begins speaking in tongues. Her eyelids flicker while grim clouds move in, greying the bright afternoon.

Lisette stops her tears, her face stricken with horror at Marie. She climbs over Lee's body, pulling and prising her from Marie's clutches. 'Marie, stop! You can't do this!'

Marie's lids fly open to reveal milky whites, her irises paled by ghosts. She fights Lisette off with a supernatural strength, grappling to return her grip to Lee. 'I promised her I would bring her back.' The voice emanating from Marie is not her own. It echoes around the garden, the uncanny voice of many spirits pulled as one. Possession.

'What's happening?' Lorna loosens her grip on me.

Lisette continues the tussle, while Marie's grip on Lee increases and her chanting continues.

'Help me,' Lisette cries. 'The clock is gone seven minutes.' She gives Marie a useless shove. 'Resurrection is dark, dangerous magic.' She glares at me. 'Do you want your girl to be a zombie?'

Lorna and I move together, although with contrary aims. I want Lee in this world by any means, so I wrap my arms around Lisette, aiming to remove her from Marie, whose face is turned, unseeing, to the skies. Simultaneously, Lorna attacks me, trying to pry me from her girlfriend.

Eventually I'm successful, and the three of us land in a heap. Marie speaks in whispered chants, her fingers digging into the cold flesh of Lee's chest, which convulses as if shocked by a defibrillator.

Lisette scrambles to turn her phone over. 'Lor, it's past eight minutes. No soul will be returning to that body. We have to stop her.'

The air crackles around Marie as the girls get to their feet. I watch, somehow knowing what comes next.

Marie's chant crackles, and with another convulsion, Lee's eyes flutter open.

The air grows silent all around us as Lee inhales a giant breath and blinks in the living world once again.

In two breaths, the milky-eyed possession eases its grip on Marie, and her irises return to their usual dark brown. Slowly, she removes her palms from Lee's chest.

My own heart pounds, my arms aching with the need to hold her.

In the third blink, Lee hurls herself away, landing on her elbows. Hard breaths escape her, her eyes wide with terror. She stares at us as if we're strangers, her hand moving to clutch her chest, her stance akin to that of a wild and cornered animal.

I move with caution, lowering myself to her level and keeping my palms raised to show her I'm no threat. 'Lee. It's okay. You're okay.' I smile.

Her eyes settle on me, confusion spinning through them. 'Tino? How?' She glances around again. 'How did I get here? I don't understand.' Her vision locks on to mine once more. 'Tino.'

She staggers to her feet and into my arms. I wrap myself around her. Everything's going to be okay. She'll be fine while she's in my arms, and I'm never letting her go again. I give her a squeeze, then remember her cracked ribs and ease my grip.

I pull away a touch to drink her in, relief flowing through me as the colour returns to her cheeks. 'Let's get you to the hospital.'

'No.' She moves her hand back to her chest. 'No hospital. I'm fine.'

Lisette approaches her, gentle and cautious. 'What do you remember? You were dead for almost ten minutes.'

'Ten minutes,' she whispers, twirling a lock of wet hair in her fingers.

'Your memories,' Marie urges, catching her wrist.

Lee recoils, unwilling to be touched. 'Sorry.' She pulls the sodden material of her top to cover her exposed skin. 'It's just, I'm not ready for that pain.' She shrinks to my side.

'Of course,' Marie acquiesces gently. 'But do you have any memories?'

Lee shakes her head, her fingers clutching my sleeve. 'It all feels black. Sludgy.'

Marie purses her lips. 'Let's hope they find their way back to you and this wasn't in vain. I'm exhausted. If you don't mind, I'm going to lie down.'

Marie walks towards the house, Lisette monitoring her progress with keen eyes. She whispers to Lorna, 'The type of power she invoked.... There's always a price to pay.'

Lee flinches. 'Price?'

'It's not your fault, honey. Marie made her choice, and we're all glad to have you here.' Though Lisette's tone is sympathetic, her smile is a wooden one.

Lee turns to me, her expression filled with uncertainty. Her clothes are still sodden.

I frown a little. There's something I should be remembering. 'Let's get dry.' I wrap my arm round her, careful not to touch skin, and lead her to the house.

'I'm starving,' she says.

'Now that sounds like you,' I chuckle, trying to let her words assure me that this is very much Lee, my Lee, who has returned to me.

CHAPTER
THIRTY-ONE
LOVELY

After an age in the shower, my skin is finally reheated, wrapped in the warmest clothes I could find. Thick leggings, slouchy socks, my hair tied in a bun, and snug in Tino's jumper. The expanse of food in front of me is vast.

I pretend not to notice the concerned stares from Lisette, the uncomfortable itch in my shoulder blades, or wonder what kind of price Marie will pay for pulling me out. Instead, I focus on more pleasant things like drinking beer, Tino's arm that hasn't moved from my waist, blueberry pancakes slathered in syrup, the warmth of Lisette's parents' home, and Lorna's happy chatter.

The night wears on, and still I haven't had my fill of food. Lisette, who previously indulged me, now looks a little unnerved, though she tries to hide it. Perhaps she sees right through me, and she can tell that her previous assumption that I would be the light is so very, *very* wrong. Only madness runs through my veins now. Does she understand how I long to gorge myself on this world to be rid of the other?

'Come to bed,' Tino coaxes from my side, giving me what should be a knee-weakening grin.

'Soon,' I tell him, munching my third cherry pie.

'I did say that when you came back, I would never let you go.'

I laugh, eyeing his hand around my waist with a raised brow. 'I didn't think you meant literally.'

He squeezes a little. 'Anything come back to you yet?'

I shake my head.

'You've just died—again.' His brow furrows, his tone turning serious. 'Promise me that was the last time you die, Lee.'

'I promise,' I say with a dazzling smile of my own.

'I'll go easy on you tonight. But it's very hard not kissing you.'

'Tomorrow. I promise that we can do that too.'

He heads to bed. Now on my own, I drink down the melted cookie dough ice cream.

Absolute fucking bliss.

I take another swig of beer, which refuses to get me drunk, and then start on some Oreos. Is it possible to die from eating too much? What a glorious way to go. Would The Ferryman welcome me with open arms if I was the size of a house? A glorious fat wraith to battle with.

Let's face it—he was never that welcoming to begin with.

The floor creaks behind me. I would chastise myself for forgetting I'm sitting in a haunted house, but this creak is no ghost.

'I'm sure you have many questions, Marie.'

She gives me a wide berth, observing me as if I'm a dangerous creature as she moves at a snail's pace until she's sitting opposite me. I, meanwhile, continue to crunch through cookies.

She observes the mess in front of me from enough food to feed ten people.

Her fingers tremble with nerves, so I start. 'Thank you—for doing whatever it was you did to return me to the land of the living. I hope you won't pay dearly for it.'

'I spoke with Carline. Not long ago.'

'Oh?' I reach for another cookie and snap it between my teeth.

'She aided me in bringing you back. She and another. A powerful spirit by the name of Kane.'

I stop my crunching to glance at her, and a wave of self-satisfaction settles in her expression. 'So, you do recall more than you're letting on.'

I put the remaining Oreo carefully on the table's surface. 'If it was Kane you made your bargain with, I'm afraid you'll pay most dearly.'

'Is that a threat?'

'It's a fact.'

Her eyes shine in the low artificial gloom of

midnight. 'A fact? Much like the fact that your heart hasn't taken one beat since I resurrected you?'

A nefarious grin stretches the width of my face. 'What is it that you want, Marie?'

She leans forward, anticipation drowning the moments that stretch between us. 'You've seen the other side.' There's a questioning desperation in her voice.

She cares not for my atrophied heart, only the secrets of death. My smile deepens.

Leaning in, my voice the barest whisper, I reveal the knowledge she so longs for. After all, she's earned it. 'There's a city carved by the hands of the ruler of the Underworld. An in-between where lost souls may become wayward from their journey on.'

'On?'

'Sweet Marie, yes, *on*. There's a river. One that ferries souls to the source of all things, where they may be recycled, changed yet still the same. The lives we live are infinite. The waters that carry us there are enriched with our most golden moments. It is beauty personified. Memories painted with every shade of the most glorious sunset. The only light in the grey Underworld. Marie, everything lasts forever. *We* last forever.'

Lifetimes ago, the thud of a drip would fill me with dread, yet as Marie's tears pitter-patter onto the table's surface, calm fills me.

'T-Thank you.' She trembles. 'What are you now?'

'You now hold the secret of the Underworld.' I sigh. 'What I am, or am not, is no longer your concern. I'm alive because of you, or at least in the land of the living because of you. You'll always have my gratitude. We're even.' Tilting my face in the direction of a slumbering Tino, I say, 'It's time for me to go home.'

Home.

BE ON THE LOOK OUT FOR PART TWO, *SHE OF THE SHADOWS*.

THANKS

Thanks for reading *DAUGHTER OF THE DROWNED*. I do hope you enjoyed my story. I appreciate your help in spreading the word, including telling a friend. Before you go, it would mean so much to me if you would take a few minutes to write a review and share how you feel about my story so others may find my work. Reviews really do help readers find books. Please leave a review on your favorite book site.

ACKNOWLEDGMENTS

When writing and editing *Daughter of the Drowned*, my thoughts often drifted to my nan, who is living with advanced dementia. Dementia is such a cruel disease; it strips a person of everything they were and leaves them lingering in this halfway place. My nan, in her true life, was an avid reader and the matriarch of our family, a family of love and quiet strength. These past years have been some of the toughest our family has endured, but we do it unfailingly at each other's sides. She would have loved that I'm writing books now. Nan, this one is for you.

First of all, thank you so much for reading my book. Everything I write has a piece of my soul (in this case, the creepy part), and I'm so grateful that you came on this journey with me. I hope you loved it and are all in for book two!

I have to give the biggest thanks to my wonderful editor, McKinley. Who would have thought that the editing process would bring me to a true kindred spirit who fully understood and relished the inner workings of this world? You made editing such a pleasure, and the book that's in readers' hands today is so much stronger for each one of your thoughtful suggestions.

Of course, also a huge thank-you to the whole team at Hot Tree Publishing. Your organisation and professionalism have blown me away from day one. Kristin, I can't thank you enough for taking a chance on me and for always being a short email away with any questions I have. I don't know where I would have been without your reassurance. You made me feel like part of a family from the off, always with a kind word and even sending me the cutest pictures of your squirrels! You guys make this crazy industry a joy to be part of.

Claire, you blew me away with your talent in designing the perfect cover for *Daughter of the Drowned*. I didn't quite know what I wanted, only what I didn't want! Thank you oh so much for designing the cover of my dreams—I get chills every time I look at it. And a huge thanks to Becky from Hot Tree Publishing for being excellent and accommodating at every turn.

Thank you to my lovely beta readers, Jessica and T.H., for your wonderful feedback and suggestions. I'm so thrilled you both enjoyed the ride!

And, finally, to Kim for being my final eyes on this project and ensuring *Daughter of the Drowned* is as perfect as it can be.

A special shoutout to my awesome author friend Maria Dean, who is not only my rock but is always there through the writing ups and downs. I never would have submitted to HTP without you—so really, all the thanks in the world!

Thanks to my aunt Diane Harvey Reeves for helping me get my manuscript shipshape for the submission process. To my sister Roxy and my mom for being my test readers and always believing in me—love you both so much. And to my fiancé, Ben, thanks for putting up with my head always being in the clouds—even if that means I never listen to you!

A final word for my beloved daughter, Ivy. You are five right now, this wild bundle of energy who makes me laugh an insane amount. Keep sparkling, treasure.

About the Author

Kerry Williams is a UK author based in the heart of England and writer of romantic fantasy novels.

Copywriter by day, she gets lost in a world of magic at night, either in her writing or in what she reads. Her creative roots were cultivated by the writing of the unforgettable Anne Rice, and she also adores the work of Erin Morgenstern, Holly Black, and J. K. Rowling. These days you will often find her with her nose buried in a romantic fantasy book.

She graduated from Brunel University with a 2:1(hons) in Creative Writing. She is an avid cat lady, die-hard tea drinker, and eternal stargazer. Always known to her family as a daydreamer, she and her young daughter, Ivy, can often be found looking at the moon.

Join Kerry's newsletter: https://bit.ly/KerryWMailList
Visit Kerry's website for her current booklist: https://kerrywilliamsauthor.co.uk/

instagram.com/kerrywilliamsauthor
tiktok.com/@kerrywilliamsauthor
goodreads.com/kerrywilliamswrites

ABOUT THE PUBLISHER

Hot Tree Publishing loves love. Publishing adult romantic fiction, HTPubs are all about diverse reads featuring heroes and heroines to swoon over. Since opening in 2015, HTPubs have published more than 300 titles across the wide and diverse range of romantic genres. If you're chasing a happily ever after in your favourite subgenre, HTPubs have you covered.

Interested in discovering more amazing reads brought to you by Hot Tree Publishing? Head over to the website for information:

WWW.HOTTREEPUBLISHING.COM

facebook.com/hottreepublishing
x.com/hottreepubs
instagram.com/hottreepublishing
tiktok.com/@hottreepublishing

www.ingramcontent.com/pod-product-compliance
Ingram Content Group UK Ltd.
Pitfield, Milton Keynes, MK11 3LW, UK
UKHW040133260225
455541UK00001B/7